C000049090

CRIMEWORKS BRUIN

FLESH OF THE ORCHID

Published by
Bruin Books, LLC
April, 2010

© James Hadley Chase 1948

All rights reserved. No part of this book may be reproduced or
transmitted in any part or by any means, electronic or
mechanical, without written permission of the Publisher, except
where permitted by law.

This book was designed and edited by Jonathan Eeds

Graphics design by Michelle Roper

Photograph of James Hadley Chase by Max Feissel

Printed in the United States of America

ISBN 978-0982633908

Bruin Books, LLC
Eugene, Oregon, USA

www.bruinbookstore.com

FLESH
OF THE
ORCHID

crazy \'krā-zē\ *adj*, 1 : affected
with madness or insanity; "a man who
who had gone mad" [syn: brainsick,
demented, distracted, disturbed, mad,
sick, unbalanced, unhinged] 2 : foolish; totally unsound; "an impractical
solution"; "a crazy scheme"; "a half-
baked idea"; "a screwball proposal
without a prayer of working" [syn:
half-baked, screwball, a...

creak

JAMES
HADLEY
CHASE

BRUIN BOOKS
THE EMERALD EMPIRE
EUGENE, OREGON

CHAPTER I

SOMEWHERE in the building, above the roar of the wind that rattled doors and windows, a woman's scream filtered through padded walls. It was an eerie sound of idiot degeneracy rather than of pain or fear, and it swelled to a muffled crescendo before dying away in a whimper of lunatic self-pity and remorse.

A young and attractive-looking nurse, carrying a supper-tray, walked down the broad corridor that ran the length of the building. She paused outside a door, set the tray on a white enameled table against the wall.

As she did so a squat dark man with two gold teeth came round the bend in the corridor. He grinned cynically when he saw the nurse, but another scream from the woman upstairs twisted the grin into a wry grimace.

"That yelling sets my teeth on edge," he said as he came to a slouching halt by the nurse. "I'd like to give her something to yell about."

"Oh, that's number ten," the nurse returned, patted the corn-colored curls that framed her pretty face under the edge of the stiff white cap she wore. "She's always like this in a storm. It's time they put her in a soundproof room."

"They ought to give her a shot," the squat man said. "She gets on my nerves. If I'd known it was going to be like this I'd've never taken the job."

"Don't be so fussy, Joe," the nurse said, and laughed unfeelingly. "This is the nut-house, remember? What do you expect, working in a mental sanatorium?"

"Not this," Joe said, shaking his head. "It gets on my nerves. That screw in number fifteen tried to hook my eyes out this morning. Did you hear about it?"

"Who didn't?" the nurse said, and laughed again. "They said you shook like a leaf."

"Couldn't think of any other way to get a nip of brandy out of Doc Travers," Joe said with a grin. "And the punk gave me a dose of *salvolatile.*" The word was difficult for him to pronounce and he sounded foolish saying it. He brooded for a moment, went on: "And listen to that wind. It's creepy enough here without the wind moaning like a lost soul."

"You got that out of a book," the nurse said. "I like the sound of the wind."

"Then you can have it," Joe said shortly.

The woman's screams changed suddenly to clear, high-pitched peals of mirthless laughter, eerily unhurried and in control: a weird, frightening sound against the background of the storm raging outside.

"Maybe you like that giggle too?" Joe said, his mouth tight, his eyes uneasy.

"You get used to it," the nurse said callously. "Lunatics are like children: they want to express themselves."

"She's doing fine, then," Joe said. "She ought to be proud of herself."

There was a pause, then the nurse asked, "Are, you going off duty now?"

Joe eyed her thoughtfully, a half jeering, half friendly expression on his face.

"Is that an invitation?" he asked, sidled closer.

The nurse laughed.

"I'm afraid it isn't, Joe," she said regretfully. "I've eight more suppers to serve. I won't be through for another hour."

"Oh, the hell with that!" Joe said. "I'm going to bed. Sam's turned in already. We've gotta be up at four. Besides, I don't want to listen to that nut sounding off. I've had enough of her."

"All right, go to bed," the nurse said, tossing her head. "I'm not hard up for company. Dr. Travers wants me to play gin-rummy with him."

Joe sneered.

"That's about his top ambition: cards. You won't learn anything fresh from Doc Travers. He's as cold as his stethoscope."

"I know that... Dr. Travers isn't fresh like you, Joe."

Joe sniffed, eyed the supper-tray on the table.

"They feed 'em good, don't they?" he said, took a stick of celery from the glass holder on the tray. "Before I came here I thought they shoveled raw meat at 'em through iron bars."

He bit into the celery, chewed.

"Hey, you leave my patient's supper alone," the nurse said, indignantly. "Where are your manners? You can't do that sort of thing here."

"I've already done it," Joe said with simple truth, "and it eats swell. Besides, she won't miss a bite of celery with all that dough to keep her warm."

"Oh, so you've heard about that, have you?"

Joe leered.

"I don't miss much. I had my ear clamped to the keyhole when Doc Travers was shooting his mouth off on the phone. Six million bucks. That's what Blandish left her, ain't it?" He pursed his lips into a soundless whistle. "Think of it! Six million bucks."

The nurse sighed. She'd been thinking about it all day.

"Well, some people have all the luck," she said, leaned against the wall and studied Joe with an appreciative eye. She thought he was attractive in a brutish way.

"What's she like?" Joe asked, waving the celery stalk at the door. "I've heard things about her. Sam says she's juicy. Is she?"

"I've seen worse," the nurse said noncommittally. "But she's not your style, Joe."

"That's what you think," Joe said, grinning. "With six million bucks as a sweetener Mrs. Astor's horse would be my style. I'd marry that dame tomorrow if she'd let me dip into her purse. Maybe you could talk her into the idea. You could be maid of honor."

"You wouldn't like her for a wife, Joe," the nurse said, and giggled. "You'd be scared to close your eyes. She has homicidal tendencies."

"Don't most women?" Joe returned. "If she's as good as Sam says I wouldn't want to close my eyes. Besides, I'd take my chance for all that dough. I guess I could handle her at that. I gotta hypnotic eye." He patted the nurse's flank. "I'll hypnotize you one of these days."

"I don't have to be hypnotized," the nurse said, laughing. "You know that, Joe."

"Yeah, that's right," Joe said.

The nurse picked up the tray.

"I'll have to get on. Won't I see you tonight?" She looked archly at him. "Are you really going to waste time in bed?"

Joe eyed her over. He contemplated his prospects while he gave her a knowing grin.

"O.K. Eight o'clock, then," he said. "But don't keep me waiting. We can go to the garage and sit in a car. If we don't do anything else, I can learn you to drive—maybe let you play with my stick-shift." He closed a jeering eye. "More useful than playing gin-rummy." He went off along the corridor, a shambling, squat figure, wrapped up in himself, indifferent to his conquest.

The nurse looked after him, sighed, as she fumbled for the key that hung from a thin chain at her waist. The woman on the second floor began to scream again. She seemed to have found a new source of inspiration, for her screams rang out high above the noise of the rain as it lashed against the stucco walls of the asylum. The wind, dying before a fresh blast, moaned in the chimney-stacks. A door slammed violently somewhere at the back of the building.

Unlocking the door, the nurse entered a plainly furnished room. There was a steel table by the window, an armchair facing the door. Both pieces of furniture were bolted to the floor. High up in the ceiling was a bare light bulb, guarded by a wire basket. The walls of the room, a soft shade of blue, were quilted; padded and thick. By the wall, away from the door, was a bed, and in the bed was the outline of a woman, apparently asleep.

The nurse, a little absentminded, her thoughts on Joe, set the tray on the table and crossed over to the bed.

"Wake up," she said briskly. "You shouldn't be asleep at this time. Come along, I've brought your supper."

There was no movement from the form under the blanket, and the nurse frowned, uneasy suddenly for no reason at all.

"Wake up!" she repeated sharply, prodded the form. As her fingers sank into the cushiony softness she realized that this was no human form she was touching. She felt a prickle of alarm run through her as she snatched back the blanket. Her eyes had scarcely time to register the pillow and the rolled blanket where her patient should have been when steel fingers coming from under the bed closed round her ankles, wrenched them up and forward.

Terror choked the scream that rose in her throat as she felt herself falling. For what seemed a long moment of time she struggled frantically to regain her balance, then she crashed over backwards, her head and shoulders meeting the carpeted floor with a violence that turned her sick and faint. She lay there for a moment too stunned to move, then the realization that she was helpless and alone with a dangerous lunatic made her struggle desperately to get to her feet. She was dimly aware that a shadowy figure was standing over her and she gave a thin wail of terror as her muscles refused to respond. Then the tray with its contents of crockery and food smashed down on her upturned face.

~§~

The woman on the second floor began to laugh again. It was still as mirthless and idiotic as the laugh of a hyena.

Joe, lifting his shoulders as if he expected a blow at the back of his head, hurried down the dark passage, down a flight of stairs to the basement of the building. He was glad to reach his bedroom, which he shared with Sam Garland, Dr. Travers's chauffeur. Garland, still in his shirt and trousers, lay under a blanket on his small cot. His broad, good-tempered face was up-tilted to the ceiling; his eyes were closed and his fingers were neatly interlaced across his chest.

"What a night," he said when Joe came in. "I don't remember it so bad in years."

"And creepy, too," Joe said, going over to the fireplace and sitting in the armchair. "There's a Judy upstairs laughing and screaming her head off. Got on my nerves. I keep imagining myself locked in the room with her."

"I heard her. Suppose she got loose and crept down here while we were asleep?" Garland said, hiding a grin. "Ever thought of that, Joe? She might come in here in the dark with a carving-knife and cut our throats while we slept. That'd give her something to laugh at, wouldn't it?"

"Shut up!" Joe said with a sudden shiver. "What are you trying to do—give me goose bumps?"

"A dame did that once here," Garland lied, relaxing on his soiled pillow. "She got into one of the nurse's rooms with a razor. They found her playing kickball with the nurse's head up and down the corridor. That was a few months before you came—a dirty little secret they didn't tell you during your job interview, I'll bet."

"You're lying," Joe said angrily. "Pipe down! I tell you my nerves are shot tonight."

"I was only telling you," Garland grinned, closed his eyes again. "You want to take it easy. This is a good job if you take it easy."

"My luck," Joe said, scratching his head. "I gotta date with that blonde nurse on floor one at eight. I don't reckon I'll be happy with her out in the dark."

"Oh, that one," Garland said scornfully. "She makes dates with all the new hands. She ain't so hot."

"She's got a sweet disposition in the back of a car," Joe said. "I had a dress rehearsal a couple of nights back. That dame's keen."

"That's her trouble," Garland said. "She's too keen."

But Joe wasn't listening. He sat forward, stared at the door.

"What's biting you now?" Garland asked, puzzled.

"There's someone outside," Joe whispered.

"Maybe it's a mouse or your blonde destiny getting impatient," Garland said with a grin. "Why shouldn't there be someone outside, anyway?"

But the look of uneasy fear in Joe's eyes startled him and he sat up and listened too.

Outside a board creaked, then another. A sliding sound, a hand touching the wall, came nearer.

"Maybe it's Boris Karloff," Garland said, but his grin was fixed. "*Booga-booga.* Have a look, Joe. See who it is."

"Have a look yourself," Joe whispered. "I wouldn't go out there for a hundred bucks."

Neither man moved.

A hand fumbled at the door, a board creaked again, then a sudden patter of feet on the wooden floor outside brought both men to their feet: Garland throwing off his blanket, and Joe kicking back his chair. A moment later the back door slammed, and a great rush of cold air came up the passage.

"Who was it?" Joe said, starting back.

"Only someone going out, you dope," Garland growled, sitting on the bed again. "What's the matter with you? You're making me jumpy now."

Joe ran his fingers through his hair. There was a slight jerkiness in his movements.

"I've got the jitters tonight," he said. "It's that dame yelling her head off and the storm." He still listened, still stared at the door.

"Quit getting your vitamins in an uproar," Garland said sharply. "They'll be putting *you* in a padded cell next."

"Listen!" Joe said. "Do you hear that? It's the dog. Listen to him."

Somewhere in the garden a dog began to howl mournfully. The sound was caught up and swept away by the wind.

"Why can't the dog howl if it wants to?" Garland demanded uneasily.

"Not like that," Joe said, his face set. "A dog only makes a noise like that when he's scared bad. Something out there's frightening him."

They listened to the mournful howling of the dog, then Garland gave a sudden shiver.

"You're getting me going now," he said angrily, got up, peered out of the window into the wet darkness. "There's nothing to see. Shall we go down and give him something to howl about?"

"Not me," Joe said and sat down again. "Not out there in the dark; not for any money."

A new sound—the shrill ringing of a bell—brought him to his feet again.

"That's the alarm!" Garland shouted, snatching up his coat. "Come on, Joe, we gotta get up there quick. Something's breaking loose!"

"Alarm?" Joe said stupidly. He felt a chill run up his spine into the roots of his hair. "What alarm?"

"One of the nuts is loose," Garland bawled, pushing past Joe to the door. "Whether you like it or not, you're going out there into the dark now."

"That's what we heard. That's why the dog's howling," Joe said, hanging back.

But Garland was already running down the passage, and Joe scared to be on his own, blundered after him.

Above the flurry of the wind and the rain the dog howled again.

~§~

Sheriff Kamp swooshed water from his black slouched hat and followed the nurse into Dr. Travers's office.

"Hear you have trouble up here, Doc," he said, shaking hands with a tall, angular man who crossed the room to meet him. "One of your patients got loose, huh?"

Travers nodded. His deep-set eyes were anxious.

"My men are out looking for her as we speak," he said, "but we'll need all the help we can get. It'll be nervy work; she's extremely dangerous."

Sheriff Kamp pulled at his straw-colored, tobacco-stained moustache. His pale eyes looked startled.

"Is that right?" he said slowly.

"I'm in a very awkward position," Travers went on. "If this gets into the newspapers it could ruin me. She was the one patient I had no business to lose."

"I'll help if I can, Doc," Kamp said, sitting down. "You can rely on me."

"I know," Travers said, pacing up and down, and went on abruptly: "The patient is John Blandish's heiress. Does that mean anything to you?"

Kamp frowned.

"John Blandish? The name's familiar. You don't mean the millionaire fella whose daughter was kidnapped some twenty years ago?"

"That's right. We've got to get her back before anyone knows she's escaped. Look at the publicity that followed Blandish's death last year. If this leaks out it'll start all over again and I might just as well close down."

"Take it easy, Doc," Kamp said quietly. "We'll get her back." He pulled at his moustache, went on: "You say she's Blandish's heiress? What was he doing leaving his money to a lunatic? Doesn't make sense."

"She was his illegitimate grand-daughter," Travers said, lowering his voice. "And that's for your information only."

"Can I have that again?" Kamp asked, sitting bolt upright.

"Blandish's daughter was kidnapped by a homicidal mental degenerate," Travers said, after a moment's hesitation. "She was in his hands for months before she was found, and you'll remember she committed suicide—threw herself out of a window before her father could reach her. She died of her injuries."

"Yeah, I know all that," Kamp said impatiently.

"This is what you don't know: she didn't die right away. She went into a coma that she never came out of. Before she died she gave birth to a daughter by caesarian. She died in surgery. Here's something else you don't know: the father of the child was the kidnapper, Grisson."

Kamp blew out his cheeks.

"And this child is your patient—grown up now? Is that what you're telling me?"

Travers nodded.

"The child, Carol, was exactly like her mother in appearance, and Blandish couldn't bear to have her near him. Carol was brought up by foster-parents. Blandish never went near her, but she lacked for nothing. The fact that her father was a mental degenerate made Carol suspect, but for the first eight years of her life she showed no signs that she had inherited anything from her father. But she was watched and when she was ten she ceased to mix with other children, became morose, developed violent tempers. Blandish was informed and engaged a mental nurse to watch her. Her tempers became more violent and it soon became obvious that she wasn't to be trusted with anyone weaker than herself.

By the time she was nineteen it was necessary to have her certified. For the last three years she has been my patient."

"Just how dangerous is she?" Kamp asked.

"It's difficult to say," Travers returned. "She has always been under observation, and in the hands of trained specialists who know how to look after themselves. I don't want you to think she is violent or dangerous all the time—far from it. In fact, she is, most of the time, a very lovely, sweet-natured girl. She will go for months behaving normally, and it seems a wicked shame to have to keep her under lock and key. But without warning she'll attack anyone within reach. It's an odd kind of mental sickness: a form of schizophrenia." Seeing Kamp's face go blank, he went on: "A split mind if you prefer it: a Jekyll-and-Hyde mentality. It is as if there's a mental shutter inside her head that drops without warning, turning her into a dangerous homicidal lunatic. The trouble, as I have said already, is that there are no warning signs of the attack. It just happens and she goes for anyone with great violence and strength. She is a match for any man when she gets out of control."

"Has she ever killed anyone?" Kamp asked, pulling at his moustache.

"No, but there were two very ugly incidents which led to the certification. The final incident occurred when she came upon a fellow beating a dog. She is fond of animals, and before her nurse could make a move she had flown at the man and slashed his face with her nails. She has great strength in her hands and the fellow lost the sight of one eye. It was only with the greatest difficulty that the nurse and passers-by got her away from him. It is certain that she would have killed him if she had been on her own. He brought an action, and this led to her being certified. It was hushed up, and cost Blandish a pretty hefty sum." Travers ran his fingers through his hair, shook his head. "But now she is free to go where she likes, any unsuspecting person who happens to run into her could be in serious danger."

"Well, that's a bright lookout," Kamp said. "And hunting for her in this pesky storm isn't going to make things easier."

"She must be found quickly and without publicity," Travers said. "You may have heard that Blandish's will has just been proved and that the estate is to be administered by trustees. It involves a sum of over six million dollars. But if it is known that she has escaped and is wandering about the countryside, some unscrupulous person may try to get hold of her and exploit her for her money."

"But if there are trustees the money's safe enough, isn't it?"

"Not necessarily. We have a law in this State concerning certification. If a certified person escapes from an asylum and remains at liberty for fourteen days, recertification is necessary before that person can be put under restraint again. I understand also that the terms of Blandish's will direct that if the girl should leave here, and is no longer certified, she gains complete control of the money, and the trusteeship is automatically cancelled. You see, Blandish would never believe the girl was incurable, and that's why he worded the will like that. I believe he regretted that he washed his hands of her in her early childhood, and this was his way of retribution."

"So if she's not found within fourteen days you can't bring her back?"

"Not unless a judge issues an order for her detention and the order is supported by two doctors' certificates, and they won't consider her case on her past record. She'll have to give them proof that she is certifiable before they'll act, and that may be impossible if she moves from one State to another."

"Looks like we've got to find her quick," Kamp said. "Did she have any money on her?"

"Not that I know of. I'd say no."

"Got a photograph of her?"

"I don't believe there's one in existence."

"Then let's have a description," Kamp said, pulled out a tattered notebook from his pocket.

Travers frowned. "She's not easy to describe: not to do her justice. Let's see. I'd say she was about five foot five; red hair and big green eyes. She's an extraordinarily beautiful girl: good figure, graceful. At times she has a peculiar habit of looking at you from under her eyelids, which gives her a calculating, distinctly unpleasant expression. She has a nervous tic on the right side of her mouth, the only outward sign of her mental disorder."

Kamp grunted, scribbled in his notebook. "Any distingui-shing marks?"

"She has a two-inch jagged scar on her left wrist," Travers told him. "She got that when she tried to open a vein in a fit of temper when she first came here. The most obvious thing about her is her hair. It is the reddest hair I've ever seen: real red, not red-brown. It's most unusual and attractive."

"And how was she dressed when she escaped?"

"A dark blue wool dress and stout walking shoes are missing. My chauffeur reports that his trench coat, which was hanging in the passage outside his door, has gone. I think we can assume that she took that with her."

Kamp stood up.

"O.K., now we can make a start. I'll notify the State Patrol and get them to watch all roads, and I'll organize a search-party to comb the hills. Don't worry, Doc, we'll find her."

But as Travers listened to the Sheriff's car roar down the drive he had a presentiment that they wouldn't find her.

~§~

The truck drifted to a stop before Andy's Café. Dan Burns climbed wearily from the cab of the truck, stumbled through puddles, his head bent against the driving wind and rain, pushed open the door. He fumbled his way through the overpowering heat and thick haze of tobacco smoke to a table away from the stove. He didn't want to get too cozy. In fact, he thought of going into the restroom and splashing icy water on his face.

Andy, big, fat, boisterous, came over. He wiped his greasy hands on the dirty apron that seemed to be plastered onto his doughy girth.

"Hello, Dan," he said. "Glad to see you again. You look whacked, son. Not heading on tonight, are you? Most of the boys are staying over. There's room for you."

"Got to head on," Dan said. "No choice." His face was stiff with fatigue and his eyelids kept drooping. "Let's have a cup of coffee, Andy, and make it snappy. I gotta make Oakville by tomorrow."

"You're crazy," Andy said in disgust. He went away, came back almost immediately with coffee. "You truck drivers are all crazy. Why don't you catch up sleep in your cab first? I bet you ain't been to bed for days."

"Think I do it for fun?" Dan growled. "With the freight rates as they are and me ten weeks behind in the truck payments, what the hell else can I do? I don't want to lose the truck, Andy."

"You watch out. You look bad. You ain't in a condition to take that heavy truck over the mountain."

"Cut it out!" Dan said shortly. "You'll only jinx me. I tell you I gotta get on." He sipped the scalding coffee, sighed. "I got five hundred cases of grapefruit and the damn stuff's going rotten on me. I gotta deliver it, Andy. It's all the dough I've got coming to me."

Andy grunted

"Well, if it's like that... How's Connie and the kid? Hope you'll bring them over next trip. I'd like to see them again."

Dan's face lit up. "They're fine. Can't bring them on a trip, Andy. It's too tough. I gotta hustle all the time." He finished his coffee. "I reckon to get home for a night before long. I ain't been home in weeks."

"You'd better. That kid of yours will be socking you in the eye when you kiss Connie if you don't see more of him."

"You're right about that," Dan said and got to his feet. He flipped his jacket collar up. "This rain gives me colic. Look at it come down."

"It won't stop tonight," Andy said. "Watch yourself, son."

"Sure. Well, so long. See you next trip if I'm lucky enough to get a load."

"You'll get one," Andy said cheerfully. "Keep awake over the mountain." He picked up the money Dan had dumped on the table. "So long."

It was cold in the cab after the warmth of the café, and Dan felt more awake. He gunned the engine, pulled out into the road, sent the truck roaring into the darkness and the rain.

Away to the right, off the highway, he could see the lighted windows of the Glenview Mental Sanatorium. He wrinkled his snub nose in an uneasy grimace. The place gave him the willies.

Each time he passed the Sanatorium he had the same morbid thought: if he didn't run off the road, hit something, get burned up in the truck, he'd land up in a nut-house. The long hours at the wheel, the monotonous roar of the truck engine, the constant lack of sleep were enough to drive anyone crazy in time. He looked again at the receding lights of Glenview. Well, he wouldn't be locked up there: only rich nuts could afford Glenview.

The wind slammed against the truck, and the rain beat down on the hood. It wasn't easy to see the road, but he drove on, his hands clenched on the wheel so tightly that they hurt.

Suddenly he leaned forward, peered through the windshield. His headlights picked out a girl standing by the side of the highway. She seemed oblivious to the rain that poured down on her. She weakly raised her arm as the truck approached. Headlights swept across her sodden figure.

Dan automatically kicked his brake pedal, skidding the back wheels. He pulled up beside the girl, hung out of the cab. She was now out of the beam of the headlights and he couldn't see her clearly, but he could see she was hatless and her hair was plastered flat by the rain.

He was puzzled and a little startled.

"Want a ride?" he shouted, pitching his voice to get above the roar of the wind. He swung open the door.

The girl didn't move. He could see the white blur of her face, felt unseen eyes probing at him.

"I said do you want a ride?" he bawled. "What are on doing out there, anyway? Don't you know it's raining?"

"Yes, I want a ride," the girl said. Her voice was flat, casual. He reached down, caught her hand, swung her up into the cab beside him.

"Pretty wet," he said. "Pretty damn wet night."

He leaned across the girl, slammed the cab door shut. In the dim light from the dashboard he saw she was wearing a man's trench-coat.

"Yes, isn't it?" she said.

"Yeah, pretty damn wet," Dan repeated, not sure of her, puzzled. He released his brakes. The engine roared as he changed up and he drove on into the darkness.

In the distance there came a faint sound of a tolling bell. "What's that?" Dan asked, cocking his ears. "Sounds like a bell."

"It's the asylum alarm," the girl said. "It means someone's been lucky to get away," and she laughed softly, an odd metallic little laugh that somehow set Dan's teeth on edge. The mournful sound of the bell, carried by the wind, pursued them.

"You mean one of the loonies has escaped?" Dan asked, startled. He peered into the darkness, half expecting to see a wild, gibbering figure spring out at the truck from the thick bushes lining the road. "I bet you're glad I came along when I did. Where are you heading for?"

"Nowhere," the girl replied. She leaned forward to peer through the rain-lashed windshield. The light from the dashboard fell on her long narrow hands, and Dan noticed a deep puckered white scar on her left wrist. *Near the artery,* he thought; *must have given her a scare at the time.*

"Nowhere?" he repeated and laughed. "That's a hell of a long way away."

"I've come from nowhere and I'm going nowhere and I'm nobody," the girl said. There was a strange bitter note in her hard flat voice.

Telling me to mind my own business and not pulling any punches, Dan thought, and said: "I didn't mean to be curious. I'm going to Oakville if that's any use to you."

"It'll do," she said indifferently and fell silent.

They were climbing now and the engine grew hot, filling the cab with warm fumes, making Dan sleepy. His body ached for sleep and his brain grew numb, so that he drove automatically and forgot the girl at his side swaying like a rag doll to the lurching of the truck.

He had had only six hours' sleep in four days and his resistance was now stretched to breaking-point. Then he suddenly couldn't keep awake any longer and he fell forward, his head striking the steering-wheel. He awoke immediately, straightened up, cursing himself under his breath. He saw the edge of the road rushing towards him: the grass vividly green in the headlights. He dragged over the wheel, and the truck skidded round with a screaming of tortured tires. The off-wheels mounted the grass verge, thudded back on to the tarmac. The great towering load of cased grapefruit, lashed down by a tarpaulin, creaked and shuddered, swayed dangerously. For one sickening moment Dan thought the truck was going to turn over, but it righted itself, continued to crawl up the twisting road.

"Gee! I'm sorry," he gasped, his heart banging against his ribs. "I guess I must have dozed off." He glanced at the girl, expecting to see her shaking with fright, but she sat peering through the windshield, calm, quiet—as if nothing had happened. "Weren't you scared?" he asked, a little irritated at her calmness. "We nearly went over."

"We'd've been killed, wouldn't we?" the girl said softly. He scarcely heard her above the noise of the wind as it slammed against the cab. "Would you be afraid to die?"

Dan wrinkled his snub nose.

"It's unlucky to talk like that in a truck. Guys get killed every day in trucks," he said, and rapped with his knuckles on the wooden dashboard.

He slowed to take a sharp bend which would bring them on to the mountain road. He felt the strain in his shoulders as he steered the truck around a shelf of rock.

"This is where we climb," he went on, shifting in his seat to bring himself closer to the steering wheel. "You watch it—it's some road."

They were hedged in now; on one side by the towering granite mountain and on the other side by a sheer drop into the valley. Dan geared down. The truck began to crawl up the steep gradient, its engine roaring.

"The wind'll be bad half-way up," he shouted to the girl. And already the wind seemed to increase in violence, and somewhere ahead heavy falls of rock crashing into the valley added to the din. "It blows across the plain and smashes itself against the mountain. I did this trip last year in a wind like this and I got stuck."

The girl said nothing, nor did she look at him.

Some kid, he thought. *I wish I could see more of her. She's shaped like a looker.* He yawned, gripped the steering wheel tightly. *"I'm nobody from nowhere..." Funny thing to have said. Maybe she's in trouble: running away from home.*

He shook his head, worried about her.

But as he turned into the next steep bend he forgot everything but the handling of the truck. The wind suddenly pounced with the ferocity of a wild beast. The engine stalled and the truck came to a shuddering standstill. It was as if they'd run into a brick wall, and they were headed right into the teeth of the wind and received its full blast. Rain like a jet from a hydrant made the windshield creak. It was impossible to see through the torrents of water that hammered down on the truck.

Cursing, Dan started the engine again, let in his clutch. The truck jerked forward, shuddered against the wind, then suddenly began to rock violently. There was a crash as cases of grapefruit, torn from under the slapping tarpaulin, thudded on to the road.

"Christ!" Dan gasped. "The load's going!"

More cases crashed on to the road as he threw the truck into reverse, began to back down the incline to the shelter of the mountain-side round the bend.

The truck wobbled and he felt the off-side wheels lift.

We'll flip over, he thought, stiff with fear. He wanted to open the cab door and jump clear, to save himself, but he couldn't bring himself to abandon the truck and his load.

The truck began to slide towards the edge of the road, and, struggling desperately to steer against the skid, Dan gunned the engine, shooting the truck backwards, took the bend with the rear wheel almost over the edge, reached shelter. He braked, cut the engine, scarcely believing they were safe, and sat back, every muscle in his body fluttering, his mouth dry.

"That was something," he said, shoved his cap to the back of his head, wiped his streaming forehead with his sleeve. "That was certainly something."

"What are you going to do now?" the girl asked. She was as calm as a patchwork quilt.

He couldn't bring himself to speak, but climbed down into the rain to inspect the damage. Icy rivulets of rainwater dribbled down the back of his neck.

In the light of the headlamps he could see the wooden cases scattered all over the road. Some of the cases had broken open; bruised yellow balls glistened in the rain. He would have to wait for daylight now, he thought, too bitter even for anger. There was nothing else for it. He was stuck on the mountain with a lost load the way he'd been stuck last year.

Soaking wet, tired beyond endurance, he dragged himself into the cab.

The girl was sitting in his place behind the steering-wheel, but he was too tired to ask her to move. He slumped in the other corner of the cab, closed his eyes.

Before he could think of any plan for the next day, before he could estimate what he had lost, he was asleep, his head falling on his chest, his eyelids like lead weight.

Then he dreamed he was driving the truck. The sun was high above the mountain and a soft wind sang as the truck skimmed down the downhill stretches. It was fine, driving like that. He didn't feel tired any more. He felt fine and he gunned the engine and the speedometer needle showed seventy, flicking back and forth. His wife, Connie, and his kid were at his side. They were smiling at him, admiring the way he handled the truck, and the kid yelled for him to go faster, to outrace the wind, and the truck seemed to fly over the road with the grace and speed of a swallow.

Then suddenly the dream became a nightmare. The steering wheel crumpled in his hands as if it were made of paper and the truck gave a great bound in the air, swerved off the road and plunged over and over and over, and he woke with Connie's screams in his ears, shaking, ice round his heart.

For a moment he thought the truck was still falling because the engine was roaring and the truck was lurching, then he realized that the truck was rushing madly downhill, its headlights like a flaming arrow flying through darkness.

Stupefied with shock and sleep, he automatically grabbed for the handbrake, shoved his foot down on the brake pedal. His hand and foot found nothing, and then it dawned on him he wasn't driving at all, but that the girl had charge of the truck.

Before his befuddled brain could grasp what was happening, he became aware of another sound: the wailing note of a police siren behind them.

He was awake now, alarmed and angry.

"What the hell do you think you're up to?" he shouted at the girl. "Stop at once! My load's loose and the cops are after us! Can't you hear them? Stop, I tell you!"

She paid him no attention, but sat behind the wheel like a stone statue, her foot slowly forcing the gas pedal to the boards, building up the speed of the engine, forcing the truck faster and faster until it began to sway dangerously. The wooden cases behind clattered and banged under the tarpaulin. The tires sprayed jets of water as high as the cab.

"Have you gone crazy?" Dan bawled, frightened to touch her in case he caused her to swerve off the road. "You'll have us over in a moment. Pull up, you little fool!"

But she was deaf to him, and the truck hurtled on through the rain and the wind into darkness.

Behind, the siren screamed at them, and Dan leaned out of the cab window, stared back the length of the swaying truck, rain beating on his face and head. A single headlight flickered behind them. Dan guessed they were being chased by a State cop on a high-speed motorcycle. He turned back to the girl, shouted: "That's a speed cop behind. He's signaling us. You can't get away from him. Pull up, will you?"

"I'm going to get away from him," the girl said, her voice pitched high above the roar of the engine and the wind. And she laughed that odd metallic little laugh that had already set his teeth on edge.

"Don't be a fool," Dan said, moving closer to her. "We'll only hit something. You can't beat a cop in this truck. Come on, pull up."

Ahead the road suddenly widened.

This is it, Dan thought. *The cop will shoot past and turn on us. Well, it's her funeral now. She'll have to stand the rap. They can't touch me. I had no part in it. The mad, stupid, irresponsible little fool!*

It happened the way he thought. There was a sudden roaring of an engine, a dazzling searchlight of a headlamp and the speed-cop was past them; a broad squat figure in a black slicker, his head bent low over the handlebars.

"Now you've gotta stop," Dan shouted. "He'll sit in the middle of the road and cut speed. You'll have to stop or you'll hit him."

"Then I'll hit him," the girl said calmly.

Dan peered at her, had a sudden feeling that she meant what she said.

"Are you nuts?" he bawled, then his heart gave a lurch. *Glenview! The tolling bell, someone's been lucky to escape, the odd metallic laugh, I'm nobody from nowhere. Then I'll hit him. She was crazy! A lunatic! The cop was after her to take her back to Glenview!*

Dan drew away from her, his eyes wide with fear. He'd have to do something. She'd kill the cop, kill him and herself. She wouldn't care what she did. If he could get at the ignition switch! But dare he try? Suppose the move upset her, caused her to pull off the road? He looked through the cab window, his breath labored, his heart hammering wildly against his ribs. They were climbing again. To their left was a white wood fence, guarding the long drop to the twisting road they had left miles behind. If she pulled to the left they were finished, but if she turned right they had a chance: a slim one, but they might get out before the gas tank went up.

He became aware that the cop was signaling them to stop. The sign on the back of his carrier was flickering: *Police Stop!*

"You've gotta stop, kid," Dan shouted desperately. "He doesn't want you, he wants me. You've got nothing to be scared of."

The girl laughed to herself, leaned forward to peer at the flickering sign. She seemed to be aiming the truck at it.

Dan saw the cop was reducing speed. The truck creeping up on him. The great beam of the headlights was centered on his back.

"The fool!" Dan thought. "He must know she's nuts. He must know she'll run him down." And he leaned out of the cab and screamed at the crouching figure just ahead.

"Get on! She'll nail you, you goddamn fool! Get out of the way! She's going to run you down!"

The wind snatched the sound from his mouth, flung it uselessly away. The cop couldn't hear anything above the roar of his engine and the wind. He was still reducing speed, set solid in the middle of the road. The truck's lights beat on him, the roaring hood of the truck no more than twenty feet from his rear wheel.

Dan turned frantically, made a grab at the ignition switch, but the girl slashed at him with hooked fingers. Her nails ploughed furrows down his cheek and he cannoned against the steel side of the cab as the truck swerved, ran up the grass verge, straightened, slammed back on to the road again. He held his face in his hands, blood running between his fingers, his skin crawling with horror and pain.

Then, as he looked up, it happened. The cop glanced over his shoulder, seemed to sense his danger. Dan saw the mud-splashed, goggled face for a brief second, saw the mouth open in a soundless shout. The girl rammed down the gas pedal. The two machines seemed suspended in space: the motor-cycle struggling to get away, the truck racing to destroy it. Then with a tremendous surge of power, the truck hit the motorcycle and contemptuously tossed it high into the air.

Above the roar of the wind Dan heard the cop's yell of terror, heard the crash as the motorcycle hit the moun-tainside, saw the flash of fire as it burst into flames. Then he saw a dark form come down heavily in the road, right in the path of the truck's headlights.

"Look out!" he screamed, threw up his hands before his face. *This can't be happening!*

The cop struggled to his knees as the truck smashed into him. The off-side wheel bumped up, thudded down. The off-side rear wheel skidded and slithered in something soft. Then they had an empty road ahead of them once more.

"You've killed him!" Dan yelled. "You mad, wicked bitch!"

Without thinking, he flung himself forward, snatched at the ignition key, ducked under a flying claw. He managed to turn the switch and then seize the wheel. He tried to wrench it to the right to crash the truck into the mountainside, but the girl was too strong. The truck swayed madly on the road while they fought for the possession of the wheel.

His face was close to hers. He could see her eyes like lamps behind green glass. Swearing at her, he hit out, but the truck swayed and his fist scraped the side of her face.

She drew in a quick hissing breath, released the wheel and went for him. Her nails ripped across his eyeballs, splitting his eyelids, blinding him He felt hot blood drowning his eyes and he fell back, crying with pain, hitting madly at nothing, seeing nothing: a nightmare of pain and movement.

The girl slipped from under the wheel and threw herself at him, her hands fastening on his throat; her long fingers sinking into his flesh.

The truck swung off the road, crashed through the white wood fence. The headlights swung aimlessly out into a black empty pit. Stones rattled inside the mudguards as the tires bit uselessly on the gravel verge. There was a crunching, ripping noise and the truck hung for a second in mid-air, then went down through the darkness into the valley below.

~§~

The big Buick utility van, its long hood glistening in the morning sunshine, swept effortlessly up the road that rose steeply towards the mountains.

Steve Larson sat at the wheel; his brother, Roy, lounged at his side. There was nothing to tell that these two men were brothers. Steve was big, muscular and fair, with good humored eyes gently creased by laugh lines. His skin was burned a deep mahogany color from the wind and the sun and he looked younger than his thirty-two years. He had on corduroy trousers and a cowboy check shirt and his rolled-up sleeves revealed thick brown arms.

Roy was older, dark, almost a head shorter than his brother. His thin lips were nervous, his agate eyes narrow. His movements were sharp, jerky; his reflexes ragged, those of a high-strung man whose nerves are beginning to snap under some constant strain. His smart city clothes looked out of place in the mountain country.

Steve had driven down from his fox farm up on Blue Mountain Summit to meet his brother, who had traveled by train cross country from New York. The brothers hadn't seen each other for years, and Steve was still puzzled to know why Roy had suddenly decided to visit him. It was not as if they'd ever got on well together, and Roy's surly greeting when Steve met him at the station came as no surprise. The two men scarcely spoke a dozen words for the first two miles of the journey. Roy seemed nervous and kept looking back through the rear window as if to make sure they were not being followed. This unexpected furtiveness began to get on Steve's nerves, but knowing how touchy his brother was, he hesitated to ask what it was all about.

"You look pretty well," he said, attempting to get a conversation started. "Doing all right in New York?"

"So-so," Roy grunted, twisted round once more to peer through the rear window of the van.

"Well, it's nice to see you again after all these years," Steve went on, not sure whether he was being sincere or not. "What made you suddenly decide to come out and see me?"

If there was anything on Roy's mind—and Steve was pretty sure that there was—this was an obvious opening for his confidence.

But Roy hedged.

"Thought a little change of scenery might do me good," he said, shifting in his seat. "New York's too hot in the summer, anyway." He stared morosely at the huge rocky peaks that cut up the distant skyline. Whichever way he looked mountain rose above mountain, some jagged and sharp, some softly rounded, their crevices and fissures filled with snow, which gave off a dazzling brightness under the sun. "Lonely as hell here, isn't it?" he went on, impressed in spite of himself.

"It's grand," Steve returned, "but you'll find it quiet after New York. I'm twenty miles from the nearest cabin and I'm lucky if I have a visitor in weeks. The only sound you'll hear is the wind through the trees."

"That'll suit me," Roy said. "I aim to relax." He twisted round in his seat to stare through the rear window again. The long empty road unwinding like a grey ribbon behind them seemed to give him satisfaction. "Yeah, this is going to suit me fine." He brooded for a moment before continuing: "But I wouldn't like it for always. How do you get on, being all alone? Don't it make you restless?"

"It suits me," Steve returned. "Of course it does get lonely at times, but I'm pretty busy. I have over a hundred foxes to look after, and I'm self-supporting."

Roy shot him a hard, curious look.

"How do you get along for a woman up here?" he asked.

Steve's face tightened.

"I don't," he said, staring ahead. He knew what Roy was like with women. He was a ladies' man from way back. Even when they were kids he was girl-crazy. He felt the ridicule coming.

"You always were a limp-dick wallflower," Roy said, tilting his hat to the back of his head. "You mean you stick it out here year after year without seeing a woman?"

"I've been here a year, anyway, and I don't bother with women," Steve returned shortly. "I like a simple life."

Roy grunted.

"I wish I'd imported a floozy," he said. "I thought you'd got a supply laid on. What do you use—a knothole?"

Ahead the road forked to right and left.

"We go right," Steve said, changing the subject. "Left takes you to Oakville, over the mountain and down into the valley. You'd see plenty of traffic on that route. All trucks heading from California use the Oakville road. This way we go up into the mountains."

"Looks like a wrecked truck up there," Roy said suddenly, and pointed.

Steve's eyes followed the pointing finger and he stamped on his brake pedal, stopping the Buick. He leaned out of the window to look up the sloping hill that rose to meet the Oakville road a couple of thousand feet above him. It was a wrecked truck all right. It lay on its side, pinned between two pine trees.

"What the hell are you stopping for?" Roy asked irritably. "Haven't you seen a wrecked truck before?"

"Sure," Steve said, opening the door and sliding out on to the road. "I've seen too many of them. That's why I'm going up there to look it over. Some poor devil maybe hurt. After the storm last night it's possible no one's spotted him."

"Little comrade of the mountains, huh?" Roy sneered. "OK. I may as well come along: haven't stretched my legs in years."

They reached the truck after a stiff climb through thick grass and broken slabs of rock.

Steve climbed up on the side of the overturned cab, peered through the broken window, while Roy leaned against the truck and tried to control his labored breathing. The climb had exhausted him.

"Give us a hand, Roy," Steve called. "A driver and a girl. It looks like they're dead, but I want to be sure." He reached down, grabbed hold of the man's hand. It was cold and stiff, and Steve released it with a grimace. "He's dead all right. Poor sucker."

"I told you how it'd be," Roy said. "Now let's get the hell out of here." From where he stood he had an uninterrupted view of the road that stretched for miles. Nothing moved on it. It was empty: a glistening ribbon that wound into the mountains. For the first time in weeks he felt safe.

Steve reached down and touched the girl who lay across the driver. Her hand was warm.

"Hey, Roy! She's alive. Don't go away. Help me get her out. Come on!"

Muttering under his breath Roy climbed on to the cab, peered over Steve's shoulder.

"Well, all right," he said, with an uneasy glance along the mountain road. "We don't want to stick around here all day."

Steve gently lifted the girl, passed her through the cab doorway to Roy. As Roy laid her on the side of the cab he caught sight of the dead driver.

"Good grief!" he exclaimed, startled. "Take a look at that guy's face."

"Looks like he's been scratched up by a cat, the poor devil," Steve said, hurriedly climbing out of the cab.

Roy lifted one of the girl's hands.

"And here's your cat," he said. "There's blood and skin under her nails. Know what I think? The driver made a pass at her and she slashed him. She got his eyes and he drove off the road." He studied the girl. "Nice bit of homework, isn't she?" he went on. "I bet that poor punk thought he'd picked up a pushover. Say, she's a real looker, isn't she? I don't blame the punk trying to make her, do you?"

"Let's get her down," Steve said shortly, and together the two men carried the girl from the cab down on to the thick grass. Steve knelt beside her while Roy stood back and watched.

"She's got a nasty wound at the back of her head," Steve said. "We'll have to get that attended to right away."

"Forget it," Roy said, a sudden snarl in his voice. "Leave her here. She'll be all right. A floozy who bums rides can take care of herself. We don't want to be cluttered up with a twist, anyway. Some guy'll find her and will be glad of it."

Steve stared at him.

"We're certainly not leaving her here," he said sharply. "The girl's badly hurt."

"Then bring her down to the road and leave her there. Someone'll be along in awhile," Roy said, his white face twitching. "I don't want to be mixed up in this."

"She needs medical attention," Steve said quietly. "There's no place between here and my farm where I can leave her. That means I'm taking her home and I'm going to get Doc Fleming over to fix her. Anything to say against that?"

Roy's face was ugly with controlled rage.

"You can't kid me," he sneered. "You're like all the other hicks who live too long in the mountains. You're a horn-dog hermit. One look at a dame who's got something on the ball and you shoot your top."

Steve jumped to his feet. For a moment he looked as if he was going to hit his brother, but he choked down his anger, gave a twisted grin instead.

"You haven't changed much, have you?" he said. "And you're not going to get my rag out. Why don't you grow up? You've still got a mind like a schoolboy." He turned away and bent over the girl. As he moved her limbs, making sure she had no broken bones, she stirred.

"Why don't you undress her," Roy sneered, "instead of just pawing her over?"

Steve ignored him, although the back of his neck turned red. He felt the girl's pulse. It was strong under his fingers and her skin felt feverish.

"You'd better leave her, Steve," Roy went on. "You'll be sorry if you don't."

"Oh, shut up," Steve snapped, lifted the girl.

"O.K., but don't say I didn't warn you," Roy returned, shrugging indifferently. "I've got a hunch she's going to cause a hell of a lot of trouble. But why should I care? It'll be your headache."

"You've got to care about something," Steve said as he passed him and began his slow, careful walk to the van.

~§~

Silver Fox Farm was set in an enclosed valley of mountain peaks on Blue Mountain Summit, eight thousand feet above sea level. It was reached by a dirt road that branched off the highway and wound for four or five miles through big boulders and pine trees until it terminated at Steve's log cabin by the side of a lake, a pale blue sheet of water packed with rainbow trout.

A year back Steve had decided to throw up his job as an insurance salesman and breed foxes. He had saved money, discovered Blue Mountain Summit, bought the deed and moved in. The farm was still in its infancy, but Steve hoped it wouldn't be long before he could afford to hire help. The worst part of the life was the utter loneliness of the place; to have no one but his dog to talk to from one day to the next. When Roy called him a hermit he wasn't far from the truth.

Roy's coming should have solved the problem, but Steve was quick to realize that Roy was likely to be more of a nuisance than a companion. He was already beginning to regret the visit.

Roy had looked the cabin over with sour eyes and then had slouched down to the lakeside without a word, leaving Steve to carry the unconscious girl into the cabin without any help.

But as soon as Steve was out of sight, Roy retraced his steps, ran to the Buick. He looked furtively towards the cabin, then raised the hood and unscrewed the head of the accelerator switch, snapped the leads, pocketed the switch. Closing the hood, he lounged up to the wide verandah.

He could hear his brother moving about somewhere in the cabin and he sidled into the big living room, took in its rough comfort at a glance, crossed over to the gun rack, which was equipped with an iron bar on a hinge and a padlock that, when locked, secured the guns in their rack. Roy fastened the padlock, pocketed the key.

Steve came into the room a moment later.

"Put your floozy to bed?" Roy asked jeeringly.

"Cut it out," Steve snapped. "I don't like it, Roy, so pack it in, will you? Jesus!"

Roy eyed him over, grinned.

"That's too bad," he said; took out a cigarette and lit it.

"I can't figure out what's wrong with you," Steve said. "What gives? You've acted odd ever since we met."

"That's too bad, too," Roy said. "I am what I am."

Steve shrugged.

"I'm going over to Doc Fleming," he went on. "It'll take me the best part of two hours. Keep an eye on her, will you? She's got a concussion, I think, but she'll be all right until I return. Make sure she's comfortable."

"That certainly makes my day," Roy sneered. "What do I do? Hold her hand and fan her with my hat?"

"Come on, Roy," Steve said, keeping his temper with difficulty. "I'll get the Doc to bring his car and we'll get her out of here. But while she is here you might try to be a little helpful."

"Sure I will," Roy said. "You get off. I'll keep her amused. Dames like me."

Steve gave him a hard look, went out.

Roy watched his brother get into the van and try to start the engine. He grinned to himself.

He was still lounging against the verandah doorway when Steve, hot and furious, came bounding up the steps.

"You've been fooling with the van," Steve snapped, planting himself in front of his brother.

"Sure," Roy grinned. "What of it?"

Steve steadied himself.

"You've taken the accelerator head. Better hand it over, Roy. I'm not kidding."

"I'm keeping it. I told you to leave the twist, didn't I? Well, you've got her on your hands now. No one's coming here while I'm around, and no one's leaving here until I say so."

Steve clenched his fists.

"Look, Roy, I don't know what's on your mind, but you're not getting away with this. Hand over the switch or I'll take it. I don't want to get tough, but I'm not standing any more nonsense from you."

"Yeah?" Roy said, stepping back. "Then what do you think of this?" A gun suddenly jumped into his hand: an ugly-looking, blunt-nosed .38 automatic. "Still got the same ideas?" he asked, pointing the gun at his brother's chest.

Steve stepped back, his mouth tightening.

"Have you gone crazy?" he demanded. "Put that gun away."

"It's time you got wise," Roy said, speaking in a harsh low voice. "Get this straight: I'd think no more of plugging you than I'd think of treading on a beetle. Nuts to this brother stuff. To me you're just another dumb hick. One move out of turn and you'll get it." He backed away, hoisted himself up on the verandah rail, holding the gun loosely in his hand. "You may as well know it now. I'm in a jam: that's why I'm here. This dump's tailor-made as a hideout. No one would think of looking for me here. And no Doc Fleming is coming out here to tell all his goddamn patients he's seen me. That's the way it is, and you're going to like it. You and the twist will stay here until I'm ready to pull out. And don't try any tricks. I'm fast with this rod. Bigger guys than you have found that out."

Steve had recovered from his first startled surprise, but he could still not believe his brother was serious. How could he be so selfish?

"Why, this is crazy, Roy," he said. "I've got to get the Doc to the girl. Now come on, give me the switch and let me get off."

"Still playing stupid?" Roy sneered. "Listen: I've worked for Little Bernie's mob. Mean anything to you?"

Steve had read of Little Bernie: he was the modern day Dillinger.

"What do you mean?" he asked. "Little Bernie's a killer—wanted by the police. What the hell's come of you?"

Roy laughed.

"For the last year I've been sticking up banks," he said. "Made a lotta dough. I carried a gun for Bernie. It paid well. I made good."

"So that's it," Steve said, shocked and disgusted. "I might have guessed you'd hook up with a gang. You always were a weak fool, Roy."

Roy slid the gun back into his shoulder holster.

"I've done all right," he said. "Maybe I'm in trouble now, but it won't last long and then I'll spend the dough I've put by. I'm not like you, you hick, buried out in the wilds, surrounded by a lot of foxes. I know how to live."

Steve moved slowly towards him.

"You'd better give me that gun," he said quietly.

Roy grinned; his hand suddenly flashed to the holster and there was a spurt of flame. The sharp crack of the gun set up echoes across the lake. Something buzzed past Steve's ear.

"I could pop one through your thick skull just as easy," Roy said, "and I'll do it if you try anything funny. So now you know what's come of me."

He turned and slunk into the living-room, shaking the tension from his fingertips before dropping into an easy chair with an irritated groan.

Steve stood hesitating in the sunshine. He realized now that Roy meant what he said, but his thoughts were not for himself, but for the girl lying unconscious on his bed. He'd have to do something for her at once now Doc Fleming wasn't to come, and he was thankful he had a first-aid outfit and knew how to use it.

As he passed through the sitting-room, Roy drawled: "And I've locked up your pop-guns. I'll do all the shooting around here from now on."

Steve ignored him, went into his bedroom where the girl was lying. He examined the cut at the back of her head, then fetched his medical kit, a bowl of water and towels. He was just fixing the last safety-pin when the girl gave a little sigh and opened her eyes.

"Hello," he said, smiling at her. "Feeling better?"

She stared at him, her hand going to her head.

"My head hurts," she said. "What happened? Where am I?"

"I found you on the mountain road. You were in a truck accident. There's nothing to worry about. You have a cut head, but it's not bad."

"Truck?" she murmured, her eyes blank. "What truck? I can't remember…" Suddenly she struggled to sit up, but Steve gently pressed her back. "I can't remember anything. I can't think. Something's happened to my head!"

"It's all right," Steve said soothingly. "It'll come back. Just try and sleep. You'll be all right after a little sleep."

"But I don't know what's happened to me," the girl cried, catching his hand in hers. "I'm frightened. I don't know who I am. It's like I'm caught up in somebody else's dream."

"But it'll be all right," Steve said. "You must relax and not worry. When you wake up again you'll remember and you'll be all right."

She closed her eyes.

"You're kind," she said softly. "Stay with me. Please don't leave me."

"I'll be right here," Steve said. "Just take it easy."

She lay still for a few moments, then went limp, drifting once more into unconsciousness.

In the other room Roy sat in the armchair, a thoughtful expression on his face. If it hadn't been for the twist he could have stayed here and kept his brother in the dark, but now he'd have to watch out. Steve was a tough egg, and if he caught him off guard he wouldn't stand a chance. A sudden movement in the doorway made him jump round, his hand flying to his gun. A big mongrel dog came in, wagging his tail and sniffing Roy's shin.

"You punk," Roy said, grinning sheepishly. "You scared me silly. What a mangy mutt."

He shoved the dog away impatiently with his foot, watched it amble down the passage in search of its master.

Steve was grappling with a new problem as the dog peered round the door. He had just decided that he couldn't leave the girl lying on the bed like that. He hesitated to undress her, but there was nothing else he could do about it. The nearest woman was thirty miles down the other side of the mountain and he couldn't fetch her, anyway.

The dog entering the room relaxed his embarrassed tension. "Hello, Spot," he said. "You've arrived at the tricky moment." But the dog whined, backed to the door, its hair bristling.

"What's bugging you, buddy?" Steve asked, bewildered. The dog had only eyes for the girl on the bed. It slowly backed out of the room, then with a low whining howl it bolted down the passage into the open.

I guess we're all going screwy, Steve thought as he crossed the room to his chest of drawers and hunted for his best pajamas, a suit of white silk. He cut the sleeves down, tacked around the edges, performed on the trouser legs. He measured the finished effort against the girl, decided they'd do in a pinch.

Well, here goes, he thought, and hoped she wouldn't recover consciousness. He began to unhook the fastening on the girl's dress. In one of the sleeves he found a handkerchief; embroidered in a corner was the name Carol. He turned the handkerchief over in his fingers. Carol. Carol who? Who was she? Where did she come from? Was it possible that she had lost her memory, that she didn't know what had happened to her? Didn't know who she was? He looked down at her. She was lovely, he thought. Not the kind of girl who'd thumb a truck ride. There was some mystery behind all this.

He removed her shoes, then, raising her gently, slid her dress up her body, worked it carefully over her head. Under the dress she had on a simple, tailored one-piece garment, and he could see the lovely lines of her body as if she were naked.

For a brief moment he stared down at her. There was a tightness in his throat. Her beauty and helplessness filled him with pity and wonder. Seeing her like that, he lost his sense of embarrassment; it was like looking at a work of art and not at a living woman.

He did not hear Roy come in, nor was he aware that Roy, too, was staring with intent, hard eyes at the half-naked girl as she lay on the bed.

Steve lifted the girl to slip on the pajama coat.

"Not so fast," Roy said. "I want to look some more. What a stack-up! Why, damn it, she's even better than I thought."

Steve laid the girl down quickly, turned.

"Get out!" he said furiously.

"Hey, take it easy," Roy said, grinning, his eyes still on the girl. "Why should you have all the fun? I'll give you a hand. This is right up my alley."

Steve advanced on his brother, his eyes furious.

"Get out," he said, "and keep out."

Roy hesitated, then shrugged.

"O.K.," he said, and laughed. "You can have her until she's well, then I'll take over. I've got a way with women. She won't claw my eyes out. I know how to tame a wildcat like her. You watch and see, and don't think you'll stop me, you big hick. I'm going to have a lot of fun with this beauty," and still smiling he slouched down the passage and out on to the verandah.

CHAPTER II

A WEEK passed.

It was a bewildering week for Steve, kept hard at work running the farm, cooking the meals and nursing Carol. Roy made no effort to help him, and spent most of his time sitting on a high crag overlooking the mountain road and staring with fixed intensity into the empty valley.

Steve guessed that something or someone was terrifying his brother, and decided that Roy's fear and jumpy nerves were partly responsible for his vicious mood. This conclusion seemed right, for after the third day of nothing happening Roy became less nervy and hostile and finally ceased to watch the road. By the end of the week he was almost friendly—at least, as friendly as his sneering, selfish nature would permit. But he was still determined that Steve shouldn't leave Blue Mountain Summit while he was there, and Steve was forced to accept the situation.

Now that Carol had Steve's room, the two brothers shared the only other bedroom, and Steve had further proof of his brother's nervousness. Roy scarcely slept, tossing and turning through the night; and when he did doze off it was only to start up at the slightest sound.

Carol, however, was making rapid progress. She had been very ill for the first two days of her stay at the cabin, and Steve had to be constantly with her. But once the fever had left her, the wound began to heal, and she quickly gained strength.

But her mind remained a blank after the accident. She had no recollection of anything that had happened or of Glenview, nor who she was. She had complete and child-like faith in Steve, and as the days passed, the accepted conventions between man and woman swept aside by her helplessness, there grew up between them an odd and intimate relationship that bewildered Steve and awakened in Carol a deep feeling of affection for him which quickly turned to love.

Steve had always been shy with women. When Carol was ill and helpless he regarded her the way he would have regarded a sister (if he had had a sister), and attended to her needs impersonally and with no feeling except that of embarrassment. But when she was convalescing and showed so obviously that she was in love with him he did not know how to cope with the situation.

As soon as Carol was able to get up, she trailed rather helplessly after him wherever he went, and she was never happy unless she was with him. He was the pivot around which her life now revolved.

Not knowing of her mental history, Steve assumed that the head injury she had received had not only obliterated her memory but had, in some inexplicable way, broken down her adult reserve, giving her the mentality of a child. It would be out of the question, he argued to himself, to respond to her love for him or to take advantage of it, and be kept a tight reign on his feelings for her, refusing to believe that this love was anything more than an odd mental twist that would pass when her memory returned.

On the other hand, Roy was quick to realize that she might be easy prey, and she was seldom out of his mind. Although she paid him no attention, her mind being continually focused on Steve, he was confident that, given the right opportunity, he would make her yield to him.

One morning, as he was lounging by the lake, he saw her coming down the path through the pine trees. Steve was busy in the cabin and out of sight, and seizing this opportunity of having her to himself, Roy stepped squarely in her path.

"Hello," he said, eying her over. She looked radiant in the pale sunshine and her beauty quickened his blood. "Where have you been?"

"To feed the foxes," she said, her voice flat and casual. "I want to find Steve," she went on, adding, "You're in my way. Please step aside."

"But I want to talk to you," Roy said, moving closer. "It's time you and me got to know each other."

"I want to find Steve," she repeated; tried to step round him, but he prevented her.

"Never mind Steve. Come on, be nice. I like you, kid. I could go for you in a big way." He caught hold of her, pulled her to him. She stood against him, unresisting, uninterested, her eyes still looking towards the cabin. His hands went round her back and he held her close, feeling her soft hair against his face. It was like holding a tailor's dummy, but Roy was scarcely aware of her apathy. He had been without a woman for three weeks, and to Roy that was three weeks too long. He didn't care how apathetic a woman was so long as he could have his hands on her body and she didn't resist him.

"Please let me go," Carol said seriously. "I want to find Steve."

"He won't run away," Roy said thickly, swung her round, bending her back. He looked into her blank serene eyes, then crushed his mouth down on hers. Her lips were hard and tight under his, but her hands hung limply at her sides. She neither resisted nor complied.

Blood hammered inside his head as his hands slid over her, and he bent her further back, holding her close to him.

Then suddenly he was dragged round, and releasing Carol with an oath he caught a glimpse of Steve's infuriated face. Before he had a chance to reach for his gun Steve's fist crashed to his jaw and he fell heavily and lay on the pine needles, stunned.

"Do that again and I'll break your neck," Steve said evenly; put his arm round Carol, drew her away. "Come on," he said to her. "Let's get back to the cabin."

"Why did you hit him?" Carol asked, walking contentedly by Steve's side. "I didn't mind."

"I didn't want him to frighten you," Steve returned, giving her a quick, puzzled glance.

"I wasn't frightened. But I don't like him," Carol said. "If you don't want him to do that to me again I won't let him. I didn't know if that's what you wanted."

"No," Steve said, bewildered by this reasoning. "I don't want him to do that again."

Roy watched them go, then he got slowly to his feet. He was so elated that Carol hadn't resisted him that he almost forgot that Steve had knocked him down. He had kissed her! It had been like taking candy from a kid. If Steve hadn't shoved his oar in... why, she was a pushover!

That night, when Roy was in bed, Steve came into the bedroom after locking up. Roy had kept out of the way all day, but now, face to face once more with Steve, he decided to take the initiative before his brother slugged him.

"You watch your fists, you big hick," he said, scowling. "The next time you start something like that you'll pick lead out of your belly."

"Then keep your hands off the girl," Steve said, sitting on the edge of his bed. "Can't you see she's not normal? That bang on the head's done something to her. She's like a kid. So lay off, Roy. There can be no fun in fooling around with a girl in her mental state."

"Can't there?" Roy grinned. "All cats are grey in the dark whether they're nuts or normal. She's just a woman to me, and I like women."

"Lay off or we'll have a showdown," Steve said, his face grim. "I don't care if you are my brother."

"You've some hopes," Roy said. "What's to stop me knocking you off? No one would find you here for months, and by that time I'd be miles away. You watch your step. I can do what I like here, and the sooner you realize it the better."

Steve kicked off his shoes, began to undress.

"I'm telling you. Keep your hands off Carol."

"She likes me. She let me kiss her, didn't she? You can't kid me a girl with her stack-up doesn't like being kissed. If you hadn't shoved your oar in we'd have got along fine together."

"I won't tell you again," Steve said quietly. "If I have to take you, I'll take you, gun or no gun."

The two men stared at each other for a long moment. Roy's eyes were the first to give ground.

"Aw, nuts to you," he said, rolled over.

Steve got into bed.

"What are you scared of?" he asked abruptly. "You think I don't know something's going on? Who's after you?"

Roy whipped round, half sat up.

"Shut your mouth. I'm not scared of anyone."

"But you are. You're as jumpy as a flea. Who are you running away from—the police?"

Roy jerked up the ugly blunt-nosed automatic.

"I'll blast a hole in you if you don't shut up," he snarled, his face white and twitching. "Why I haven't knocked you off before—"

"Because you're afraid to be left alone," Steve said quietly. "You want me behind you when what you're expecting to happen happens."

Roy dropped back on his pillow, slid the gun out of sight under the blanket.

"You're crazy," he said, turned off the light. "You don't know what you're talking about. I'm going to sleep."

But he didn't. He lay awake for hours, listening to Steve's heavy breathing, seeing the moonlight on the big pine trees through the open window.

The night was quiet and still. A soft breeze rustled in the trees and the water swirled gently round the jetty.

Roy thought of Carol, wondered if he could leave the room without waking his brother. If he could get into Carol's room, the rest would be easy; he was sure of that. The idea of holding Carol once more in his arms suddenly galvanized him into action. He half raised himself, looked across at Steve. As he did so a movement outside the cabin caught his eye. His desires drained from him and he sat up, his heart racing.

A shadow crossed the open window: a gliding, silent shadow that had come and gone before his eyes had scarcely time to register it.

Fear gripped him and he lay transfixed in bed, staring at the window.

A light step sounded on the verandah, then another. A board creaked. The sound came nearer.

Roy grabbed hold of Steve, shook him violently.

Steve woke instantly, sat up, feeling Roy's frenzied fingers digging into his arm. He stared at Roy's white face, sensed immediately that something was wrong.

"What's up?" he asked, keeping his voice low.

"Someone's outside," Roy said. His voice was shaking. "Listen. Hear that?"

Somewhere down by the lake Spot began to howl mournfully. The low baying echoed off the trees on the opposite shore.

Steve swung his legs out of bed, paused as he saw the shadow once more at the window. He leaned forward.

"It's Carol, you fool," he said. "Pull yourself together."

The breath whistled through Roy's clenched teeth.

"Carol? What's she doing out there? You sure?"

"I can see her," Steve said, crept to the window.

After a moment's hesitation Roy joined him. Carol was pacing up and down the verandah. She had on Steve's cut-down pajamas and her feet were bare.

"Damn her," Roy said softly. "She scared the pants off me. What's she doing?"

"Quiet," Steve whispered. "Maybe she's walking in her sleep."

Roy grunted. Now he had recovered from his fright the picture Carol made, bare-footed, in the white silk pajamas, her red hair loose on her shoulders, fired his blood.

"She's a looker, isn't she?" he said, speaking his thoughts aloud. "What a shape she's got!"

Steve made an impatient movement. He was puzzled, wondering what the girl was doing, pacing up and down out there.

Suddenly Carol paused, looked in their direction as if sensing she was being watched. The moonlight fell directly on her face, and both men saw a change in her expression that startled them. The muscles in her face seemed to tighten, the lines contort, giving her a sly look of animal cunning. There was a nervous tic at the side of her mouth and her eyes were like pieces of glass and as soulless. Steve scarcely recognized her. Doubt flooded his mind.

Spot howled miserably from his hiding-place across the yard, and Carol turned swiftly to look in that direction. Her whole bearing was as quick and lithe as the movements of a jungle cat, and as dangerous. Then, as Spot howled again, she disappeared through the open window of her room.

"What the hell do you make of that?" Roy asked uneasily. "Did you see the way she looked just now? Did you see that expression?"

"Yes," Steve said, worried. "I'd better find out what she's doing. I think she's having a fever dream."

"Take care she doesn't scratch your eyes out," Roy said with an uneasy laugh. "She could do anything the way she looked just now."

Steve pulled on a dressing-gown, took a flashlight and went down the passage to Carol's room. He opened the door quietly.

Carol was in bed, her eyes closed, the moonlight on her face. She looked as lovely and as serene as she always did, and when Steve called to her, she didn't move.

He stood for a moment watching her, then quietly shut the door and returned to his room.

He slept as badly as Roy that night.

~§~

Sam Garland and Joe were cleaning an ambulance in the big garage at the rear of Glenview Mental Sanatorium.

"Don't look now," Sam said, polishing away, "but that news hawk's heading this way."

Joe showed his two gold teeth.

"I like that guy. He's persistent. Think we could bite his ear for a few potatoes?"

"Good idea," Sam said, stood back to admire the glittering chromium headlamps.

Phil Magarth, lean, tall, carelessly dressed, sauntered up to them. He had been around for the past week trying to get some worthwhile information about the patient who had escaped from the sanatorium, but apart from a short, useless statement from Dr. Travers and a curt "Get the hell out of here" from Sheriff Kamp, he had got nowhere.

Magarth, the local reporter for the district as well as a special correspondent for a number of Mid-West newspapers, had an instinct for news, and he was sure there was a big story behind the escape if he could get at it. Having tried every other avenue for further information without success, he decided to see what he could learn from Garland and Joe.

"Hello, boys," he said, draping himself over the hood of the ambulance: "Found that loony yet?"

"No use asking us," Garland said, resuming his polishing. "We're just hired helps, ain't we, Joe?"

"That's right," Joe said, winked at Magarth.

"I was reckoning you boys knew something," Magarth said, jingling his loose change suggestively. "Who the dame is, for instance. My expense account is fat with inactivity, if that interests you."

Both Garland and Joe lost their indifferent expressions.

"How fat would it be?" Garland asked cautiously.

"Well, maybe 'fat's' the wrong word. I should have said bloated. If you know anything don't be scared to open your little mouths."

"We won't," Garland said, looked cautiously over his shoulder. "A hundred bucks would buy it, wouldn't it, Joe?"

"Just about," Joe said, rubbing his hands in anticipation of a big pay-off. "A hundred each."

Magarth winced.

"I guess I'll try that blonde nurse. By the circles under her eyes she'd give herself away as well as information for two hundred bucks."

Garland's face fell.

"He's right," he said to Joe.

"But you'd never be the same guy again," Joe said seriously. "I've tried her. It's like wrestling with a bear-trap."

"I like 'em that way," Magarth said simply. "Ever since I was knee-high to an ant I've been handling energetic women. You don't have to worry about me." He tilted his hat over his nose, squinted at Garland. "Of course, if you'd like to make it a hundred bucks I'd play along with you. I'm the self-sacrificing type."

Garland and Joe exchanged glances.

"O.K.," Garland said. "It's a deal."

"It'll have to be good for the dough," Magarth reminded him.

"It's better than good—it's sensational," Garland said. "Front page stuff in six-inch type."

"Bigger than Pearl Harbor," Joe said.

"Bigger than the Atom Bomb," Garland added, not to be outdone.

Magarth produced a roll of notes, peeled off five twenty-dollar bills.

"I came heeled guessing you two would sing," he said, dangling the bills. "Let's hear it."

"John Blandish's heiress," Sam said, grabbed the notes. "How do you like that?"

Magarth took a step forward.

"What do you mean?" he said, a rasp in his voice. "What kind of fluff's this?"

"What I say," Sam said. "Ain't you heard of John Blandish? Well, this guy had a daughter and she was kidnapped..."

~§~

Steve and Carol breakfasted alone together the next morning. Roy had gone out early after trout. His absence eased the tension in Steve's mood.

"Did you sleep all right last night?" Steve asked casually as he poured coffee.

"I dreamed," she returned. "I always dream."

"But did you get up in the night?" Steve smiled at her. "I thought I heard someone moving about in the cabin. Maybe I was dreaming, too."

"Oh, no," she said, touched her temples with slim fingers. "But something did happen. I can't remember. I can't remember anything. It frightens me." She reached across the table for his hand. "I don't know what I would do without you. I feel so safe with you."

Steve grinned uncomfortably, patted her hand.

"You'd be all right," he said. "What do you dream about, Carol? Maybe your dreams can help us learn more of your past."

"I don't really remember. I seem to dream the same dream over and over again. It's something to do with a nurse. I don't know what she does, but it's always the same nurse. She has a horrible look in her eyes and she stands over me. I am so frightened in my dreams, and I wake up frightened, my heart beating, and the dark frightens me."

Steve worried about her all day, and he was still worrying when Roy returned after dark.

Roy was silent and surly until bedtime, his eyes continually on Carol. He was already in bed when Steve came in after locking up, and he pretended to be asleep.

Steve glanced at him, shrugged, and then got into bed. He was tired of his brother's surly behavior. He longed to be rid of him and reclaim his peace and quiet.

Later in the night Roy sat up, called softly, and when Steve made no reply he cautiously pushed off his blanket. He was trembling with excitement and desire. All day he had brooded about Carol, working himself up, determined that tonight when Steve was asleep he'd go to her. She had let him kiss her: showed no fight. It should be easy so long as he could get out of the room without waking Steve. Quietly he slid out of bed.

Steve stirred in his sleep and Roy waited, tense, ready to slip back to bed, but Steve slept on. Moving softly, Roy left the room, closed the door, stood listening.

Carol's room was at the end of the passage. There was no sound but the wind rustling in the trees and the lake water swirling against the jetty.

Roy crept down the passage, listened at Carol's door, heard nothing, turned the handle and went in.

He could see Carol lying in the bed, her arms uncovered, her hair like a red halo on the pillow. She looked very beautiful with the moonlight failing directly on her face, and as he came in she opened her eyes. She didn't seem alarmed. Her eyes were wide but serene.

"Hello, kid," Roy said. His tongue felt a little too big for his mouth and his skin was feverish. "I've come to keep you company."

She didn't say anything but watched him cross the room, her eyes on his.

"You're not scared of me, are you?" he asked. Her beauty made him shiver.

"Oh, no," she said quietly. "I thought you would come tonight. I've been dreaming about you."

Roy started.

"You mean you wanted me to come?" he asked, sitting on the bed by her side.

She looked gravely up at him.

"I felt your eyes on me all this evening. Wherever I went you watched me. I felt you'd come tonight."

Roy grinned.

"And I've thought about you all day, too," he said, put his hand on hers. Her hand was warm and limp, unresisting. "I wanted to kiss you again."

"Steve doesn't want you to do that."

"Steve won't know. He's asleep. You liked it, didn't you?"

His face was close to hers now and his hand touched her breasts. She didn't flinch, but stared at him abstractedly.

"Undo that," he went on, touching the buttons on the silk jacket. "Come on, Carol, come on. I'm not going to hurt you."

The girl mechanically, to his astonishment, undid the pajama buttons, and he touched her bare skin.

"You're beautiful, kid," he said, not knowing quite what he was saying. "Your skin is like porcelain," and his hands eagerly covered her breasts.

There was a blank fixed look in her eyes and she seemed to listen only vaguely to what he said.

His hands moved round her back and he lifted her. And then suddenly she gave a soft metallic little laugh that startled him.

"What's so funny about this?" he asked, angry, and hungrily crushed his mouth down on hers.

For a brief moment she lay motionless in his arms, then her arms, like steel bands, slid round his neck and gripped the back of his neck and shoulders and her teeth sank into his lips.

In the other room Steve woke suddenly. One moment he was asleep, the next wide awake and sitting up, staring round the room, a startled, puzzled expression on his face.

What woke me like that? he wondered, looked across at Roy's bed, which was in the darkest part of the room. He thought he could make out Roy's outline, looked at the window. *Was Carol out there again? Was that why he had awakened so suddenly?*

He got out of bed, went to the window. There was no one on the verandah. He could see Spot down by the outhouses. The dog was looking towards the cabin, but it made no sound.

Steve shook his head, yawned, turned back to bed.

Guess I was dreaming, he thought, then something prompted him to go over to Roy's bed: it was empty. Instantly he thought of Carol and ran to the door.

A wild, agonized scream rang through the cabin. There was a moment's silence, then a sobbing, croaking voice yelled: "Steve! Quick! Help me!"

The hair on Steve's neck bristled at the sound of Roy's voice, and he flung open the door, stepped into the passage.

Roy was coming towards him, bent double, his hands hiding his face. Blood ran between his fingers, dripped on to the floor.

"What's happened?' Steve gasped, standing frozen.

"It's my eyes!" Roy sobbed. "She's blinded me! Help me! For God's sake, do something!"

Steve caught hold of him.

"What have you done to her?" he cried, pushed the groaning man aside and ran into Carol's room. The room was empty. He ran to the window and came to an abrupt stop.

Carol was standing on the top verandah step looking towards him. She was naked to the waist, and her eyes glowed like cat's eyes in the moonlight.

He stood transfixed. He had never seen a wilder, more beautiful creature as the one he looked at now. Her red hair, gleaming like beaten bronze in the white light of the moon; the satin-white luster of her skin, cold-looking against the dark shadows of the cabin wall; the curve of her breasts; her tense, dangerous attitude like a jungle cat, and the way she held her hands before her like two claws, startled him, and yet strangely excited him.

Then she turned and ran down the steps and across the yard.

"Carol!" Steve cried, starting forward. "Carol, come back."

But she had already vanished into the pine wood. She had moved with incredible swiftness.

Not knowing what to do, Steve stood hesitating, then the sound of his brother's groans made him return to the passage.

"Pull yourself together," he said impatiently. "You can't be so badly hurt."

"She's blinded me, damn you!" Roy screamed frantically, and took his hands from his eyes.

Steve stepped back, sick and cold.

Roy's eyes swam in blood. Cruel long nail-marks ran down his forehead, across his eyelids, down his cheeks. He was on the point of collapse and sagged against the wall, moaning, his body shivering.

"Save my eyes," he begged. "Don't let me go blind. Don't leave me, Steve. She'll come back. She's mad... a killer... look what she's done to me."

Steve took hold of him, half carried, half dragged him into the bedroom.

"Take it easy," he said curtly as he laid the sobbing wreck on the bed. "I'll fix you up. Just take it easy." He ran from the room for his medical chest, snatched up a kettle from the stove.

"Don't leave me!" Roy wailed. "I can't see! She'll come back!"

"All right, all right," Steve shouted from the kitchen, unnerved himself. He returned to the bedroom. "I'm here now. Let me bathe your eyes. I think it's only because they're bleeding so badly you can't see."

"I'm blind! I know I'm blind," Roy groaned. "Stick by me, Steve. They're after me... they'll kill me if they ever find me. I'm helpless now. I can't save myself."

"Who're after you?" Steve asked sharply as he poured the warm water into a bowl.

"The Sullivans," Roy said, his hand groping vainly for Steve's. "They mean nothing to you. No one knows them. They work secretly... professional killers. Little Bernie's hired them to get me."

"They won't get you here," Steve said shortly. "You're safe here. Lie still. I'm going to bathe your eyes. It may hurt."

"Don't touch me!" Roy cried, cowering back. "I can't stand any more pain."

Steve waited.

"What did you do to her?" he asked when Roy had calmed down a little.

"Nothing!" Roy groaned. "She wanted me to come to her. She said so. She let me kiss her. Then I couldn't get away from her. She's strong. She had me round the neck. She bit my mouth. It was hell... her eyes were like lamps. I fought her off, and as I got away she slashed me. It was like a tiger striking. She's mad... a wild beast."

"She was frightened," Steve said, chilled. "I warned you to leave her alone."

"If the Sullivans come now... what shall I do? Steve! You won't let them kill me?" Roy sat up, groped wildly under his pillow. "Here, take the gun. You must shoot on sight... you can't mistake them."

"Take it easy," Steve said impatiently. "You're safe here..."

"You don't know them. They're professional killers. They never let up once they're hired to kill. They go on and on. Little Bernie's paid them well. They'll find me. I know they'll find me."

"But why?" Steve demanded. "Why should they want to kill you? What are you to them?"

Roy caught hold of his coat.

"Bernie and I pulled a big bank robbery. I skipped with the dough. Bernie had been cheating me, and I wanted to get even. Twenty thousand dollars, and I've salted it away, but Bernie went to the Sullivans. He knew they'd fix me, and they will!"

"They won't find you here," Steve repeated. "You might as well be on the moon."

"They'll find me," Roy groaned. "Keep the gun handy. Shoot on sight... they're like two black crows... that's what they look like... two black crows."

"Lie down. I'm going to bathe this blood away," Steve said, forcing his brother back on the pillow. "Lie still."

Roy screamed when the wet cotton-wool touched his eyes.

~§~

Two black crows.

The description fit the Sullivans. They were a sinister looking couple in their black, tight-fitting overcoats, black slouch hats, black concertina-shaped trousers and black-pointed shoes. Knotted round each short thick throat was a black silk scarf.

A few years ago they had been the star act of a small traveling circus, and they had been billed as the famous Sullivan brothers. But they were not brothers: their real names were Max Geza and Frank Kurt. By profession they were knife-throwers and trick marksmen. The finale of their act was to throw phosphorus-painted knives at a girl who stood against a black velvet-covered board. The stage was in darkness and the audience could see only the flying knives, which gradually outlined the figure of the girl as the knives slammed into the board an inch from her shivering skin. It was a sensational act and might have gone on for years, only the Sullivans got bored with the circus and with the girl.

It was the girl really that made them want to break up the act. She was a nice little thing and willing enough, but she just didn't understand the Sullivans' technique after business hours; besides, she fell in love with a clown, and that added to her difficulties, too.

The Sullivans tried to get another girl, but for the money they paid they couldn't find a girl willing to risk the flying knives and also be accommodating after 'business hours.' So they got fed up with the circus and told the manager they wanted to quit, but the manager refused to release them from their contract. Their act, he reckoned, kept the show together—and it did.

So one night Max solved all their problems by throwing a knife with deliberate aim and it pinned the girl through her throat to the board, and that finished the act, got rid of the girl and broke the contract. Max couldn't understand why he hadn't thought of the solution, which was simple enough, before.

It was Max's idea for them to become professional killers, Death interested him. Taking human life seemed to him to be God-like, and he liked to regard himself as a man set above and apart from other men. Besides, he wanted big money; he was tired of the peanut stuff they were making in the circus.

There were hundreds of men and women wishing to get rid of someone, he reasoned. A professional killer would be a benefit to Society. Since no motive could be proved, the killer had an excellent chance of avoiding detection, and if the killing was carefully planned and executed there was no reason why they should ever be caught. Frank welcomed the idea. Frank was never strong on ideas himself, but he was a natural enthusiast. Max knew he couldn't wish for a better partner. So these two passed the word round that they would undertake any killing for the fee of three thousand dollars and a hundred dollars a week expenses. Even the Sullivans were surprised how quickly the idea caught on in certain circles, and how many commissions came their way.

They traveled all over the country in a big black Packard Clipper: two black crows who brought death silently and secretly and were never detected. The police didn't know about them, for their victims feared the police and couldn't go to them for protection. There were times when word would reach the intended victim that the Sullivans were after him and he'd go into hiding. It was a matter of complete indifference to the Sullivans whether they had to hunt out their victim or whether they had merely to drive up to his house and shoot him as he opened the door. All they required was a photograph of the victim, his name and last address. Finding him was part of their service. They were men of few needs. The hundred dollars they charged for their weekly expenses amply sufficed. The three thousand dollar fee was never touched, but salted away against the time when they should retire. Both Max and Frank were passionately fond of birds, and they planned to buy themselves a bird business when they had saved sufficient capital to set up in a big way.

Little Bernie got in touch with them a day after Roy had gypped him out of the proceeds of the bank robbery. The Sullivans undertook to murder Roy for five thousand dollars. They felt that as Little Bernie was a big shot and had plenty of hired help to do his own killing he wouldn't come to them unless he anticipated the job would be long and difficult. To be on the safe side they jacked up the fee.

The difficulty, of course, was to find Roy. He had been warned that the Sullivans were after him and had immediately vanished from his usual haunts. Enquiries showed that he had left New York and had covered his tracks so well that his trail ended at the Pennsylvania station: the task of picking up the trail again appeared to be a hopeless one, a dead end.

But not to the Sullivans. They were expert man-hunters. To find your victim quickly, they reasoned, you must know his habits, where his relations are, whether he has a girlfriend, and if so, where she is. Once you have that data all you have to do is to exercise a little patience: sooner or later you find your man.

It was an easy matter for them to discover that Roy had a brother, who, a year ago, was an insurance salesman in Kansas City. They wasted time going to Kansas City, for there they learned that Steve Larson had quit the insurance business and was believed to be fox-farming somewhere, but where no one seemed to know.

A week passed while the Sullivans sat in their hotel bedroom and took it in turns to call every fox farm equipment store in the district and beyond, asking for the address of Steve Larson. They gave the name of a reputable firm of solicitors when making their call and stated that as Larson had come into a large sum of money they were anxious to get in touch with him. After making many calls their patience was finally rewarded. A firm in Bonner Springs had supplied Steve Larson with equipment and was delighted to give his address. It was all they needed to know.

Three days later a big black Packard Clipper slid into Point Breese, a little valley town twenty miles or so from Blue Mountain Summit.

The Sullivans parked outside a saloon, left the Packard and entered the deserted bar. They had become so accustomed to their routine entrance into the circus ring that they unconsciously walked as one man, each taking the same short quick step, each swinging his arms the same length; one looking like the other's shadow. In their black clothes, moving as they did, they immediately attracted attention, and people stared after them, conscious of a feeling of uneasiness, of being spooked, as if they had seen an apparition.

Because in their circus days they had been supposed to be brothers, they had endeavored to look alike, and the habit stuck. They both wore penciled-line black moustaches and their hair cut very close. But here the similarity ended. Max was a couple of inches shorter than Frank. His face was small and white and he had tight lips. Frank was fat and soft. His nose was hooked, his mouth was loose, and he had a habit of moistening his lips with his tongue before he said anything. His eyes were as animated as glass marbles.

The Sullivans pulled up two high stools close to the bar and sat down, resting their gloved hands on the counter.

The barman eyed them over, thought they looked a dangerous, ugly pair, but he smiled because he was anxious to have no trouble.

"Yes, gentlemen?" he said, wiped the counter before them.

"Two lemonades," Max said. His voice was high-pitched, soft and lilting as a canary's.

The barman served them, his face expressionless; then as he moved away Max crooked a finger at him.

"What goes on in this town?" he asked, sipped his lemonade, stared at the barman with dead eyes. "Tell us the news. We're strangers here."

"Right now there's plenty of excitement in town," the barman said, quite eager to talk about the topic of the hour. "We'll be on the front page of every newspaper in the country tomorrow. I've just heard it from a newspaper reporter. He gave me the whole story straight from his notes."

"What's all the fuss?" Max asked, raising his eyebrows.

"A mental patient escaped from Glenview Sanatorium," the barman explained. "It's only just leaked out she's the heiress to six million bucks."

"And where's Glenview Sanatorium?" Max asked.

"Up the hill; five miles from here on the Oakville road," the barman told him. "This dame got a ride in a truck as far as here. They found the wrecked truck a mile or so up the road. They reckon she killed the driver."

"But did they find her?" Frank asked, sipped his lemonade, then blotted his lips with the back of his glove.

"I guess not. They're still looking for her. We had the cops in here this morning. I've never seen so many cops."

Max's eyes flickered.

"How come a nut has all that dough?"

"She got it from John Blandish, the meat king. Maybe you remember the Blandish kidnapping? She's his grand-daughter, and she's the sole heir to the family fortune."

"I remember," Frank said. "Must be twenty years ago."

"That's right," the barman said. "The kidnapper was the father. He was crazy in the head. So's the daughter. If they don't find her in fourteen days they won't be able to take her back. That's the law of the State. Then she'll come into the dough and no one can control it. That's why there's all this uproar. Everyone wants to get their mitts on the dame."

The Sullivans finished their lemonade.

"She's a real nut—dangerous?" Max asked.

The barman nodded his head vigorously.

"You bet... a killer."

"Just in case we run into her, how does she look?"

"They say she's a redhead and peach to look at. She's got a scar on her left wrist."

"We'll know her," Frank said. He put down a dollar bill on the counter. "Would there be a fox farm around here some place?" he went on casually.

The barman gave him change.

"Sure. Larson's Silver Fox Farm up on Blue Mountain summit."

"Far?"

"Best part of twenty miles."

Max looked at his watch. It was 9:30 pm.

"We're interested in foxes," he said carefully. "We thought we might look 'em over. Is he in the market?"

"I guess so," the barman said, surprised. These two didn't look like fur men.

They nodded, turned to the door, turned back again.

"Is this fella up there alone?" Max asked softly.

"You mean does he run the farm alone? Sure, but there's a guy staying with him now. I saw them go through a week ago."

The Sullivans' faces were wooden.

"So long," Frank said, and together they walked out of the bar to the Packard Clipper.

Phil Magarth, lounging against a tree, watched them drive away. He pulled his long nose thoughtfully, tilted his hat further to the back of his head and wandered into the bar they had just left.

"Hi, Tom," he said, dragging up a stool and folding himself down on it wearily. "Let's start a famine in whisky."

"Hello, Mr. Magarth," the barman said, grinning. "Any more news of the nut?"

"Not a sound," Magarth returned, helping himself from the black bottle the barman had set before him.

"I was telling those two guys about your story. Did you see them? Two guys in black."

"Yeah."

The barman hesitated, scratched his head.

"Nasty-looking couple; said they were in furs."

"Did they?" Magarth looked interested. "Don't look like fur men, do they? I've seen 'em before. In fact I've seen them three times over a period of a couple of years, and each time a guy died suddenly and violently. Make anything of that?"

The barman stared at him.

"What do you mean, Mr. Magarth?"

"I don't know," Magarth said truthfully. "Only you wouldn't forget a couple of guys like those two, would you? Ever heard of the Sullivan brothers?"

"I guess not."

"Maybe they don't exist, but there's a story going round that the Sullivans are professional killers. They call on a guy any-where in the country and he turns his toes up quick. I wonder if those two are the Sullivans." He was now talking his thoughts aloud. "What did they want?"

"They were asking for Steve Larson," the barman said, worried. "Asked if he was alone."

"The fox farmer?" Magarth asked. "Up on Blue Mountain Summit?"

"Yeah, that's the fella. Nice guy. Buys his whisky from me. I see him once a month. Saw him a week ago, but he didn't look in. He was going through with another guy."

"He was? And these two were asking for him?"

The barman nodded.

"You don't think—"

Magarth cut him short with a dismissive wave of his hand.

"I never think," he said. "I find out; and when I've found
out I sit at my typewriter and hammer out a lot of crap that
you read at breakfast. Hell of a life, isn't it?" He turned to the
door, turned back again. "I hope I don't need to tell you, Tom,
but keep this under your bonnet."

~§~

Roy's eyelids were so swollen that it was impossible to tell
yet whether or not serious damage had been done. Steve had
stopped the bleeding, and working quickly he made his
brother as comfortable as he could.

"I'm going after Carol," he said when he had finished. "I
can't—"

But Roy's wail of protest cut him short.

"No!" Roy cried, starting up. "You can't leave me like this.
She may be hiding out there, waiting for you to come after
her. That's what she wants... she wants to finish me! She's a
maniac."

"Oh, shut up!" Steve exclaimed savagely. "I'm going; so
stop whining."

"Don't be a fool, Steve," Roy gasped and reached out
blindly. "She's dangerous... she'll kill you... claw you up the
way she clawed me."

Steve looked out into the moonlit night. He didn't want to
go out there in the dark, but he couldn't let Carol roam
around without making an effort to find her. He thought of
the truck driver's lacerated eyes, remembered the sly animal
cunning he had seen in Carol's face as she paced the verandah
the previous night, looked down at the sobbing wreck who
whined not to be left alone, and a chill ran through him.
*Suppose she was dangerous... a lunatic? Suppose that bang
on the head had done something to her? But that wasn't
possible. You were born a lunatic. Bangs on the head didn't
make you homicidal. She had been scared silly. That was the
explanation. First the truck driver had tried to assault her;
then Roy. Well, they had got what was coming to them. She
wouldn't do that to him. So long as he didn't frighten her it'd
be all right.*

"I'm going, Roy," Steve said, and shoved the gun into his brother's hand. "Hang on to that. If she does comes back, fire into the ceiling. I'm not going far."

He struggled into his clothes, deaf to Roy's protests.

"You won't come back," Roy moaned. "I know you won't. She'll lie in wait for you. You don't know how strong she is She'll kill you Steve, and then what'll happen to me? I'm helpless! I can't see!" His voice rose and he sat up in bed. "I'm blind! Stay with me, Steve! Don't leave me!"

"Will you shut up?" Steve exclaimed, exasperated: "You asked for it and you damn well got it. So stop squealing."

He snatched up his flashlight, went out into the yard. All was quiet. The moon rode high above the pine trees, casting deep shadows.

There was no sign of Spot, and Steve felt unpleasantly alone. He walked down to the lake, stood at the water's edge, listening, his eyes trying to pierce the thick darkness of the woods. *That's the way she went,* he thought uneasily. *Was she hiding there, watching him?*

He began to walk along the path by the lake. A sudden flurry in a nearby tree brought him to an abrupt stop. His heart began to thud against his ribs. A bird crashed through the branches of the pines, flew away across the lake. Steve drew in a sharp breath. He hadn't realized how strung up he was. His nerves were shot.

Ahead, the path curved away from the lake and wound into the wood. It was dark there and he stopped again, hesitating to leave the moonlit path and enter the blackness that yawned before him.

"Carol!" he called sharply. "It's Steve. Where are you, Carol?"

The faint echo of his voice floated across the lake.

Where are you, Carol?

It had a spooky sound, like a voice without a body, jeering at him.

He moved on and darkness closed in on him. He could see nothing now and he turned on his flashlight. The powerful beam lit up the narrow path. Overhead the branches of the pines seemed to be reaching down, threatening him. He kept on, pausing every now and then to listen. He became suddenly aware that he was not alone, that he was being watched, and turning quickly, he flashed the beam of the flashlight around, lighting up bushes and trees, but he could see no one.

"Are you there, Carol?" he called. His voice was a little shaky. "It's Steve. I want you, Carol."

Behind him a shadowy figure rose out of the bushes, crept silently upon him.

In front of him a dead branch snapped loudly. He swung the beam of his flashlight in that direction, caught his breath sharply. A man stood in the bright beam of the flashlight: a man dressed in black; a heavy .45 revolver in his hand.

"Reach up, Larson," Max said softly.

Two hands patted his pockets from behind. He glanced round, a chill crawling up his spine, saw a second man in black: Frank.

The two black crows: the Sullivans! Steve thought, and his mouth went dry.

"Who are you?" he demanded, keeping his voice steady with an effort.

"Button up," Max said, shoving the barrel of the .45 into Steve's ribs. "We'll do the talking. Who's Carol? And what are you doing out here?"

"She's a friend, staying with me," Steve said shortly. "I was looking for her."

Max and Frank exchanged glances.

"Roy up at the cabin?" Max asked softly.

Steve hesitated. There was no point in lying. They had only to go up there and see for themselves.

"Yes," he said.

"You watch this guy, Frank," Max said. "I'll handle Roy."

"And the girl?"

"If she doesn't show up, it don't matter. If she does, we'll fix her," Max said. "Better bring him along. Make sure there aren't any heroics. He looks like he's chopped a lot of firewood."

He walked away towards the cabin.

Frank pushed his gun into Steve.

"Get moving," he said, "and don't try any tricks. I know 'em all. And don't shout when you get near the cabin. You'll only be throwing your life away."

Steve walked after Max. He was pretty sure that when these two had killed Roy, they'd kill him, too. But he wasn't worrying about himself. He was thinking of Carol. What would happen to her? He was surprised to find that he had a sudden tightness in his throat when he thought of her. Whatever happened, he decided, she can't fall into the hands of these two.

"Can't you fellows leave us alone?" he said. "We're not doing you any harm."

"Give it a rest," Frank said. "You don't want to make it any harder for yourself. We ain't worrying about you: it's Roy we're after."

"But what's he done to you?" Steve asked. "If it's money you want, I've enough. You don't have to kill him."

"We've got our dough," Frank returned. "Once we take a guy's dough we give him satisfaction. That's the way we do our business."

There was a note of flat finality in his voice that told Steve it would be useless to plead for his brother. He walked on, a sick feeling in his stomach. It was like living through a realistic nightmare.

At the head of the road leading to the cabin he saw the big black Packard. It had been reversed up the road; its long hood pointing to the valley.

If I could reach that, he thought, *I might ditch these two, but there's nothing I can do for Roy.*

There was nothing he could do for Roy. Max was already looking through the open French windows at Roy, who lay on the bed, his hand grasping the gun.

Max came up the verandah steps like a shadow, his rubber-soled shoes soundless on the wooden boards.

Roy had been listening all the time, his nerves tight, fear gripping his throat. He listened with an intentness that made his head ache, expecting any moment for Carol to come in out of the night and finish him. He didn't think of the Sullivans. He was now sure he was safe from them, believed because they always worked so quickly that, as they hadn't found him before, they would never find him.

He wondered how long Steve would be: whether he would return. The pain in his eyes had turned to a dull ache. He was sick with self pity and fear.

Max moved silently into the room, saw the gun in Roy's hand and grinned sourly. He crept across the room until he was by the bed. It would have been easy to have finished Roy now: too easy. Max was bored with easy death. A death without suffering was humdrum. He liked to innovate and squeeze every drop of excitement out of the process.

Roy groaned to himself, let go of the gun to hold his aching head between his hands. Max picked up the gun, shoved it into his hip pocket. He waited, watching the blind man, wondering how he would react when he had found the gun gone.

After a moment or so, Roy put his hand down on the exact spot where the gun had been. His fingers moved to the right and then to the left. Then he muttered under his breath, moved his hand further along, the bed. His movements were at first controlled. He thought the gun had slipped along the blanket. But as he touched nothing but the bedclothes he began to scrabble feverishly, then sat up, using both hands, sweat beading on his face.

Max lifted a chair very gently, set it down soundlessly by the bed, lowered himself into it. It amused him to see Roy's growing panic, to be so close to his victim knowing he was unaware of his presence.

"Must have fallen on the floor," Roy muttered to himself, leaned over the side of the bed and groped blindly on the strip of carpet.

Max still sat, his gloved hands folded in his lap, his chin sunk into his black scarf, and he didn't move, but waited, an interested, bland expression in his eyes.

Roy's groping fingers touched Max's pointed toecap, passed on, then paused. Back came the fingers, slowly now, hesitant. Again they touched the toecap, moved up, touched the frayed trouser cuff. Then Roy shivered. His breath came through his clenched teeth like an escape of compressed steam.

Someone was sitting by his bed!

He snatched his hand away, wedged himself back against the wall.

"Who's there?" he croaked. His voice sounded less human than a parrot's.

"The Sullivans," Max said softly.

For a long moment of time Roy crouched against the wall, scarcely breathing, his face livid, sweat soaking the bandage across his eyes.

Then:

"Steve!" he screamed wildly. "Quick, Steve! Save me!"

"He can't help you," Max said, crossing his legs. "Frank's watching him. Nothing and nobody can help you now. We've come to take care of you."

"You wouldn't kill a blind man," Roy implored. "I'm blind! Look at me. I'm through... can't you see I'm through? I'm no use to anyone."

Max was staring at the bandage across Roy's eyes.

"Take that rag off," he said. "I don't believe you're blind."

"I am," Roy said, beating his clenched fists together. "I can't take it off . . . my eyes will bleed."

Max grinned, reached out, hooked his fingers under the bandage and jerked.

"Then let 'em bleed," he said.

Roy screamed.

"Enjoy yourself," Frank called from the verandah. Max was gaping at the ruin of Roy's eyes.

"Hey, Frank," he said. "Look at this punk's mug. He's had his eyes scratched out."

"That's fine," Frank said languidly. "Saves us doing it."

"You should see him," Max urged. "It's a sight for sore eyes," and he laughed.

"Can't be bothered," Frank returned. "Me and my pal are comfortable out here."

"Well, he's sure in a mess," Max said, tapped Roy's shoulder. "How did it happen, ol' man?"

Roy caught at the gloved hand, but Max shoved him off.

"She did it. She's crazy and ...a lunatic."

"Who is?" Max asked, his dead eyes coming to life and fiercely gazing at him.

"The girl... Carol... we found her up on the hill. There'd been a truck smash... Steve nursed her... and she turned on me."

Max leaned forward.

"What's she like to look at?"

"A redhead," Roy gasped. His face was a shiny mask of blood: blood ran into his mouth, stained his teeth. He looked inhuman. When he spoke he sprayed blood into Max's face.

Max gave a little sigh, wiped his face with the back of his glove, went out on to the verandah.

"You're taking your time, ain't you?" Frank asked, surprised. "What's up?"

"That nut with the six million bucks," Max said tersely. "The one the barman told us about: she's here."

Frank gave a sharp giggle.

"Don't we get all the luck," he said, poked Steve with his gun. "Pal, if only you knew what lucky guys we are. Where is she? Where have you hidden her?"

"I don't know what you're talking about," Steve said, bewildered.

"Yes, you do. The redhead... Carol, isn't that her name? Where is she?"

"She's run off. I was looking for her when you arrived."

"Did she scratch him up like that?" Max asked.

Steve nodded.

"But she's not mad. She was scared."

"O.K., so she's not mad," Max said, winked at Frank. "But we'd better find her." He looked across the lake at the distant mountains. "Six million dollars is a lot of dough-re-me to be roaming around those peaks."

"Yeah," Frank said, "but first things first. What about the punk?"

"Sure; I haven't forgotten him. We'll fix him now. How shall we do it?"

"Little Bernie wanted it nice and slow," Frank said. "He wants him to suffer. We could drown him in the lake—make it look like an accident."

Max shook his head.

"You've got drowning on the brain," he said. "You always get wet when you drown anyone. When will you learn?

Remember that twist we surprised in her bath? That was your idea: flooded the goddamn bathroom, spoilt a nice looking ceiling and I got a cold. It hung around for weeks. No drowning for me."

"I forgot," Frank said apologetically. "Suppose we open his veins and let him bleed out?"

"Too easy for him; besides, it's messy. I thought if we got rid of these two we might stay here for a few days. I like it up here. We don't want to mess up the cabin."

"Keep the redhead until the fourteen days are up, is that what you mean?" Frank asked.

"That's the idea. We could look after her—and her dough."

Frank brooded for an inspiration.

"We could shove his face in a bucket of molasses. He'd suffocate slow that way," he said at last, looked enquiringly at Steve. "Got any molasses, pal?"

Steve shook his head. Out of the corner of his eye he had seen Roy creeping along the verandah.

"Why don't you give him a break?" he demanded loudly. "What's he done to you?"

Roy had stopped and was crouched against the cabin wall, his head turned in their direction. The Sullivans had their backs to him, but he didn't know that.

"We could make a bonfire of him," Max suggested, ignoring Steve.

"Now that's a swell idea," Frank said. "Saves us burying the bum, too."

At that moment Roy made his bid for freedom. He crept across the verandah, swung his leg over the rail, dropped to the ground. Then he began to run blindly, his arms wildly flailing in front of him.

The Sullivans glanced round, saw him.

"Keep to your left Roy," Steve bawled, seeing his brother was running towards the lake.

Roy swerved, bounded towards the pine woods.

"Now I wonder what he thinks he's doing?" Max asked, and laughed. He raised his gun.

Steve made a movement, but Frank's gun rammed into his ribs, winding him.

There was a sharp crack and a flash and Roy pitched forward on his face. He lay there for a moment, then began to crawl over the ground, his left leg limp.

"I'll fix him now for good," Max said, and walked down the steps of the verandah, across the yard. He overtook Roy, kicked him savagely, walked on to where the Packard was parked.

"You're going to see something in a minute," Frank said to Steve. "He's got brains, that boy; and style—you've never seen such style."

Roy was still crawling desperately towards the lake. He left a thin trail of blood behind him on the sandy ground.

Max reached the Packard, took from the boot a can of gasoline, walked after Roy.

Roy heard him coming, cried out, tried to crawl faster, fell over on his side.

"Don't touch me," he moaned as Max came up. "Leave me alone... for God's sake, leave me alone...!"

"Little Bernie says he hopes you rot in hell," Max said, poured the gasoline over Roy's shuddering body.

"No!" Roy screamed as the gasoline ran over his head. "You can't do this to me! Steve! Help me! No... no, no...!"

Max fumbled in his pocket, found a match, struck it alight on his shoe.

"Here it comes, ol' man," he said, and laughed.

"Ever seen a guy burn?" Frank asked Steve. "Even when they're dead they jump and twitch... like a chicken with its head chopped off. We burned a guy a couple of weeks ago. He went up like a firework and the crazy lug ran right back into his own house and set that on fire, too... burned his wife and kids." Frank shook his head. "Take a look at that," he went on, suddenly excited. "That's what I call a blaze. He's cooking fine now, ain't he? Now watch him run... they always run. There! Didn't I tell you? Watch him!"

Steve shut his eyes and put his hands over his ears.

~§~

Something happened inside Carol's head. It was as if her brain had turned completely over with a deafening *snap!* and at once the shadowy dream world in which she had been living suddenly came to life. Things which a moment before had blurred edges, dim colors and faint sounds became sharpened and vivid: like a film out of focus on the screen that has been suddenly adjusted. It was like bursting up into fresh air after diving too deeply in green silent water.

Carol thought she must have been dreaming that she was out in the pine woods, but now she realized that she had walked there in her sleep; it seemed to her to be the only explanation. She was surprised she could accept the shock of awakening so calmly and looked around for a familiar landmark to lead her back to the cabin. She saw through the trees the lake glittering in the moonlight and she walked towards it using a narrow deer path. The dry grass brushed her calves.

As she walked she tried to remember what she had been dreaming about before awakening. She had a vague recollection she had dreamed that Roy had come into her room, but it was nothing more than a vague recollection. She thought it was when Roy had come into her room that she had heard the snap inside her head. She wasn't sure about this, but she knew some time recently a shutter or something like that had fallen inside her head. It had happened in the past, but she could not remember exactly when. When she thought about it she had a vague recollection of a room with blue-quilted walls and an electric lamp high up in the ceiling which was covered by a wire basket. It must have been something that had occurred in a dream, because the nurse was there: the nurse with the horrible look in her eyes who said nothing, did nothing, but stared and pointed at her. Carol knew she had many such dreams, although she couldn't remember them clearly. They were a jumble of dissociated figures and faces and rooms.

She wondered why she had come out here into the pine woods, and realized, with dismay that she was half naked. She wondered if Steve had missed her and was looking for her, and she became anxious to get back to the cabin and find her pajama jacket that had so mysteriously disappeared. She experienced a strange confused feeling of tenderness and embarrassment at the thought of him finding her like this. She wanted to tell him about the noise inside her head. That worried her. He might know what had happened: might be able to explain it to her.

It was when she was walking up the path from the lake that she saw the Sullivans. They were standing by the lake, looking away from her, talking. In the moonlight she could only see their black sharp-etched outlines, but it was enough.

She had no idea who they were, but they frightened her—as they would have frightened anyone who came upon them suddenly in the dark. So she stepped behind a tree, her arms across her breasts, and watched them walk quickly and silently into the woods, past her, down the path along the lake.

She saw their white, hard faces: faces that looked as if they had been carved out of cold mutton fat, and she shivered, knowing instinctively that they were dangerous and evil. Her thoughts flew to Steve, and she felt weak, wondering if they had harmed him.

When they had gone, she ran towards the cabin, her heart beating so fast that the beat was like a hammer-stroke against her side.

As she crossed the yard she came upon what was left of Roy: something that twitched and was arched back from the heat; a burned up, shriveled object that was human only in outline. To her this scorched nameless thing was just another dream figment, and she scarcely looked at it, believing it existed only in her mind, and anxious only to reach the lighted cabin to make sure that Steve was safe.

She ran up the steps, stood in the doorway and looked into the lighted sitting room.

The faint light revealed that a reading lamp had been upended and that Steve was lying on the floor, tied hand and foot. He tried to sit up when he saw her.

She came to an abrupt stop, forgetting she was half naked, staring at the cords that bound him, horror in her eyes. Seeing her like that: wild, beautiful, her skin like the smooth luster of a pearl, Steve realized how much he loved her: that he had loved her almost from the moment he had found her, lying in the wrecked truck: that he wasn't going to restrain his feelings for her any more: that she was the only woman he could ever love.

"Carol!" he said. "Quick, darling. Get me free."

She ran to him, dropped on her knees beside him, her arms going round him.

"Are you hurt?" she asked, her face close to his. "Tell me you're not hurt."

"It's all right, but get me undone quickly. We're in bad trouble, kid."

"Dear Steve," she said, her lips brushed his cheek. "I was so frightened."

"It's all right," he assured her, "but get me undone."

She pulled at the cords, but the knots were too tight and she ran to the kitchen, snatched up a knife. On her way back to the sitting room she picked up Steve's jacket, struggled into it, buttoned it across her.

"Hurry, Carol," Steve called as she ran into the room. "They'll be back."

She slashed the cords and Steve struggled up, rubbed his wrists, smiled at her.

"It's going to be all right," he said. "But we've got to be quick. Come on!"

She went to him, her arms going round his neck.

"I love you, Steve," she said. "I was so frightened when I saw those two. I thought... I don't know what I'd do without you..."

He drew her to him and kissed her.

For a moment of time they stood close, their lips touching, then he gently pushed her away from him.

"I've loved you all along, kid," he said. "But we mustn't waste time. Come on, we've got to get away. Get your clothes on and be quick."

She ran into her bedroom, and Steve went out on to the verandah, looked across the yard. There was no sign of the Sullivans. He stood there, waiting, and in a moment or so Carol joined him. She was wearing her wool dress and there was a serene trusting look in her eyes as she ran to him.

"We've got to get their car," Steve said, slipping his arm round her. "Keep in the shadows and run ..."

Together they ran down the verandah steps and across the yard. They could see the outline of the big Packard at the top of the road.

"We're going to do it," Steve said, slipped his arm round Carol and rushed her across the open ground into the moonlight.

The Sullivans, coming out of the wood at that moment, saw them running across the yard.

Max shouted.

"Quick, Carol!" Steve panted. "Can you drive?"

"Yes," she returned, "but we go together. I won't leave you."

"I'm coming, but go ahead. I'll try to stall them. Get the engine started. Run like hell, kid!"

"Stop!" Max shouted, a sharp threatening note in his voice. Steve paused, turned to face them.

The Sullivans began to run towards him. He heard Carol start the Packard, and he spun on his heel, ran to the car.

Max shot from his hip.

Steve lurched, stumbled, reached the open door of the car as Max fired again.

"I'm hit, kid!" he gasped, pitched forward into the car, falling across Carol.

Blood from him ran across her hand.

Frantically she pushed him upright, saw the two Sullivans coming across the moonlit yard very fast. She roared the engine, released the clutch and the car swept forward.

Max stopped, raised his gun, but Frank grabbed his arm.

"Have a heart," he said. "Not at her... not at six million bucks."

"But she's getting away," Max said, lifting his shoulders in a disgusted shrug.

"We'll find her again," Frank returned. "We always find 'em. She's worth a little trouble... she and her dough."

They watched the tail light of the Packard flash down the mountain road to the valley.

CHAPTER III

To the north of Point Breese, spotted among the low-lying hills at the foot of the mountain range, are the country estates of the wealthy.

Phil Magarth drove recklessly along one of these hill roads, swung his battered Cadillac with a scream of tortured tires off the road and down a long twisty carriageway that led to Veda Banning's spacious Spanish-style house with its white stucco walls and red tiles.

Veda was known as the bad girl of Point Breese, but in spite of her reputation she was liked and she had a lot of fun. She was rich; ran a five hundred acre orange plantation with smart efficiency, and was crazy about Magarth. She wanted to marry him.

As Magarth stopped the Cadillac before the ornate front door he glanced at his watch. It showed *3:50* a.m. He opened the car door and slid out on to the white-tiled terrace. The house was in darkness, but he knew where Veda slept and walked quickly across the flower scented patio, climbed four broad steps to the verandah, stopped short before open French windows.

"You awake?" he called, peered into the dark room, where he could just make out the huge ornate bed in which Veda slept.

No movement came from the bed and he entered the room, sat on the bed and slid his hand under the bedclothes. There was a sudden flurry, a stifled shriek and Veda sat up, snapped on the light.

"For heaven's sake!" she exclaimed, flopped back on her pillow. "This is too much... how dare you come in here at this hour?"

"What's too much?" Magarth asked, grinning at her. "You always say you'll be glad to see me... well, here I am; be glad."

Veda struggled up in bed, stretched, yawned. Magarth admired her figure, which was exceptional.

"You look swell; good enough to eat, but things are popping. Is that little thing you call your brain awake yet?"

"There are times when I wonder what I see in you," Veda said, reached for a hand mirror on the table beside her, studied herself. She had green-blue eyes, thick lashes, gold-brown hair, hanging straight down past her shoulders and curling under at the ends: hair that looked like burnished copper. She was beautiful, and she knew it. There was a sultry, sulky look to her mouth and dark smudges under her eyes. She could have been younger than twenty-six, but not much.

"At least I don't look a fright," she said, yawned again, flopped back on her pillow. She had on a low-cut nightdress of blue crêpe-de-Cine and black lace. "You are hell, Phil," she went on. "You might have awakened me in a more gentlemanly manner: I bruise so easily."

"You should worry; it won't show," Magarth grinned, got up and walked over to the cupboard. He found a bottle of Canadian rye and a glass. "The stock's running low, sugar. You'd better get in some more."

"I will," Veda said, watching him and thinking how handsome he was. "Give me a cigarette, you beast."

Magarth came back with the bottle, gave her a cigarette, took a drink, lit a cigarette for himself.

"I'm on to something big," he said, sitting on the bed close to her. "I could make a fortune out of it if I handle it right. And if I do I might marry you, so listen carefully."

Veda eyed him from over the top of the blanket.

"I've heard that so many times I could play a flute obbligato to it," she said scornfully.

"But this is the McCoy," Magarth told her. "I'm after the Blandish girl."

"You're... what?" Veda demanded, sitting up, her eyes glaring at him.

"Now don't get your nightie in a knot," Magarth said hurriedly. "This is strictly business. Six days from tomorrow morning she comes into her money... if she isn't caught before then. I thought at first it'd be smart to help capture her and get an eyewitness account for my syndicate. But now I've a smarter idea. I'm going to help her avoid capture, help her get her money. If I steer her right she'll be grateful, won't she? I'll be in on the ground floor. The great American public will want to know what she'll do with all that dough... six million dollars! And I'll be there to tell them. I'm going to bring her here. Then when we've got the money, we'll take her around, get her a car, buy her a house, buy her clothes, take a cameraman around with us. It'll be terrific! Exclusive to my syndicate. I can ask my own terms."

Veda closed her eyes.

"I guessed it," she said wearily. "Of all the dumb ideas this is the dumbest. The girl's a lunatic, my pet. Remember? She's dangerous. She might kill us. Do you think I want to be killed?"

Magarth snorted.

"You wouldn't let a little thing like that stop me getting some money, would you?" he asked reproachfully. "Besides, I can handle her. Remember the time I spent two hours in an orangutan's cage to get a sensational story?"

"Well, the orangutan wasn't in the cage, so I don't see that makes you very brave," Veda said.

"Never mind," Magarth said impatiently. "It must prove something. Anyway, I'm not scared of a girl. Ever since I was knee-high to an ant—"

"I know. I've heard it all before. But this is different—"

"No, it isn't. I've had a word with the girl's nurse. What a cute little number she turned out to be! She has a figure like a Coney Island switchback."

"You once told me switchbacks made you feel sick," Veda said coldly.

Magarth leered at her.

"That depends how fast you go over them," he said.

Veda kicked him through the blanket.

"Well, what did the nurse say?"

"She told me Carol's got a split mind. She gets these attacks now and then—and more then than now. She'll go for months being a sweet, normal girl, and all she needs is watching." He sighed. "Watching a sweet normal girl is right up my alley."

Veda kicked him again.

"You're a rat," she said simply.

"Don't keep interrupting," Magarth said severely. "One of the trustees, an old crumb with a face like a squeezed lemon who calls himself Simon Hartman, has shown up at the Sanatorium. And the nurse tells me he's half crazy with rage that Carol's escaped. He sees the trusteeship going up in smoke and six million dollars sliding through his fat little paws." He gave himself another drink. "And I'll tell you something else. I don't believe the girl is anything like as dangerous as they make out. I don't believe she should have been certified. I think she's been railroaded into that nuthouse so old Hartman could collar the six million."

"Don't talk such drivel," Veda said sharply. "John Blandish had her put away... three or four years ago."

"Blandish knew nothing about her. He wasn't interested in her. Hartman did it all. Hartman looked after Blandish's affairs. The girl was put away because she went for a lug who was beating a dog. Wouldn't you go for a lug who beat a dog?"

Veda stared at him.

"But she's dangerous. Look what she did to that poor truck driver. He was probably only trying to help her."

Magarth waved that aside.

"She was protecting her honor," he said airily. "You wouldn't know what that means, but let me tell you some girls take that sort of thing very seriously."

"All right," Veda sighed. She didn't feel like arguing. "Have it your own way. You haven't found her yet."

Magarth tapped the side of his nose.

"But I'm coming on. I've found where she's been hiding these past days. I've just been there."

"For heaven's sake," Veda groaned; went on: "I think I'll have a little whisky after all. My nerves are beginning to fray."

"Not a chance. I wouldn't waste the stuff on you. Just relax and listen. I saw a couple of guys tonight in a big black Packard. They were asking for Steve Larson, who has a fox farm up on Blue Mountain Summit."

"I've seen him," Veda said enthusiastically. "He's big and fair and cute and made my heart go pit-a-pat."

"Never mind how cute he is," Magarth said sourly. "Your mother must have been frightened by a pair of trousers just before you were born. You have men on the brain. Let me get on, will you?"

"Well, it won't kill me to listen, I guess," Veda said, closed her eyes again.

"These two were asking after Larson and I recognized them. I think they're the Sullivan brothers—professional killers."

"What do you mean?" Veda asked, opening her eyes and staring.

"If you wanted to get rid of anyone you'd get into touch with the Sullivan brothers, give 'em some dough and they'd do the rest; and that's no fairy tale," Magarth said. "Anyway, I thought I'd sniff around and I went up to Larson's place. It was deserted. The lights were on, the doors open, the Buick van was in the garage and the dog, scared silly, in its kennel. I went through the cabin and found this"—he dropped a handkerchief on the bed. "I bet that's Carol Blandish's property. See, it has her name in the corner. And another thing: I found the trench coat belonging to Doc Travers's chauffeur; the one Carol took when she escaped from Glenview."

Veda looked intrigued.

"But where does all this get you?"

Magarth scratched his head.

"I wish I knew," he said, "but it's a start. Larson has been hiding her at his fox farm. These two—the Sullivans, if they are the Sullivans—have smoked them out into the open. That's the point. They're out in the open. Maybe the Sullivans are after them. I don't know. If I can get to her before anyone else I'll bring her here. No one would think of looking for her here. If I don't find her, then I'm out of luck and our marriage is as far off as ever."

Veda pulled him down, slid her arms round his neck.

"It doesn't have to be that way, Phil," she said softly, nibbling at his ear. "I'll give you all my money and then we can live happily ever after."

Magarth pushed her away, stood up.

"I may be a rat, but even a rat has its pride," he said, began to loosen his collar and tie. "Do you think I'm going to stand for everyone saying I married for money? Not a chance. Now move over. I've got to get me some rest before daylight, and when I say rest, I mean rest."

~§~

Carol gripped the steering wheel of the Packard, stared through the windshield at the bright blob of light coming from the headlights that raced ahead of her, lighting up the twisty mountain road.

Her heart seemed frozen, her brain numbed with shock and fear. In the light of the dashboard she could see Steve's white face as he lay crumpled up on the floorboards, his eyes closed. She wanted to stop, but the thought of the Sullivans forced her on. She would stop in a little while, when she was sure that the Sullivans couldn't reach them, and she prayed it would not be too late; that she would be able to do something for Steve.

The narrow, twisting road made speeding impossible, but she drove as fast as she could, skidding at corners, jolting the big car recklessly over potholes and ruts, her only thought to put as much distance between the Sullivans and herself as she could in the shortest time.

A few more minutes' driving brought her out on to the State Highway and she sent the Packard hurtling forward. A mile or so farther on she slowed down, looked for a place where she could stop. Ahead she saw a clearing, leading to an abandoned logging camp, and she drove the car off the road, bumped over the rough track which led to a number of half-ruined shacks that had, at some time or other, given shelter to the lumberjacks.

Hidden now from the road, the Packard slid to a standstill and Carol bent over Steve.

"I must keep calm," she said to herself. "I must control myself." The thought that he was dead or even badly hurt filled her with such dread that every muscle in her body was trembling and her teeth chattered.

"Steve, darling," she said, her hand touching his face. "What is it? Tell me. How badly hurt are you?"

Steve made no movement, and when she lifted his head it felt heavy and lifeless.

For a long moment she sat still, her fists clenched, controlling the scream that rose in her throat; then she opened the car door, got out, stood on the pine needles, holding on to the door for support. She thought she was going to faint; her heart was beating so hard she felt suffocated. She stumbled round the car, opened the offside door, supported Steve as he rolled through the doorway. He was heavy, but she managed to get him from the car and on to the soft pine needles. She adjusted the spot-lamp, switched it on, caught her breath when she saw the blood on his coat. She ran to him, opened his coat, saw the blood-soaked shirt.

She put her hand over his heart, felt the faint, uneven beat, and choked back a sob of relief. He wasn't dead! But unless she got help he might easily die. He was still bleeding, and that would have to be stopped.

She turned back to the Packard. In the back of the car, on the floor, she found two suitcases. Feverishly she opened one of them, found shirts and handkerchiefs, began ripping the shirts up for bandages.

"*Carol!*" Steve called faintly.

She gave a little cry, ran to him. He was blinking in the strong light of the spot-lamp, but he didn't move: his eyes looked dull and lifeless.

"Oh, my dear," she said, falling on her knees beside him. "What am I going to do? Does it hurt? I can't stop the bleeding."

"Easy kid," Steve muttered, and his face twisted with pain. "It's pretty bad, Carol. Somewhere in my chest."

For a moment she lost control of herself and sobbed wildly, hiding her face in her hands.

What am I going to do? she thought hysterically. *He mustn't die... I couldn't bear for him to die... and I'm the only one who can save him...*

"Come on, kid," Steve gasped. "Don't get scared. I know how you feel. But don't lose your nerve. See if you can stop the bleeding."

"Yes..." she brushed her tears away, bit down on her lip. "I'll stop it, darling. It's—it's just... Oh, my dear, I feel so helpless."

She ran back to the car for the makeshift bandages, returned and undid his shirt. The caked blood and the feel of the soaked material sickened her, but her fear that he might die stiffened her nerve, but when she opened his shirt and looked at the two small black holes oozing blood in the centre of his chest, darkness came down on her and she sat hunched up, her head in her hands, shivering.

"Don't let it scare you," Steve said, raised his head with difficulty and looked at the wounds. His mouth tightened—it was worse than he thought. There was a cold feeling creeping up his legs, and pain, like white-hot wires, stabbed his chest. "Carol! Come on, sweet. Stop this bleeding."

"I can't do it!" she cried. "I've got to get help. Where can I go, Steve? Where can I take you?"

Steve lay still, tried to think. He felt as if the whole of his chest had been laid open and that a salt wind was blowing down on the exposed nerves and flesh.

"Doc Fleming," he managed to say. Carol could scarcely hear his murmur. "Straight down the road through Point Breese, the second turn on the left. A small house off the road, stands by itself." He struggled against the faintness, forced it away, went on: "It's a good twenty miles, but it's a straight shot once you're on the road. There's no one else."

"But twenty miles..." Carol beat her clenched fists together. "It'll take too long."

"There's no one else," Steve said, and his mind swam away in a liquid pool of pain.

"I'll go," she said, "but first I'll do what I can." Then she thought: *I must take him with me. Of course; I can't leave him here. I should never have got him from the car.* She bent over him. "We'll go together, darling," she said. "If you can help yourself just a little, I'll get you into the car."

"Better not," Steve said. He felt blood in his mouth. "I'm bleeding a bit inside. Better not move me now." And the blood ran down his chin, although he tried to turn away, not wanting to frighten her.

Carol caught her breath in a sob.

"All right my dear," she said. "I'll be quick." She began to make pads with the handkerchiefs. "And, Steve, if anything... I mean... oh, darling, I love you so. I want you to know. There's no one but you, and I'm so frightened and lonely... Do try... don't leave me..."

He made an effort, smiled, patted her hand.

"I won't... that's a promise... only be quick..."

But when she lifted him to take off his coat, his face suddenly turned yellow and he cried out, his fingers gripping her arm, then he slumped back into unconsciousness.

She worked feverishly, strapping the pads tightly against the wounds. Then she ran to the car; found a rug, rolled shirts and pajamas into a pillow and made him as comfortable as she could.

She hated leaving him, but there was nothing else to do. She bent over him, touched his lips with hers, then with one last look back she climbed into the car.

She never remembered much of the drive to Point Breese. She drove the car recklessly, her one thought was to get Doc Fleming back to Steve. The road was broad and good, and she was only conscious of the noise of the wind as the car flew along. At that hour in the morning—it was a little after two o'clock—the road was deserted and her speed seldom dropped below eighty. Once rounding a bend she narrowly missed another car (it was Magarth coming up to Larson's place), but it all happened so quickly that she was only half aware that another car had passed her. She arrived at Point Breese as an outside clock chimed the half hour past two. The journey had taken her just under the half hour.

She found Doc Fleming's house easily enough, and brought the Packard to a stop outside. She ran up the garden path and hammered on the front door, and kept up the persistent hammering until the door was opened.

A middle-aged woman with a mean lined face and untidy hair stood in the doorway. She had on a drab dressing gown which she held across her flat chest with a hand like a claw.

"Making a noise like that," she said furiously. "What do you think you're doing?"

"Please," Carol said, trying to control her voice, "I want the doctor. Someone is very ill... hurt... where is the doctor?"

The woman ran her skinny fingers through the tangle of unwashed, graying hair.

"It's no use coming here," she said, preparing to slam the door. "The doctor's ill. Banging and banging like that. Who do you think you are?"

"But someone is hurt," Carol said, wringing her hands. "He's dying. Please let me see the doctor. I have a car... it won't take long."

"I can't help that," the woman said, her face red with anger. "The doctor's an old man and he's got a cold. He's not going out at this hour. You must go elsewhere."

"But someone's bleeding to death. Don't you understand? Dr. Fleming would come if you only told him. He's bleeding." Carol began to cry, "and I love him so."

"Get off," the woman said harshly. "We can't help you here. Go elsewhere."

Carol controlled her rising panic.

"But where?" she asked, clenching her fists. "There's no time... he's bleeding."

"There's a hospital at Waltonville and there's Dr. Kober at Eastlake. He'll turn out. He's a Jew. They always turn out."

"I see," Carol said. "I'll go to him. Where's Eastlake? How do I get there?"

The woman was staring at the puckered scar on Carol's left wrist, then she quickly averted her eyes.

"It's five miles," she said. "I'll show you on a street map ...perhaps you'd better come in."

"Please be quick," Carol said. "I shouldn't have left him. He is badly hurt."

"Come in, come in," the woman said. "I can't show you if you stand in the dark. Let me put on a light."

She turned away and a moment later the dark little passage was dazzling with a hard naked light hanging from the ceiling.

Carol stood just inside the front door and faced the woman as she turned.

"What lovely hair you have!" the woman said, her small eyes gleaming with excitement. "Perhaps I could persuade the doctor to go with you. Come in, come in. He might if he... he's not been very well. I'll tell him if you'll wait in here."

The sudden shifty change of expression, the sudden false friendliness, frightened Carol, but there was nothing she could do. She had to save Steve. So she followed the woman into a small waiting room, consisting of three chairs, a round table on which were tattered copies of old periodicals. There was an atmosphere of decay and neglect in the room.

"I'll tell him, dear," the woman said. "You sit down. He won't be long."

"Please hurry," Carol begged. "He's bleeding so badly."

"I'll hurry," the woman said, went to the door, looked back at Carol and then left the room. There had been a look in her eyes that sent a shiver up Carol's spine. She listened to the woman hurrying up the stairs and felt instinctively that she was trapped... that this woman meant her harm.

Quietly she opened the door.

"It's the lunatic from Glenview," she heard the woman say. She was speaking loudly and clearly. "She's downstairs."

"What? Speak up," a man said angrily. "Why do you always whisper? Who from Glenview?"

"The lunatic... Carol Blandish... the one they're looking for... go down and talk to her... I'll call the Sheriff," the woman said. "And hurry."

"But she's dangerous," the man said, a whine in his voice. "You talk to her. I'm too old. I don't want anything to do with her. I only want my bed."

"Go down!" the woman said angrily. "You know you can't use the telephone. There's five thousand dollars reward for her capture. Don't you want that, you old fool?"

There was a long pause, then the man said: "Yes, I'd forgotten that. Perhaps I'd better go down."

Carol closed her eyes. She must be dreaming this, she thought. It must be another of those terrifying dreams that came so mysteriously: only this time more vivid than ever before. Perhaps Steve hadn't been hurt; perhaps the two men in black were also part of the dream and she would suddenly wake up in her bed in the cabin, her heart pounding, frightened but safe.

The lunatic... Carol Blandish... the one they're looking for...

She shivered, willed herself to wake up and slowly opened her eyes, praying that she would find herself in bed, safe, but the shabby little room was still there and looked too real to be a dream figment, and she backed across the room, staring with horror at the door, listening to the slow shuffling steps on the stairs.

Somewhere at the back of the house she heard a sharp *ting!* of a bell: a telephone-bell.

Go down and talk to her...I'll call the Sheriff...There's five thousand dollars reward for her capture.

Whether or not this was a nightmare she must get away from this house. These people meant her harm. They wouldn't help Steve. They would try to keep her here, away from Steve, and he would die.

But she was now so frightened that she could not move, and crouched in a corner, her heart hammering against her side, a nerve jumping and twitching at the side of her mouth.

The door was slowly pushed open, and a vast old man came into the room: a bald-headed, tired, sagging figure with a great hooked nose and a drooping tobacco-stained mustache. But it was his eyes that filled her with unspeakable terror. His blind right eye, which was like a dirty yellow clay marble, sat fixed in his face at a skewed angle, and yet she felt it somehow probed right into her mind.

The old man was wearing a blanket dressing-gown; food stains encrusted the lapels and above the opening she could see heavy underwear: layers of old, over-washed wool.

"Go away!" she screamed to herself. "Let me wake up! Don't come near me!"

The old man closed the door and set his great bulk against it. He took a handkerchief from his dressing-gown pocket and mopped his left eye, which watered. The yellow clot over his right eye continued to stare at her, hypnotizing her.

"You're in trouble I hear," he said in a shaky, whining voice. "What do you want me to do?"

Carol squeezed herself further into the corner.

"Are you the doctor?"

"Yes," the old man said. "I'm Dr. Fleming." He touched his temples with the handkerchief. Little beads of moisture ran down his face.

He was horrible, Carol thought. She couldn't take him to Steve. She couldn't trust him.

"I've made a mistake," she said quickly. "I don't want you. I shouldn't have come here..."

Fleming cringed. She realized that he was very frightened, and his fear increased her own terror.

"Now don't be hasty," he implored. "I'm old, but I'm a good doctor. Does my eye worry you? It's nothing: a clot. I'm always promising myself to have it removed, but I never have the time." His wrinkled hands fluttered up and down the lapels of the dressing-gown; they looked like big bleached spiders. The harsh electric light picked out the black hairs on his fingers.

"But it doesn't interfere with my work. My other eye—But won't you sit down? You must tell me what's wrong..."

Carol shook her head.

"No!" she said. "I'm going. I shouldn't have disturbed you. Thank you for seeing me..." Her voice broke, rose a note. "There's nothing you can do."

Very slowly she pushed herself from the wall, took a hesitant step towards him.

"You'd better stay," Fleming said. "We want you to stay," and he spread his bulk across the door, his face grimacing at her in his fear. "Have some coffee. My wife... coffee will do you good." He waved the bleached spiders at her imploring her to be quiet, not to frighten him any more.

Carol ceased to breathe, then suddenly she screamed, feeling her lungs emptying long after all the air was expelled and her diaphragm laboring long after her chest was empty. The scream was very thin and soft: like the scream of a trapped rabbit.

"No, please," Fleming said. "It's all right. Nothing is going to happen. We're good people... we only want you to be safe from harm..."

A soft scratching sound came on the door, and the old man suddenly relaxed, his face white as chalk. He stood away from the door and his wife came in.

"What is it?" she asked, looked at Carol. "Why aren't you sitting down? Has my husband..." Her eyes went to the old man. "Won't you go with her? Someone is ill."

"Yes, yes," Fleming said, sat abruptly on one of the hard chairs. "She's change her mind." He put fingers to his throat. "This has upset me, Martha," he went on. "I shouldn't have come down. A little brandy, I think—"

"Be quiet," the woman said sharply. "Don't think so much of yourself."

"I must go," Carol said. She was standing by the table now, her mouth fixed in a cringing grimace. "I shouldn't have disturbed you so late."

"But the doctor's going up to dress now," the woman said quickly. "He won't be a minute. Your friend's ill, isn't he? Someone you love?"

Carol's heart lurched.

"Oh, yes," she said. "I don't know what I'm thinking of." She touched her temple with her fingers. "Yes... he's bleeding. But why does the doctor sit there? Why doesn't he do something?"

"Go on," the woman said to Fleming. "Get dressed. I'll make the young lady a cup of coffee."

Fleming still sat slumped in the chair. His breathing was heavy, asthmatic.

"Let her go," he said suddenly. "I don't want the money. I want peace. I'm old. Let her go before something happens. Look what she did to the truck driver..."

"Get upstairs, you old fool," the woman said angrily. "You don't know what you're saying."

"Don't disturb him," Carol said. "I'm going... I really must go," and she eased across the room with slow determination, keeping her eyes fixed upon the woman as she backed away.

Fleming hid his big floppy face in his hands. The woman hesitated, gave ground, backed against the wall, her hard eyes alight with rage and fear.

"You'd better stay," she said. "We know who you are. You'd better not make a fuss. You can't get away."

Carol opened the door.

"I don't know what you mean," she said, turning so that she could face them. "I thought you would help me." She turned quickly, ran to the front door, but it was locked. She whirled round to find the woman standing in the doorway of the waiting room, watching her.

"Open this door," Carol said, her face like a small lead-colored mask.

"It's all right," the woman said. "Why don't you come in and sit down? I'll make you a cup of coffee..."

Carol ran down the passage, past the woman, wrenched at the handle of another door that she thought might open on to the back garden. That too was locked.

Fleming had joined his wife and was standing just behind her. The yellow clot in his eye seemed to beseech her to be quiet and calm.

Trapped in the narrow passage, between the two doors, Carol paused, her brain refusing to function.

"You see?" the woman said gently. "You can't get away. Your friends are coming. There's nothing you can do."

Then Carol saw another door; a small door half-hidden by a curtain, a yard or so from where she was standing.

Without taking her eyes from the two in the doorway, she edged towards the door, then snatched at the handle. The door opened. At the same moment the woman darted forward.

Carol cried out, stepped back through the open doorway, threw up her hands to ward the woman off. The woman pushed her, and the ground seemed to give way under her feet and she felt herself falling.

~§~

Sheriff Kamp lay flat on his back in his small truckle bed. His low, rasping snores vibrated round the room. He didn't hear the shrill ring of the telephone-bell in the main office of the county jail, nor did he hear his deputy, George Staum, cursing as he pushed himself out of his desk chair.

But a minute or so later the door crashed open and Staum was shaking the Sheriff awake.

"Hey, hey, hey," Kamp growled, flinging off Staum's hand. "Can't you let a man sleep?"

"They've found her!" Staum said excitedly. His round fat face hung over Kamp like a Dutch cheese. "They've got her!" He was so excited that he couldn't get out his words.

"Got who?" Kamp demanded, still confused with sleep, then he started up, grabbed hold of Staum. "You mean—*her?* Who's got her?"

"Doc Fleming... Mrs. Fleming's just phoned..."

"Hell!" Kamp struggled into his trousers. "Fleming! That old quack! Five thousand bucks! It would be him. Never did a day's work in his life and he has to find her."

"Mrs. Fleming says to be quick," Staum spluttered, his eyes popping. "She's scared something will happen."

"Can't be quicker," Kamp growled, slipping his heavy revolver belt round his waist. "Get Hartman on the phone. Get the Press. I'm going to get something out of this! Fleming! My stars! I bet it fell into his lap."

Staum ran into the office.

"Do you want me to come with you?" he bawled over his shoulder.

"No. Follow me. Get Hartman and the Press first, then come on as fast as you can. I want a cameraman there. If I don't get that five thousand I'm going to have my picture in all the papers," Kamp said, grabbed up his hat, ran from the room.

~§~

Simon Hartman couldn't sleep. He sat in a big easy chair in his luxury hotel suite, a glass of whisky on the table beside him, a cigar clamped between his small sharp teeth.

Hartman was short and thick-set. The lines in his thin, sallow-complexioned face made him look older than his fifty-five years. There was a cold, brooding expression in his eyes, and his thin lips were turned down. Although the hour was a minute or so before 3 a.m., he had no incentive to sleep. For years now be had slept but little, and then only in uneasy catnaps.

Hartman was the senior partner of Simon Hartman & Richards, solicitors, whose reputation at one time had stood as high as any of the big New York firms. But since Richards had retired the business had gone to pieces, and Hartman, an inveterate gambler, had been tempted to use his clients' money to play the markets, and recently he had been juggling with securities that were not his own, with disastrous results.

He had almost reached breaking-point when John Blandish died and the Blandish Trust was formed. Here, then, was a chance in a lifetime, and Hartman was quick to seize the opportunity. Richards and he were appointed trustees and a Richards took no interest in business the trust was entirely in Hartman's hands.

It came as a tremendous shock to Hartman when he learned of Carol's escape. He knew that if she avoided capture for fourteen days she could claim the Trust money... what there was left of it. For even in that short space of time Hartman had already dug deeply into Blandish's fortune.

The girl had to be found! If she wasn't found, he'd be ruined, and Hartman had no intention of being ruined. He had already taken charge of the search. The Sheriff was a fool. Dr. Travers was irresponsible. The police were worse than useless. But he had galvanized them into action; had offered five thousand dollars reward for the girl's capture. Now everyone in Point Breese was searching for the girl.

His eyes strayed to the calendar hanging on the wall. Only another six days! Well, a lot could happen in six days—a lot must happen!

As he reached for his whisky the telephone rang shrilly. He paused, his eyes suddenly hooded. Then without fuss or undue haste he picked up the receiver.

"What is it?"

"We've got her," Staum shouted excitedly over the line. "Sheriff said I was to tell you."

"Don't shout: I'm not deaf," Hartman said coldly, but his face lightened: he looked younger. "Where is she?"

"Doc Fleming's got her. The Sheriff's going over there right away. He says for you to go over."

"Certainly," Hartman said. "Where exactly does Dr. Fleming live?"

Staum gave directions.

"All right. I'm leaving immediately," Hartman said, hung up.

For a moment he stared at himself in the mirror over the mantelpiece, and he smiled thinly.

The darkest hour comes before the dawn, he thought. *Trite but true.*

He pulled back the curtains and looked down at the deserted main street. Above the rooftops was a band of light stretching like a ribbon behind the distant mountains. The sky was a faint grey; the stars were losing their luster. In a little while it would be daylight.

He picked up his hat, slipped on an overcoat—it would be chilly out at this hour—walked quickly to the door.

While he waited for the elevator to take him to the street level he hummed tunelessly under his breath.

~§~

A big empty truck rattled to a standstill outside an all-night café situated near the Point Breese railway yards.

"As far as I go," the driver said. "This do you?"

The Sullivans climbed down from the cab.

"Sure," Frank said. "And thanks."

"You're welcome," the driver returned and drove on through the big wooden gates guarding the yard.

"We were lucky to get that lift," Frank said, and yawned. "My feet were getting sore."

"*Shaddap!*" Max snarled, walked across the road to the café, went in.

Frank grimaced, followed him.

The loss of the Packard had affected Max, whereas Frank was more philosophical. Possessions and comfort meant little to him. His weakness was women. His grimy pathological mind seldom thought of anything but women, and he left all the planning, the arrangements, the everyday routine, to Max.

They sat on stools at the counter, called for coffee. The girl who served them was ugly, but she had a good figure. Frank wanted to discuss her figure with Max, but he knew Max wasn't in the mood. Max didn't bother about women: he regarded them the way he regarded food: a necessity, but uninteresting and unimportant.

The girl was a little scared of the Sullivans, and when she had served them she went into the kitchen and left them alone. There was no one else in the café.

"I wish I knew if I'd killed him," Max said thoughtfully. "I know I hit him twice in the chest, but he's big and tough. I should have aimed at his head."

"Let's not worry about him," Frank said. "It's the girl I'm worrying about. She was terrific! That red hair..."

Max turned on him.

"If he's alive he saw what happened. He's the only witness we've ever let get away. He could blow our racket sky-high."

Frank hadn't thought of that.

"We'd better find him," he said, "but where?"

"I want some sleep," Max grumbled. "Hell! We can't go on and on... we're not made of iron. Where can we get a bed?"

"Ask her... she'll know," Frank said, jerked his thumb towards the kitchen door.

"Yeah," Max said, finished his coffee, slid off the stool, walked into the kitchen.

The girl was sitting on a table, talking to a negro cook. They both stared at Max, and then the negro's eyes looked down.

"Where can we get a bed?" Max asked, eying the girl.

"There's a hotel round the corner, next to the jail," the girl said. "You can't miss it."

"OK." Max flipped a couple of nickels on to the table. "Where's the hospital?"

"There isn't one. Nearest one's at Waltonville, five miles from here."

Max grunted, walked out, jerked his head at Frank.

"Let's get the hell out of here. I want to sleep."

They walked down the deserted road. The big-faced clock over the station showed three o'clock.

"There's a hotel next to the jail," Max said.

"Handy," Frank said, and giggled.

"That's it," Max said as they turned the corner, then he stopped abruptly, put his hand on Frank's arm. "What the hell's going on?"

They drew back as Sheriff Kamp came rushing down the steps of the jail. They watched him pull open the wooden doors of the garage next to the jail. His movements were those of a man in a frantic hurry. A moment later a battered Ford roared out of the garage, headed down the road.

"The Sheriff's in a hurry," Frank said, tilted his hat over his nose and squinted.

"Something's up," Max said. "Come on, we're going to see."

"Thought you wanted a bed," Frank grumbled.

"We're going to see," Max repeated.

They set off down the road, their arms swinging, a sudden new life and spring in their stride.

~§~

The bedside telephone suddenly rang.

"Let it ring," Veda said sleepily. "It's only one of my affairs with an uneasy conscience."

Magarth groaned and half sat up.

"I moved in here for a little peace and quiet," he complained. "Must you carry your love life into my life as well? What ever happened to discretion?"

"Don't be a grouch, darling," Veda said. "He'll tire of it in a moment and go back to bed."

Magarth ribbed his eyes, sat bolt upright.

"Stop chattering," he said tersely. "Maybe it's for me," and he grabbed the telephone.

"But no one knows you're here... at least, I hope they don't," Veda said in alarm.

"My editor knows everything," Magarth muttered and then spoke into the phone: "Hello?"

"That you, Magarth?"

Magarth recognized his editor's voice.

"I think so," he returned, yawned. "Anyway, it's someone very like me."

"I suppose you're in bed with that woman?"

"Who else would I be in bed with—a horse?"

"Then get out of it, you licentious rat. They've found the Blandish girl!"

"They've... what?" Magarth exclaimed.

"The Sheriff's office phoned through just now. They've got her holed up in Doc Fleming's cellar. Get going and take a camera. Kamp won't do a thing until you arrive. The old bastard wants his picture taken making the capture. Hartman's there; in fact every punk in town's there except you. So get moving."

"I'm on my way," Magarth said, slammed down the phone and jumped out of bed. "Sweet suffering cats!" he exploded. "They've found her! Found her while I'm taking a roll in the hay. That's retribution!" He struggled into his shirt, "Now what the hell am I going to do? Oh, my stars! What a break!"

"Keep calm, darling," Veda said, snuggling down under the bedclothes. "It may turn out all for the best."

"All for the best!" Magarth snorted, struggling into his coat, "If they get her back into that nuthouse my story'll go up in smoke. I've got to save her—somehow," and he rushed for the door.

"But, darling," Veda called after him, "do try to be sensible. You've forgotten to put your trousers on."

~§~

The narrow passage between Doc Fleming's back and front doors was crowded. Doc Fleming with his wife stood half-way up the stairs. Simon Hartman stood in the waiting room doorway. Magarth, a camera equipped with a flash-gun in his hand, leaned against the back door. Two State cops guarded the front entrance. Sheriff Kamp and George Staum faced the cellar door.

"All right, boys," Kamp said. "You stick around. Mind, she's dangerous." He glanced slyly at Magarth. "Get that picture as I bring her out."

"You haven't got her out yet," Magarth reminded him. "Maybe she'll bring you out. What you need is a trident and a net."

Kamp ignored this, rapped on the cellar door.

"We know you're in there," he called. "Come on out in the name of the law."

Carol crouched further back into the darkness of the cellar. When she had recovered from the fall down the cellar stairs she quickly realized that she was trapped. Groping round the cellar wall she discovered there was no way out except through the door, which was now securely locked. If it hadn't been for the thought of Steve lying helpless in the wood she would have given up, but she drew courage from her love and she told herself that she was going to get out and back to Steve and no one would stop her.

She found an electric light switch after a few minutes of groping and turned it on. The cellar was small and damp and full of rubbish, but it also contained the fuse box and main switch for the light. She discovered a rusty steel poker among the rubbish, and this she picked up, balanced in her hand. When Kamp threw open the door, she crouched down by the steps leading into the cellar, her hand on the light switch, and waited. She had already turned off the light in the cellar, and although she could see Kamp peering into the darkness, he couldn't see her.

"Come on out," Kamp called, his face red with excitement; added for no reason at all, "We've got the place surrounded."

No sound or movement came from the dark cellar.

"Be a man and fetch her out," Magarth said. "We'll give you a decent burial." While he was speaking he was racking his brains for a plan to rescue Carol, but for the moment he was foxed.

"Now come along," Kamp wheedled. He wasn't feeling too happy about tackling a dangerous lunatic. He looked over his shoulder at Hartman. "Think I should go in there after her?"

"Of course," Hartman said sharply. "But don't handle her roughly: "I won't have her ill-treated."

Magarth gave a macabre laugh.

"That's very, very funny," he said. "Never mind how she treats you, Sheriff."

George Staum edged away when Kamp beckoned to him.

"Not me," he said firmly. "Lunatics scare me. I ain't going down there in the dark. Look what she did to that truck driver."

"By rights the asylum people ought to handle it," Kamp said, hanging back. "Did anyone think to call them?"

"No one," Magarth said cheerfully. "I'll come in with you, Sheriff. I'm not scared. You go first. I'll be right on your heels."

Kamp drew in a deep breath.

"Well, let's go," he said, took a hesitant step towards the cellar, peered into the inky darkness. "Maybe someone's got a flashlight?" he went on hopefully.

No one had a flashlight, and Hartman irritably told Kamp to get on with his duty.

As he stooped to pass through the low doorway Carol snapped down the main switch, grabbed hold of his arms and jerked him forward.

Kamp gave a wild yell, plunged into space.

Magarth was quick to realize what had happened, decided to cause as much confusion as he could. He gave a ghoulish shriek, charged George Staum and hurled him against the two State Police as they crowded forward in the dark.

"Look out!" Magarth bawled. "She's right in amongst us."

Staum lost his head, hit out blindly, knocked one of the police officers cold, tried to rush up the stairs out of the way. The other police officer struck out right and left with his nightstick, but failed to hit anything. Magarth kept up his yelling and for a long moment of time confusion and panic reigned.

It was enough for Carol. She had reached the passage, heard the shouting and the sounds of a struggle going on by the front door, opened the back door, slipped into the garden.

Magarth saw her, followed her.

Carol ran blindly down the garden path, swerved to her right when she heard Magarth's thudding steps behind her. She increased her speed and seemed to fly over the ground. Try as he would, Magarth couldn't overtake her.

But he kept on, wondering how long it would be before the Sheriff came after them.

Carol was heading for a dense thicket that lay a few hundred yards ahead. Beyond the thicket was the main road into Point Breese but she didn't know this. She thought once she could get into the wood she might be able to hide, and she redoubled her speed, confidence making her careless. Suddenly she caught her foot in a thick tree root and went sprawling, rolled over, the breath knocked out of her.

For a moment or so she lay stunned, then she struggled to sit up as Magarth bent over her.

They stared at each other.

"It's all right," Magarth said. "Don't be frightened. I want to help you. It was me who helped you escape. Don't look so scared."

Although Carol shied away from him, there was something about him that reassured her.

"Who are you? What do you want with me?" she panted.

"I'm Phil Magarth— a newspaper man. You're Carol Blandish, aren't you?"

"I don't know," Carol said, holding her head. "I don't know who I am. I had an accident... I lost my memory." She sat up, clutched his arm. "Will you really help me? It's Steve... he's badly hurt... will you come with me?"

Magarth frowned.

"Steve Larson? Is that who you mean?"

"Oh, yes. Do you know him?"

"Sure. We're good friends. What happened? Those two guys in black...?"

Carol shuddered.

"Yes. He's shot. I went to Dr. Fleming. He must be mad. They locked me in the cellar..."

Magarth stared at her.

Could she be Carol Blandish? She seemed so normal: not a trace of madness. He caught hold of her left wrist. Yes, there was the scar. Then had she really lost her memory?

"You mean you really don't know who you are?" he asked.

"No.... but, please, if you're going to help me, don't waste time. He's so badly hurt. Will you come with me? Will you help me?"

"You bet I will," Magarth said, helped her on her feet. "Where is he?"

"Up on the mountain road. There's a logging camp up there. That's where I left him."

"I know the place," Magarth said, looked to right and. left. "It'll be light soon. You mustn't be seen. I'll get my ear. You'd better wait here. Go over to that wood. Just beyond it is the main road. You'll see me from the wood. Keep out of sight until I come. I shan't be more than ten minutes. Will you do that?"

"Yes," Carol said. She felt she could trust him. "But please be quick. I'm so frightened... he was bleeding so badly."

"Don't worry," Magarth said briskly. "We'll fix him up all right. You get under cover and wait for me." He patted her arm and then ran quickly back to Doc Fleming's house.

Now she was alone, Carol suddenly felt uneasy. The half light of the dawn, the cold mist that rose from the ground, the still, silent wood silhouetted blackly against the sky, produced a threatening atmosphere.

As she began to move towards the wood she had a presentiment of danger and her heart began to thud against her side.

She wished now that she had gone back with Magarth. Anything seemed better than being alone in this dim, silent wood. She worked up her courage and kept on, and some way ahead through the trees she could see the main road.

That was where she was to meet Magarth, she told herself, and fighting down this strange feeling of panic, she walked through the wood towards the distant clearing.

Then suddenly she stopped. Something moved ahead of her. She caught her breath sharply, stared. From behind a big tree trunk the brim of a man's hat appeared. She stood petrified, unable to move, even to blink her eyelids.

A man in a black overcoat and a black slouch hat slid round the tree trunk, stood directly in her path: it was Max.

"I want you," he said softly. "Don't make a fuss."

For one brief moment she stared at him, her heart freezing, then with a thin wail of terror she turned to run blindly in the opposite direction. But Frank was there behind her, and as she came to an abrupt stop he smiled, raised his hat.

Carol stood rigid. Both the Sullivans could hear her wild breathing.

"Don't make a fuss," Max said, and walked slowly towards her.

"Oh, no!" Carol cried, cringing back. "You mustn't touch me..." She felt her muscles shrinking. Her face was as wan as a small ghost. "Please go away... I'm waiting for someone. He'll be back any moment now... you mustn't stay..."

"Relax, child," Max said, reaching her. "Come on. We've been looking for you. We're your knights in shinning armor."

She backed, then suddenly whirled and ran towards Frank, who watched her with his fixed smile. He threw out his arms, barring her path.

Again she whirled, stood rigid.

"Where's Larson?" Max asked. "We want him, too."

"I don't know," she said. "I don't know anything."

"You will," Max said gently. "We know how to make girls talk. Where is he?"

"Leave me alone..." Carol said, looked round wildly, then began to scream.

Frank jumped forward, twined his short fat fingers in her hair, dragged her head back.

"Hit her," he said to Max.

Max stepped up to her. She saw him raise his fist and she threw up her hands to protect herself, screamed wildly again. Max brushed her hands aside; then four bony knuckles mashed against the side of her jaw.

CHAPTER IV

MAGARTH came out on to the sun-drenched verandah, sat down, stretched out his long legs, closed his eyes.

"A pint of black coffee laced with brandy might set me up," he said, smothering a yawn, "but it's a bed I really want. And I've got to go see the Sheriff in a moment."

"You shall have your coffee, precious," Veda said. "But you're not going to leave here until you've given me some sort of explanation. Surely it's not asking too much, since you've turned my house into a hospital. I'm sure you have your reasons, but I do feel I should be told what goes on."

Magarth opened one eye, grinned. He thought Veda looked very nice in her apricot-colored linen frock and he reached out to pat her hand.

"They holed her up in Doc Fleming's cellar," he said briefly. "When Kamp went in after her, she turned off the main switch, and I caused what is known as a diversion, and she escaped. I went after her, caught up to her, made friends. I arranged to get my car and go with her to where she had left Larson. I left her in the wood and got my car. When I returned she had vanished. So I collected Larson and brought him here. Doc Kober will let us know what he thinks of him when he comes down."

"But why didn't you take the poor lamb to hospital? Why bring him here?"

"Because he's in danger," Magarth said patiently. "You don't know what these two thugs are like."

"What two thugs?" Veda asked, bewildered.

"The Sullivans: the professional killers. If half what I've heard about them is true they've committed dozens of murders and have never left a clue or a witness. But this time they've slipped up. Larson saw them kill his brother. He managed to tell me that much before he passed out. His evidence would send them to the chair. They'll try to finish him, and the first place they'd look for him is the hospital. We'll have to keep him under cover until he's well enough to make a statement."

Veda nodded.

"But are you really sure these two won't find him here?"

"Not a chance. There's no connection between you and Larson— why should they?"

"Well, that's a relief," Veda said. "Now tell me about the Blandish girl. What happened to her?"

"I don't know," Magarth admitted, worried. "She either didn't trust me or..." He shook his head. "There was a big black Packard parked outside Doc Fleming's house when I arrived. I was so anxious to get inside the house I didn't give it a thought. But it had gone when I returned for my car, and I'm wondering. The Sullivans may have got her."

"Haven't you got the Sullivans on the brain, my pet?" Veda asked. "They can't be here, there and everywhere."

"That's just what they can be," Magarth said. "I'll have to tell Kamp. We'll need protection out here, just in case. God help the Blandish girl if the Sullivans have got her."

"But you haven't told me what she's like," Veda said with pardonable curiosity. "Have you actually talked with her?"

"Sure. She looks as sane as you do," Magarth returned. "I can't make it out. She's a marvelous-looking girl, and obviously head over heels in love with Larson. She's the kind of girl who loves but once and sticks to her man like glue."

"So am I," Veda said softly. "Only the rat I've fallen in love with doesn't know it."

"Don't let's talk about rats," Magarth said hurriedly. "They're timid creatures and don't like to be talked about."

"I've noticed they're not so timid at night," Veda said softly.

At this moment Dr. Kober joined them.

"He's bad," he said abruptly. "It'll be touch and go. The next three days will decide whether or not be pulls through. He should really be in hospital."

"It wouldn't be safe," Magarth said. "I'm seeing the Sheriff right away, Doc. These guys will have another go at him, and that's why he must stay here. Miss Banning will foot all the bills, so spare no expense. Can you stay here with him?"

"That's impossible," Kober returned. "But I'll be coming in twice a day. Nurse Davies knows what to do. There's not much we can do for him now. It depends entirely on his stamina, which is good. But he's lost a lot of blood. I shall have to report this, Magarth."

"I'll come with you," Magarth said, getting to his feet. "If you'll give me two minutes to drink this coffee," he added as the maid came out with a tray, "I'll be with you."

"I'll wait for you in my car," Kober said, and took leave of Veda.

"You'll make yourself entirely at home, precious, won't you?" she said when Kober had gone. "If there are any of your other friends who'd like rooms—"

Magarth sipped his coffee, slipped his arm round her waist.

"Don't be mad at me, sugar," he said. "You'll get your picture in the newspaper when the danger is over, and everyone will think you are a heroine. Besides, if this pans out the way I think it'll pan out, me and my friends will move in here for good. You'll love that, won't you?"

~§~

Sheriff Kamp sat in his dusty little office, his feet on his desk, a dead cigar clamped between his teeth.

Simon Hartman had just left, and it had been a difficult interview. Hartman had accused Magarth of engineering Carol's escape; he had also charged Kamp with incompetence, and had thrown out hints of going to higher authority. Kamp was worried. He now had only six days in which to find the girl, and he had no idea where to look for her.

He gave a ferocious grunt when Magarth came into the office.

"I want you," he said, bringing his feet to the floor with a crash. "You're the guy who let that damned girl escape."

Magarth drew up a chair, flopped into it.

"Not intentionally," he said, lighting a cigarette, "although maybe I did lose my head for a moment. But your fellas weren't so hot, either. You can't pick on me."

"I can and I'm going to," Kamp said grimly. "Hartman's been in here raising Cain, and he's yelling for your blood."

"And have you asked yourself why?" Magarth asked calmly. "He's scared stiff the girl will come into her money. Sitting on six million is quite a temptation. I bet he's been dipping his paws into the Trust and funks an investigation. Did you ever think of that?"

Kamp's eyes popped.

"That's a pretty serious accusation."

"I know, and I wouldn't make it to anyone but you. Maybe I'm wrong, but I don't think so. My editor is looking into Hartman's background and we'll keep you informed. But there's something more important in the wind. Ever heard of the Sullivan brothers?"

"Sure, but that's just a fairy tale. The Sullivans don't exist. They're an alibi for any unsolved murder."

"Don't kid yourself," Magarth said hitching up his chair. "They not only exist, but they're here. They killed Steve Larson's brother last night and they shot and badly wounded Steve. Now they got mop things up."

"I didn't know Larson had a brother," Kamp said, sitting bolt upright.

"If you knew everything you'd probably be President," Magarth returned. "Larson has, or rather had, a brother: a smalltime gangster who got in bad with Little Bernie. The Sullivans were hired to kill him. Roy holed himself up at Blue Mountain Summit, but the Sullivans tracked him down. And here's something else. A week before the Sullivans arrived Steve Larson found Carol Blandish in the wrecked truck and took her to his place. She's been there ever since."

"What?" Kamp roared, springing to his feet.

"Watch your blood pressure," Magarth said, grinned at the sight of Kamp's astonished expression. "Larson had no idea who the girl was. Roy wouldn't let him move from the farm and he had no means of learning the girl had escaped. Apparently she received a crack on her head and has lost her memory. She doesn't know who she is."

"How the heck do you know all this?" Kamp demanded, sinking into his chair again.

"I found Larson and talked to him. The Sullivans showed up last night, murdered Roy and were going to take the Blandish girl with them. But Larson managed to pull a fast one, and he and the girl escaped in the Sullivans' car; only Larson got shot as they were going. The girl left him at the Summit Logging Camp and tried to get Doc Fleming to come out and attend to him. Mrs. Fleming recognized her, and you know the rest. I have Larson up at Miss Banning's place. He's bad: too bad to make a statement. But when he does we'll have enough on the Sullivans to send them to the chair—if we catch them. And think what that'll mean. These two have committed murder in practically every State in the country. To catch them would put you and me right on the front page and right in the public eye. You wouldn't have to worry about Hartman's threats then."

"My stars!" Kamp said, lifted his sweat-stained Stetson and scratched his head. "And what's become of the girl?"

"I think the Sullivans have got her," Magarth said, and went on to tell Kamp of his meeting with Carol, and how, when he had returned with his car, she had vanished. "They run a big black Packard Clipper." He reached for a scrap of paper and scribbled down the registration number. "Can you start a hunt for them? You'll be killing two birds with one stone. And one more thing: I want some protection up at Miss Banning's place. I don't see how they'll get on to Larson there, but if they do they'll come after him. We can't afford to take any risks."

Kamp jumped to his feet.

"O.K., Magarth," he said. "Leave this to me. I'll get things started. I'll send Staum and a couple of deputies up there right away, and I'll throw out a dragnet for the Sullivans."

~§~

The Packard Clipper jolted over the rutty surface of the narrow by-road that led off the State Highway into a dense jungle of cane and brier and cypress.

The midday sun was hot, and the Sullivans had undone their overcoats and were sitting shoulder to shoulder in the car: Max was driving.

Behind them on the floor, under the suffocating heat of a rug, Carol lay, only half conscious. Her wrists and ankles were securely tied and a broad strip of adhesive plaster covered her mouth.

The Sullivans were now many miles from Point Breese. They had driven north and had headed for the open cotton country, avoiding the small towns; making the longer detour rather than risk defection. And now, after eight hours of furious driving, they were in sight of their destination.

Max had scarcely said a word on the journey. His mind was concentrated on Steve Larson. If Larson were allowed to talk in court, they were finished. So sure was he of his shooting ability, Max knew that Steve had been dangerously, if not fatally, injured. They wouldn't get him to testify for some time: it was even doubtful if he could make a statement for a week or so. At all costs he must be prevented from picking them out in a line-up. Statements and alibis could be fixed, but there was nothing so damning as a line-up before a credible witness. As soon as they had got the girl safely under cover they'd have to go back and finish him. It was the only safe way.

The road—if you could call it a road—began to rise steeply, and a moment later, above the jagged mass of trees, a house lifted its gaunt bulk against the autumn sky.

In this dense wilderness, miles from the nearest town, set back a mile or so off the State Highway, you wouldn't expect to find any building, let alone an old plantation house as big and as ruined as this one before which the Sullivans stopped the Packard. There was a wide verandah running round the house.

Practically every third paling in the verandah rail was missing, and the whole of the wooden building was bleached white by rain and sun over a period of many bleak winters and hot summers. To the right and rear of the building was a cultivated patch of ground, incongruous in the abandoned surroundings and overgrown foliage. A few apple and plum trees struggled for survival amongst the unclipped cypress groves. The red apples looked like the little balls you see on Christmas trees.

A dozen or so chickens scratched in the sandy soil near the front of the building, and they scattered with harsh squawks as the Packard came to a standstill.

As the Sullivans climbed out of the car a man appeared from the dark hall, came out into the sunshine and stood on the top step of the wooden stoop.

He was a man around sixty, tall, upright, pigeon-chested. He had a lean, weathered face, the jaws covered with a black stubble; his hair was grey and slicked back with strong-smelling pomade. He wore a pair of dirty overalls and his feet were bare. He was a strange looking figure. From his neck down you would have taken him for a tramp: a man who had known no success, no riches, and who, perhaps through no fault of his own, had made a complete mess of his life. But to see his face, to look into his hard cruel eyes, you realized that at one time he had been something—had wielded power: as indeed he had.

Tex Sherill had been the Ring Master of the traveling circus to which the Sullivans had been attached in their circus days. Sherill had been a spectacular Ring Master: handsome, dashing, showy. He and the Sullivans had certain things in common: in particular a need for personal freedom: to be a law unto themselves. When the Sullivans left the circus, Sherill missed and envied them. He was sick of traveling round the country, forced to live a life of fettered routine, and he wanted to get out of the business; to live his own life. He had stayed with the circus a further six months, then had quit. He now ran an illicit still, manufacturing a particularly potent moonshine which he sold locally, and which provided him with sufficient funds to run the old plantation house and to allow him his much needed freedom.

The Sullivans heard that Sherill had quit the circus and had looked him up. They decided that such a place as the old plantation house was an ideal hideout should things ever get too hot for them. They put it to Sherill as a business proposition, and he was agreeable enough provided they made it worth his while, which they did.

And so it was to the old plantation house they had driven, deciding it was an excellent place to keep Carol until the six days had elapsed when they could, through her, control the money she had inherited. It was also an excellent place to leave her while they hunted for Larson. Tex Sherill would see she didn't escape; once he undertook a job he did it with ruthless thoroughness.

"Hello, boys," Sherill said, leaned against the post of the verandah and watched the Sullivans with suspicious eyes. "What brings you here?"

Without answering Max opened the rear door of the Packard, caught hold of Carol and hauled her into the sunlight.

Sherill stiffened.

"What's this—a snatch?" he asked, took a step away from the post, hooked his thumbs in the piece of cord that was bound tightly round his waist.

"No," Max said, swung Carol off her feet and carried her up the steps. "Where's Miss Lolly?"

"Out in the garden somewhere," Sherill returned, barred the way into the house. "I'm not handling a snatch, Max. That carries the death sentence."

"This isn't a snatch," Max said shortly. "Let me put her down and then we'll talk."

"Not inside," Sherill said firmly. "Put her in that chair. This stinks of a snatch to me."

Max laid Carol in the old rotten wicker chair that had stood for years on the porch, exposed to all weathers. It creaked dismally under her weight, and when she tried to sit up Max put his hand over her face and shoved her back so hard the chair tipped up and she sprawled on the dusty planks of the verandah, the chair falling on top of her.

"Keep an eye on her," Max said to Frank as he came up the steps, then he took Sherill by the arm and walked with him to the end of the verandah.

Frank straightened the chair, lifted Carol, put her in it again.

"Stay quiet, baby," he said. "I'm your own special friend. Max doesn't like girls, but I do. I'll see you don't come to any harm." He took off his hat and ran a small comb through his oily hair and winked at her. Lowering his voice, he went on: "How would you like to be my girl? We needn't tell Max"

"Who is she?" Sherill was asking. "By God, Max; if you're trying to mix me up in a snatch—"

"Pipe down," Max said, his eyes baleful. "I'm paying you good dough for us to use this place, aren't I? Well, I'm going to use it. It's not a snatch. She's escaped from a mental sanatorium. We're protecting her from herself. That isn't a snatch, is it?"

Sherill shifted his eyes. His bare feet, hard as leather, scratched uneasily on the boards.

"You mean—she's the Blandish girl?"

Max smiled: a cold, ferocious, humorless smile.

"So you've heard about that?"

"Who hasn't? I read the newspapers. What are you doing with her?"

"What do you think? She comes into six million bucks in a week from today; that is if she's not caught. She's going to be grateful, isn't she?"

Sherill glanced back along the verandah.

"Tied like that? Damned grateful, I'd say."

"She's nuts," Max said patiently. "She won't remember anything. You treat nuts like animals. So long as you feed 'em, they're grateful." He drew off his gloves, flexed his sweating fingers. "We can talk her into anything. She has one of those suggestive minds."

"I don't think you know much about lunatics," Sherill said, leaned to spit over the rail. "Well, it's your funeral. What's it worth to me?"

"You'll get a quarter of whatever we get."

"That could be too much or nothing at all," Sherill said uneasily. "I wish you hadn't brought her here, Max. It'll be unsettling for us all."

"Aw, *shaddap*," Max said, stuffed his gloves in his pocket and stared moodily across the overgrown vista.

Sherill eyed him, lifted his shoulders.

"They say she's dangerous," he went on. "Homicidal."

Max laughed.

"Don't talk soft. You used to perform in a lions' cage. You and Miss Lolly can handle her."

Sherill's face tightened.

"I don't know if Miss Lolly will want to," he said. "She's been acting odd these past days. I guess she's going nuts herself."

"She was all right when last we were here," Max said, not interested. "What's biting her?"

"Nerves, I guess," Sherill said, shrugging. "She ain't too easy to live with."

"To hell with her, then," Max said impatiently. "Got a room where you can lock this girl up? Somewhere safe?"

"There's a top room. The window's barred. You can have that."

"O.K. then, let's lock her up. I've got to get back to Point Breese."

"Ain't you staying?" Sherill asked, startled.

"I've things to do: a job to finish," Max said, and for a moment he showed his pointed white teeth. "I'll be back in a couple of days."

He walked with Sherill along the verandah.

"Take that tape off," he said to Frank.

Frank was sitting on the floor at Carol's feet, his head resting on the arm of the chair. There was a smirking, far away expression in his eyes, but he got up as soon as Max drew near, and picking hold of the corner of the tape he gave it a savage jerk, peeling it off Carol's mouth, sending her head twisting to the right.

She gave a little gasp of pain, sat up, faced the Sullivans.

"O.K., now talk," Max said. "Where's Larson? Where did you leave him?"

"I'm not going to tell you," Carol said, her voice husky. "I'll never tell you... you can do what you like to me."

Max smiled.

"You'll talk," he said gently. "You wait and see." He turned to Sherill. "Let's get her upstairs where I can work on her."

A soft step behind them made them turn quickly. A woman, or rather a figure dressed like a woman, came towards them: a strangely startling, but pathetic-looking, freak. She—for it was a woman in spite of the long beard—was dressed in a dusty black costume that was at least ten years out of fashion; about her naked ankles a worn pair of man's boots, unlaced, flapped when she moved. The lower part of her gaunt white face was hidden behind the luxuriant beard, which grew in soft, silky waves to a point some six inches above her waist.

Although Miss Lolly was now forty-five years of age, there was not one white hair in the beard that, not so long ago, had been morbidly stared at by thousands of people in many parts of the world as she sat in her little booth in the traveling circus that had been her home for most of her lonely life.

As she walked hesitatingly towards them her eyes, which must surely have been the saddest eyes in the world, fixed themselves on Carol.

There was a sudden tense silence, then the drowsy autumn afternoon reverberated with Carol's scream.

Frank giggled.

"She doesn't appreciate your form of beauty," he said to Miss Lolly, who drew back, two faint spots of color showing on her gaunt cheeks.

"Come on," Max said impatiently, "let's get her upstairs." He bent and cut the cord that tied Carol's ankles, jerked her to her feet.

Miss Lolly watched them drag the struggling girl into the house; listened to the scuffling of feet as they climbed the stairs.

Carol began to scream as they forced her along a broad, dark passage.

Miss Lolly flinched. She hated, violence, and she moved quickly into the big barn-like kitchen. While she washed the vegetables she had gathered her mind raced excitedly. That girl was beautiful, she thought. She had never seen such beauty. Her hair, her eyes... Miss Lolly inwardly flinched when she remembered the look of dazed horror that had come over Carol's face at the sight of her. But she had no feelings of anger or hatred for the girl: it was natural that one so beautiful should have been frightened, even revolted, at the sight of Miss Lolly.

A freak, she thought bitterly, and two tears swam out of her eyes, dripped into the muddy water amongst the potatoes. *Why had the Sullivans brought her here?* she wondered. She was scared of the Sullivans... hated them. They were cruel, vicious, dangerous. They laughed at her.

The kitchen door was pushed open and Sherill came in. He stood hesitating, looking at Miss Lolly, an uneasy gleam in his eyes.

"Who is she?" Miss Lolly asked, running more water into the bowl.

"The Blandish girl," Sherill said. "The one you were reading about this morning."

Miss Lolly dropped the bowl with a clatter into the sink and turned to him.

"You mean that poor crazy thing? The young lady they're searching for?"

"Yes."

"What are those boys doing with her?" Miss Lolly asked, clasping her hands, her eyes wide with horror, "They're not fit to... a girl like that, needing care, shouldn't be in their hands... she needs someone kind; someone who knows—"

A sudden wild agonized scream rang through the old house. Miss Lolly went very pale and took a step forward. Sherill scowled down at his bare feet and ran his hand lightly over his slicked-down hair.

Again came the scream: it cut through the wooden ceiling like a whiplash; a sound that froze Miss Lolly's blood.

"What are they doing to her?" she said, started forward, but Sherill seized her matchstick of an arm, shoved her back.

"Stay where you are," he said. "Don't you know better than to interfere with the Sullivans?"

"Oh, but I can't let them hurt her," Miss Lolly said, her bony fingers fluttering in the soft silk of her beard. "I couldn't let anyone suffer..."

"Quiet!" Sherill said.

"No! Please... not again...!" Carol screamed. Her voice, hitting the sides of the wooden walls of the upstairs room, started up vibrations so that each plank in the building seemed to whisper her words.

"Go out into the garden," Sherill said suddenly. "Get out!"

He took hold of Miss Lolly and pushed her through the back doorway, into the hot sunshine.

"Come on," he said, still holding her arm. "We're not going to listen to anything. The less we know about this the safer it'll be if those two bastards slip up."

Miss Lolly went with him. She held a grubby handkerchief to her eyes and her head flopped limply as she moved.

"So beautiful," she muttered to herself. "We poor girls get trouble... always trouble."

They remained in the garden for some time, and then they saw the Sullivans come out of the house. They had changed their black suits and black overcoats. They now looked like morticians on a holiday. Each wore a light grey suit, a pearl-grey fedora and brown shoes.

As Sherill moved towards them Frank climbed into the Packard and drove it round to the barn at the back of the house.

Max sat on the last step of the stoop. Leaning to a cupped match, his profile was hard and cruel.

"Going now?" Sherill said.

"Yeah," Max returned. He dabbed his sweating face with a crisp, clean handkerchief. "He's at the Blue Summit Logging Camp. It'll be a long trip."

Sherill didn't ask who was at the Blue Summit Logging Camp. He knew better than to ask questions. He shuffled his feet in the hot sand. The dry rustling of the sand was the only sound between the two men.

Then Sherill said, "So she talked?" There was an embarrassed, furtive look in his eyes.

"They always talk," Max said in a tired, flat voice. "They never learn sense."

The soft sound of a powerful motor engine starting up came from the barn, and a moment later a big dark blue Buick swept round the corner, pulled up beside Max.

Frank leaned out of the window.

"All set," he said.

Sherill eyed the change suits, the changed car, and his eyebrows lifted.

"You boys expecting trouble?"

"We're going back to a place where we've been already," Max I said, climbing into the car. "We don't put on the same act twice. Even without their black suits there was something coldly menacing about these two.

"Will you be long?" Sherill asked.

"Two days; maybe three, not more," Max said. "Sooner if he's still there, which he probably won't be."

"That's why she talked," Frank said crossly. "I bet that's why she talked. She had that amount of sense."

"We'll go there, anyway," Max returned, pulled his hat over his eyes. "And Sherill..."

Sherill stiffened.

"Yes?"

"Watch her. And when I say watch her... I mean watch her, If she ain't here when we get back, you best not be here, either."

"She'll be here," Sherill said shortly.

"See she is," Max said. "Get moving," he said to Frank.

Frank leaned across Max, stared at Sherill with intent eyes.

"Watch her, Tex," he said. "I like that dame... I wouldn't like to lose the opportunity to know her better. I've got ideas about her."

"Move your ass," Max snarled. "You have too many ideas about too many women."

"That's not possible," Frank said, giggled, drove recklessly down the sandy, rutted by-road.

Miss Lolly crept up the stairs, entered her small neat bedroom. She was trembling and had to sit on the bed until her legs felt strong enough to carry her to the dressing table. She spent some minutes brushing her hair and beard. Then she put on stockings and shoes. She found a clothes brush and carefully brushed the dust from her aging black costume.

When she came out of her room, Sherill was standing at the head of the stairs.

"What do you think you're doing?" he asked harshly.

"I'm going to see her," Miss Lolly said firmly. "She wants a woman's care."

"You don't call yourself a woman, do you, you old scarecrow?" Sherill snarled. "You'll only frighten her."

Miss Lolly flinched.

"I'm going to see her," she repeated, and began to move towards the next flight of stairs.

"Well, see her, then," Sherill returned, "but no nonsense. You heard what Max said."

"Oh, I wouldn't interfere," Miss Lolly said hastily. "I only want to say a kind word... if the poor thing's crazy in the head, like they say, a kind word will help her."

Sherill took a key from his pocket, handed it to Miss Lolly.

"Lock her in when you're through," he said shortly. "I've got to get back to work," and he went down the stairs, his feet making a flat, slapping noise on the bare boards.

A moment or so later, with quickly beating heart, Miss Lolly unlocked the door of Carol's room and entered.

It was a small bare room and hot from the sun that baked down on the tin roof. The window that looked out on to the so-called orchard had two rusty iron bars cemented into its frame. The floorboards were dusty and bare. The only furniture in the room was a truckle bed, an old rocking-chair, a wash-stand and an enamel bowl full of water on which floated a fine film of dust.

Carol lay on the bed, her hands at her sides, her legs straight, like an effigy on an ancient tomb. Her eyes were like holes cut in a sheet and as expressionless.

Although she heard the lock turn and the handle creak she did not look in the direction of the door. She looked straight in front of her at a cobweb that festooned the opposite wall and that moved gently in the draft. But she cringed inside at the sound, and without being able to help herself, her mouth formed into a soundless scream.

"It's only me," Miss Lolly said, standing shyly in the doorway. "It's Miss Lolly..."

Carol shivered, turned her head very slowly, saw the poor freak standing there, embarrassed, nervous, her sad eyes blinking back sympathetic tears, her bony fingers fluttering in her beard.

"Please go away," Carol said, and began to cry helplessly, hiding her face in her hands.

Miss Lolly paused to look back down the stairway and to listen. The old house was silent. Somewhere in the garden she could hear Sherill sawing wood; more distant still came a sudden sharp bark of a dog.

"I didn't mean to frighten you, my dear," Miss Lolly said, added wistfully: "I'm human, really. I used to be in the circus with them ... Max and Frank."

"I'm not frightened of you," Carol said, "It's only... I must be left alone... just for a little while..."

"Perhaps you'd like some coffee.... or tea?" Miss Lolly asked. "I'm so sorry for you... we girls... it's the men, really, isn't it? We are always sacrificing ourselves for the men. I've had my lovers... you mightn't think so... they shouldn't have brought you here... a nice girl like you..."

Carol suddenly sat up.

"Who are you?" she cried. "What do you want with me?"

Miss Lolly blinked, stepped back.

"I'm Miss Lolly... you're too young to have heard of me. I'm Lolly Meadows... the famous bearded lady. I'm an artist, really... you have to be an artist to bear the cross I have to bear. I don't want anything of you... I only want to be kind. I know what kindness is; not that I've had much of it myself. When I heard you scream, saw how lovely you were... I thought I'd see if I could help you. There's not much I can do, but we girls... if we can't help each other in our troubles..."

Carol dropped back flat on the bed.

"I told them where he was," she moaned. "I thought nothing could make me tell, but I hadn't the courage... I told them and they've gone after him.... and I love him so."

Miss Lolly came nearer.

"You mustn't excite yourself," she said. "I heard them... they said they didn't expect to find him. I'll get you cup of tea."

"Help me get away from here," Carol cried, sitting up. "Please help me to get away. Don't let them keep me here. I must get back to Steve. They shot him. I left him in a wood, and they're going there to finish him."

Miss Lolly's eyes showed her shocked fear.

"Oh, I never interfere," she said quickly. "I want to make your stay comfortable. I want to do what I can for you, but I don't meddle. I couldn't help you to leave here... that would be meddling."

"I'm sure you understand," Carol said. "You said just now you had lovers. You must know what it means when you love someone and he needs you. I told them where to find him. I tried not to." She buried her face in her hands. "Oh, you don't know what they did to me."

Miss Lolly dabbed her eyes.

"Oh, you poor thing," she said. "I'd like to help you. I didn't know. Do you love him so much?" She glanced over her shoulder. "But I mustn't stay here talking... I'll get you some tea. You'll feel better after a cup of tea... it's a long walk to the main road," she went on for no apparent reason. "There'll be money on the hallstand..." and she went out, closed the door and ran down the stairs.

Carol remained motionless, staring at the door. Then her heart gave a sudden lurch. *She hadn't heard Miss Lolly turn the key.* Very slowly she got off the bed. Her legs felt weak, and the distance between the bed and the door seemed to lengthen as she struggled across the bare boards. She touched the brass door handle, turned it and pulled. The door opened. For a moment she stood staring into the dingy passage, scarcely believing that the way was open for her escape.

She crept out on to the landing, looked down the staircase well into the dark hall three flights below. She could hear someone sawing wood in the garden and the rattle of crockery in the kitchen. They were homespun, reassuring sounds in a nightmare of terror.

She moved to the head of the staircase, and holding her breath, her heart thudding against her side, she began a silent descent.

~§~

There lived in one of the ruined shacks of the abandoned logging camp on Blue Mountain Summit an old man who was known as Old Humphrey: a half-witted old fellow, very poor and dirty, and who had a remarkable power over birds. He was as timid as a field mouse, and had selected the logging camp for his home since no one ever came to the place. He had been considerably startled when Carol had driven the big shiny Packard into the clearing and had left Larson there while she drove frantically away in search of Doc Fleming.

Old Humphrey had approached Larson with the utmost caution and then had returned to his shack to await developments. He fell asleep while waiting, and awoke with a start when Phil Magarth drove up in his battered Cadillac.

Old Humphrey knew Magarth. Some months ago Magarth had tried to persuade Old Humphrey to give a demonstration of his power over birds, but the old fellow wasn't having any. So when he saw Magarth drive up he thought he had come to worry him again, and it was with relief when he saw Magarth carry the unconscious Larson to the car and drive off again.

Old Humphrey hoped that he had seen the last of these unwelcome visitors, but the following evening, as he sat before his log fire cooking his supper, the door of his shack was pushed open and the Sullivans came in.

The Sullivans hadn't expected to find Steve Larson in the camp clearing: that was too much to hope for. But following their usual method of tracking down their intended victim, they were content to start at the place where their victim had last been.

They had seen smoke coming from Old Humphrey's chimney, had exchanged glances and had walked silently to the ruined little shack.

"Hello, Dad," Frank said, and kicked the door shut.

Old Humphrey crouched over the fire. His wizened dirty old face twitched with fright; his thin, filthy hand gripped the handle of the frying pan that hissed on the fire until his knuckles showed white under the grime.

Max leaned against the mantelpiece, lit a cigarette. The light of the match reflected in his eyes: they were like glittering pieces of glass: black and expressionless.

"You talk to him," he said to Frank.

Frank sat down on an upturned box close to Old Humphrey, took off his hat to comb his hair. He smiled, and the smile struck a chill into Old Humphrey's palpitating heart. He put the comb away after picking out the hairs.

"We're looking for a guy," Frank said. "A guy who's sick. What happened to him?"

"I don't know nothing about any sick guys," Old Humphrey whined. "I just want to be left alone."

Max moved restlessly, but Frank still smiled.

"Come on, Dad," he said softly. "You know all about it. We mean business. Don't make it hard for yourself. What was he to you?"

Old Humphrey didn't say anything. He lifted his shoulders as if he expected a blow, brooded down at the mess in the frying pan, his eyes sightless with fear.

Frank kicked his ankle gently.

"Come on, Dad," he said. There was a genial note in his voice. "What happened to the sick guy?"

"I ain't seen a sick guy," Old Humphrey said. "I mind my own business."

Max suddenly snatched the frying pan out of the old man's hand and threw it across the room.

Frank giggled.

"What happened to the sick guy?" he asked again.

Old Humphrey stared at the frying pan lying in the corner, at the food that dripped down the wooden wall on to the floor, and he clawed at his beard.

"The newspaper man took him away," he said shrilly. "That's all I know."

"What newspaper man?" Max said.

"Magarth," Old Humphrey mumbled. "He's worried me before. Everyone worries me. Why can't they leave me alone?"

Frank stood up.

"No one will worry you any more," he said softly, stepped to the door.

Old Humphrey turned, sliding his broken boots over the dirty floor, clutching at his ragged overcoat.

"Close your eyes," Max said. "We don't want you to see us leave."

"I won't look, mister," Old Humphrey said.

"Close your eyes," Max repeated softly.

The grimy, wrinkled eyelids dropped: like two shutters of an untenanted house.

Max slipped his gun from the shoulder holster, touched Old Humphrey's forehead lightly with the barrel, squeezed the trigger.

~§~

Half-way down the broad stairs, on the landing leading to the final flight of stairs, stood an old grandfather clock.

As Carol crept past it it gave off a loud whirring sound and began to chime.

For an instant she stood very still and watched herself run out of her body, down the stairs, whirl and run back into her body again. Then she realized it was only the old clock chiming and she leaned against the creaking banister-rail, sick with shock. She went on down the stairs towards the dark hall and the front door that led into the open.

She reached the hall, stood for a moment to listen.

Miss Lolly poured boiling water into a teapot. She put a cup and saucer, a bowl of sugar, a jug of milk on the tray.

Carol heard all this, knew exactly what Miss Lolly was doing. In a minute or so Miss Lolly would be coming out into the hall with the tray.

The hall door was ajar and the warmth of the sun-baked garden seeped through the opening, wound like an invisible ribbon around Carol's limbs.

She moved quickly and silently past the big oak hall-stand on which lay a dirty ten dollar bill. *There'll be money on the hallstand,* Miss Lolly had said. Carol picked up the note: It felt dry and brittle in her nervous fingers. She held it tightly, not quite believing it was real, and went on to the front door.

She opened the door, which creaked sharply, making the nerves in her body stiffen like pieces of wire. She looked back over her shoulder.

Miss Lolly was watching her from the kitchen door. She was crying. Tears ran down her gaunt face and sparkled like chips of ice in her beard. She held the tea-tray before her: the crockery rattled faintly because her hands were trembling.

They stared at each other, sympathy and terror bridging the gulf between them, then Carol ran out onto the verandah, closed the front door behind her, shutting off the sight of Miss Lolly's triumphant but agonized expression.

Close by, the rasp of a saw biting into hard wood jarred the peaceful stillness. Carol paused to reconnoiter the ground.

There was an overgrown path that led from the house down to a white-wood gate. Beyond the gate was the by-road, sandy and rutty, that led into the jungle of cypress and brier. *It's a long walk to the main road,* Miss Lolly had said.

The sound of the saw abruptly ceased: a silence full of hot sunshine fell over the old plantation house. Carol walked swiftly, and carefully across the verandah to the head of the four rotten wooden steps that led to the path. There she paused again to listen.

She did not hear Sherill come round the side of the house. His naked feet made no sound in the soft, hot sand. She first became aware of him when he arrived at the bottom of the stoop and was staring at her with angry, frightened eyes as if he couldn't quite believe what he was seeing.

Beyond this tall, upright figure lay the by-road and freedom.

"Get back to your room," he said harshly.

Carol looked quickly to right and left. The rail of the verandah, rotten as it was, fenced her in. It was impossible to retreat: only the dark hall yawned behind her, but it offered no escape. Escape lay ahead, beyond this angry, frightened man who barred her path.

"Don't touch me," she said fiercely. "I'm going... you can't stop me..."

"You're not," Sherill said. "Go back to your room. I don't want to hurt you... but I will if you don't go back."

The thought of further pain made Carol cringe, but she didn't move, and when Sherill began a cautious approach she still did not move.

"Get back," he said, reached out and caught her arm.

She struck at him then. Her fist caught him high up on his cheekbone, startled rather than hurt him; then she flew at him, kicking and hitting him.

He held her close. His arms, big and hard, encircled her, crushing her to him, smothering her efforts to hit him, driving the breath out of her body. He gave her a hard chopping blow with his clenched fist that landed in the hollow of her neck, turning her sick and faint. She ceased to struggle and he half carried her, half dragged her, into the hall. Then he paused, stared at Miss Lolly, who faced him, a double-barreled shot-gun in her hand.

"Put her down," she said firmly. "Please, Tex, put her down. You're hurting her."

"Get out of the way," Sherill snarled. "Have you gone crazy, too? Listen to me!"

Carol suddenly bunched herself against him like a spring coiling, then sprang back against his encircling arms, breaking his hold. She thudded against the wall, staggered, half fell. Miss Lolly pushed the gun against Sherill's chest.

"Don't make me shoot you," she pleaded, her eyes wild. "She must be allowed to go. We mustn't stop her. We have no right to keep her here."

Sherill cursed her, but he made no move as Carol slipped past him, ran blindly into the open towards the white wooden gate.

"You know what you've done?" he said. "You damned old sentimental fool. I shouldn't have trusted you." He went to the door, looked after Carol. She was running very quickly; he was astonished that anyone could move so lightly and yet so quickly over the uneven ground. He knew he had no hope of catching her.

Then he thought of the dog, and without looking at Miss Lolly he ran down the wooden steps, round the building, to the kennels.

Carol kept to the by-road. Each side of her the dense jungle of trees and bushes and high grass shut her in like the walls of a maze. As she ran she listened and heard no sound of pursuit, but she did not slacken her pace until she had gone some distance from the old plantation house; then, panting, a pain in her side, she slowed to a walk.

She had no idea how far she was from Point Breese. She realized that the distance must be great, for she had spent a long time in the rapidly moving Packard. But she had money now: admittedly not much, but enough if she could only reach a bus stop or a railway station.

She realized with something like triumph that the Sullivans had only a few minutes' start over her. They had the car, of course, but they wouldn't find Steve quickly. She was certain that Magarth wouldn't have left Steve in that wood. With any luck she would arrive at Point Breese before the Sullivans found him: that was all she asked for.

Then suddenly she stiffened, her heart fluttering, looked back over her shoulder. Not far away came the bay of a hound; and instantly she began to run again.

If that man had set a dog after her... again she looked back along the twisting, narrow, hedged-in road. Was there any use hiding? She came to an abrupt standstill, looked wildly around for a stick—some weapon with which to defend herself.

A moment later she saw the dog. It came bounding down the narrow road: a great black brute with a spade-shaped head, close hair and a long tail. Its eyes were like little sparks of fire.

Carol caught her breath when she saw this black monster rushing towards her. There was nothing she could do. It was like being in a nightmare, and she stood still, the hot sun beating on her back, her shadow, long and thin, pointing at the dog like a weapon.

When the dog saw her it slowed to a menacing walk, its muzzle only a few inches from the ground, its tail stiff, in line with its back and head.

Carol scarcely breathed. She fixed the dog with her eyes and was as still as if she had been carved out of stone.

The dog slowed its pace, snarled at her: the great fangs as white as orange pith under the black lip. Then its hair stiffened all along its thin, hard back, and it stopped, crouched, uncertain whether to spring or not.

Knowing it was her only chance of escape, Carol willed the dog to remain where it was. She tried to see into the dog's brain, and now that she had stopped it in its tracks she moved forward very slowly and the dog began to back up like a cartoon film in reverse.

For a full minute they continued to stare at each other, then the dog's tail gradually lost its stiffness like a ship striking its flag. With its nerve broken it emitted a low howl, turned and bolted back down the narrow road. Carol turned and fled in the opposite direction.

~§~

Sherill was blundering down the hot road when the dog passed him and he stood staring after the dog, the blood draining out of his face. He knew then that Carol had escaped and there was nothing he could do to recapture her.

He stood for some moments, unable to think. *If she ain't here when we get back, you best not be here either,* Max had said. The Sullivans didn't make idle threats. Slowly he turned and walked back to the old plantation house, pushed open the wooden gate, walked stiffly up the garden path.

Miss Lolly sat in the basket chair, a wooden, frightened expression on her face. She looked at him out of the corner of her eyes, but he said nothing, walked past her into the house. He was inside some time, but Miss Lolly continued to sit in the sun, waiting. She had no regrets. She felt that in releasing Carol she had, in some way, justified her own tragic life.

Sherill came out on to the verandah. He was wearing a grey and black check suit, Mexican boots and a big white Stetson. Miss Lolly remembered that hat when, years ago, Sherill had joined the circus and it had attracted her attention: remembering how young and dashing he had looked, wearing it. But now, his face white and puffy, there wasn't any resemblance left of the young man who had fluttered her heart.

Sherill dumped down the two bags, walked down the wooden steps, then paused.

"You best pack up," he said without looking at her. "We've gotta get out," and he went on down the path, round the house to the barn. He moved slowly as if his boots were too tight.

Miss Lolly continued to sit in the basket chair. Her fingers fumbled at her beard, her eyes were bright with unshed tears.

On the upper landing of the house the grandfather clock chimed the half-hour. The clock had been in Miss Lolly's spacious caravan throughout her circus career. All the other furniture in the house—what there was of it—belonged to her, and each piece was a memory in her life.

A large red and black butterfly fishtailed in and landed on the verandah rail, close to Miss Lolly. She looked at it, watched it move its wings slowly up and down and then take off, flying through the motionless hot scented air.

The butterfly reminded her of Carol. *Beauty should not be imprisoned,* she thought. *I did right: I know I did right.*

Sherill drove round to the front of the house in a big Ford truck. He cut the engine, got out, came up the steps.

"You'll have to help," he said, still not looking at Miss Lolly. "We can take most everything in the truck."

"I'm going to stay," Miss Lolly said quietly. "This is my home."

"I know," Sherill said roughly. "Well, you've smashed it up for us now. Come on, don't talk a lot of drivel. We've got to get out...you know those boys..."

"You go," Miss Lolly said, thinking of the butterfly. "I'd rather stay, even if it's only for a day or so. I've been happy here."

Sherill eyed her, lifted his shoulders wearily.

"All right," he said. "If that's the way you feel. I'll get off then."

Miss Lolly looked up.

"I did right, Tex," she said quietly. "It was an evil thing..."

"Yes, you did right," Sherill said, defeated. "So long, Lolly."

"Good-bye," she said, "and good luck, Tex."

She watched him dump his bags in the truck, climb into the cab.

"They said they'd be back in two or three days," Sherill said as he stabbed the starter.

"It'll be long enough," Miss Lolly returned.

~§~

Carol had got to within twenty-five miles of Point Breese when her luck seemed to run out. Up to this moment she had been traveling by various routes and vehicles towards Steve, but now night had come down the cars and trucks which before had stopped willingly enough seemed shy of her.

The drivers were not chancing trouble by stopping for the rather wild-looking girl who waved frantically at them as they rushed through the darkness. A man might have got a lift, but not a girl. The drivers who passed Carol were heading for home; they didn't want trouble or excitement. One or two of them did hesitate, slow down, wondering if she was a looker, whether they might have a little fun with her, but on that patch of road there were no lights, and they decided she'd probably be a hag, so they kept on, increasing their speed, feeling suddenly virtuous.

Carol was tired. From the start it seemed to be going so well.

A truck picked her up on the State Highway and the driver was decent to her, sharing with her his ample lunch, talking cheerfully about things that happened to him in his narrow walk of life. He set her down at a cross-roads, showing her the direction she'd have to take, wishing her luck.

A traveling salesman gave her a lift only a few minutes after the truck had disappeared in a cloud of dust. No, he wasn't going to Point Breese, but he could drop her off at Campville, which was on the route.

He was more curious than the truck-driver and had asked questions. What was she doing, thumbing rides? Was she running away from home? Did she know she was pretty nice to look at? Hadn't she better let him take her home? But she evaded these questions, made him talk about himself.

At Campville he gave her five dollars.

"You'll need it, kid," he said, opening the car door for her. "Aw, forget it. I'm making good money in this racket. If I want you to have it, why shouldn't I give it to you? Get a meal. So long and good luck."

In a little restaurant in the main street she learned that the Sullivans had been in there. They had dropped in for a cup of coffee: four hours earlier. The news cheered her, and she finished her meal, went out into the street and caught the bus to Kinston, another milestone along her journey.

At Kinston she had to wait an hour or so before she found transport. Kinston, they told her, was forty-five miles from Point Breese. There was no direct bus service to Point Breese. She'd have to change at Bear Lake. There'd be an hour and a half wait at Bear Lake for the connecting bus.

A young fellow in a blue suit and stained grey hat, hearing the conversation, said he was going to Point Breese. He would be glad to take her. So she went with him, and they drove out of Kinston into the thickening dusk.

The young fellow drove very fast and said nothing and smoked cigarettes all the time. He drove with only one hand and whipped the car in and out of traffic, bearing down upon other cars until they slewed aside with brakes squealing, shooting recklessly across intersections.

He frightened Carol more by his furtive silence than his reckless driving.

When they got into the open country he slammed on his brakes, ran off the road on to the grass verge. Then he threw away his cigarettes and grabbed her.

He was very strong and handled her with practiced ease. He kept kissing her while she tried to fight him off. While they struggled, he never said a word, and Carol hadn't enough breath to scream.

He seemed to know exactly what he wanted to do to her: and he did it, and then he shoved her away from him and lit a cigarette. His hat had fallen off in the struggle and his hair had broken about his face, hair long as a girl's. He flung it back with a toss of his head.

When she opened the car door and staggered out on to the grass verge he didn't even look at her, and he drove away fast, the red glow of his cigarette like a little sneering eye where his mouth should have been.

Too numb to shiver, too weak to stand, she hunched over the broken glass and gravel along the road. A ghostly mist crept up the mountain. An hour passed before she gathered enough courage to wave again to the passing cars: but none of them stopped.

There was a long tear in her dress and one of her stockings had come down and she was crying. She looked wild all right, and the drivers were scared of her.

After a while she gave up waving and began to walk. She walked stiffly. It was dark and lonely and the night air was turning cold. But she kept on, thinking of Steve, imagining the Sullivans already in Point Breese.

Then she heard the sound of brakes and a moment later a big kind of wagon—she couldn't see much of it in the darkness—drew up and the driver switched on his spotlight and focused it on her.

She was too tired and sick to wonder at his startled exclamation.

"Hello there," the driver said out of the darkness. "I guess you could use a ride."

She said yes; not caring what happened to her so long as she could reach Point Breese.

The driver climbed down from the cab and stood beside her. She saw he was wearing a white coat.

"This must be my lucky day," he said with an excited laugh, and caught hold of her very expertly so that she was helpless without being hurt.

He ran her to the back of the wagon.

"There's another nut inside, but she's tied up," he said. "Don't you two girls get to fighting."

Carol didn't know the man was Sam Garland of the Glenview Mental Sanatorium, who had been into Kinston to collect a patient. She thought he must be drunk and she began to scream wildly.

"Don't excite yourself," Garland said genially, unlocked the door and threw her into the dimly lit ambulance. He slammed the door, went round to the cab, climbed in and drove off.

Carol half sat up, then froze into motionless terror.

A woman was lying on one of the slung stretchers. She was plain to look at and her thick black hair hung in lank coils beyond her shoulders. She was in a strait-jacket and her ankles were strapped to the stretcher rails.

She looked at Carol with bright, mad little eyes.

CHAPTER V

EXCITEMENT hung over Point Breese like a fine layer of dust. The Sullivans sensed it as they drove down the main street. It was not that there was anything to see. Point Breese was hidden under a blanket of darkness, and except for the saloon bars and the all-night café and the drug store, no lights showed. But the excitement was there: you could feel it seeping out of the dark houses and hanging in the cool night air.

The Sullivans wondered about it, but they didn't say anything to each other: not quite sure that they weren't imagining things.

They were very tired after the drive from the old plantation house. They had had no sleep worth speaking about for twenty-four hours, and although they didn't need much sleep, they were now ready for a rest.

Frank, who was driving the Buick, swung the car off the main street, round to the jail and the hotel. He slowed to a crawl when he saw the little group of men standing outside the jail.

Max's hand automatically went to his shoulder holster and his eyes grew watchful, but the men just glanced their way, turned their heads again to stare up at the jail.

"What's up?" Frank asked out of the corner of his mouth.

"Nothing we should worry about," Max returned. "There must be a garage round the back. Get the car out of sight and we'll double back."

They found the hotel garage, left the car and retraced their steps to the front entrance. They kept in the shadows, but the group of men were too intent watching the jail to notice them.

The clerk behind the reception desk was a pale little man with a moustache like a soot-mark on his upper lip. He gave Max a pen and pushed the register towards him.

"A double room," he asked, "or two singles?"

"Double," Max said, signed the book.

Frank took the pen, read the fictitious name Max had scrawled in the register, copied it.

"Send up coffee and hot rolls at half past eight tomorrow morning," Max said. "And the newspapers."

The clerk made a note on a sheet of paper, touched a bell. The bellhop was a scraggy man with bags under his eyes. The pill-box hat he wore made him look as if he was going to a fancy dress party. He took the Sullivans' pig-skin bag, led the way to a small, hand-propelled elevator.

As they were being drawn creakily upwards, a muffled hammering sound jarred the silence of the hotel.

"Fixing the scaffold," the bellhop said, and his fishy eyes sparkled with sudden excitement.

"What scaffold?" Frank asked, although he knew.

"For the hanging, of course," the bellhop returned, brought the elevator to rest, pushing back the grill. "Ain't you heard about it?"

The Sullivans looked at him watchfully, moved out of the elevator into the corridor.

A girl in a silk wrap and sky-blue pajamas, carrying a sponge bag and towel, passed them. In her lips, painted into a savage cupid bow, dangled a cigarette. She looked at the Sullivans and her eyes smiled.

She caught Frank's eye but Max didn't even notice her.

"What hanging?" Frank asked the bellhop.

"Where's our room?" Max broke in. "Come on, show us the room."

The bellhop led them down the corridor, unlocked a door, pushed it open, turned on the lights. It was the usual sort of room you'd expect a hotel like this to offer you. It had been furnished for economy rather than for comfort: not the kind of room you'd wish to stay in for long.

"What hanging?" Frank repeated, closing the door.

The bellhop rubbed his hands on the back of his trousers. He looked like a man with good news.

"The Waltonville murderer," he said. "Ain't you read about him? He killed three dames all in the same evening and then gave himself up. I guess he won't kill any more dames after nine o'clock tomorrow."

"Get out," Max said without looking at him.

The bellhop stared.

"I was only telling you, mister—" he began.

"Get out!" Max hissed.

The bellhop went quickly to the door, hesitated, looking back at the Sullivans. They stared at him, still, intent, watchful. There was something about them that scared him. It was like losing your way in the dark and finding yourself suddenly in a cemetery.

When he had gone, Max picked up the bag and tossed it onto the bed.

Frank still stood motionless in the middle of the room. The muffled hammering held his attention.

"I wonder what it feels like to be hanged," he said suddenly. "To be executed with all those eyes on you."

"I haven't thought about it," Max said, and for an imperceptible moment he paused in his unpacking.

"To be locked in, to hear that hammering, knowing it was for you; to hear them come down the passage for you, and you not able to do anything about it," Frank went on in a low voice. "Like a beast in a cage."

Max said nothing. He began to undress.

"It could happen to us, Max," Frank said, and little beads of moisture showed on his white, fattish face.

"Get into bed," Max said.

They didn't speak until they were in bed and Max had turned off the light, then Max said out of the darkness: "I wonder where we can find Magarth. It shouldn't be difficult. The thing that will be difficult is to find out where he's hidden Larson, and if Larson has talked."

Frank said nothing: he was still listening to the muffled hammering.

"How long do you reckon they'll keep pounding away like that?" he asked.

Max, who missed nothing, detected the slightest quaver in Frank's voice.

"Until they've fixed it good," he said. "Go to sleep."

But Frank didn't. He lay listening to the hammering and it got on his nerves. Max's light, even breathing also got on his nerves. To think a guy could sleep with that going on, Frank thought angrily. He was angry because his nerve wasn't as good as Max's, and because he was frightened.

After a while the hammering stopped, but still Frank didn't sleep. Later, a sudden loud crash made him start up, and he snapped on the light.

"What's that?" he demanded, his nerves crawling on the surface of his skin.

Max moved out of sleep into wakefulness as easily and as quickly as, the turning on of an electric lamp.

"They're testing the trap," he said calmly.

"Yes," Frank said, "I hadn't thought of that," and he put out the light.

Now neither of the Sullivans slept. Frank was thinking about the condemned man, and his mind slipped back into the past; the faces of the men and women he had helped to murder floated out of the darkness; surrounded him, pressed in on him.

Max didn't sleep because he was thinking about Frank. For some time now he had been watching Frank. Although Frank had shown no outward sign, Max suspected that he was losing his nerve. He wondered how long it would be before Frank would be of no further use to him. The thought disturbed him, for he had known Frank a long time. They had developed their knife-throwing act together when they had been at school.

But later they both slept, and woke at eight-thirty the following morning when the hotel maid brought them coffee, and rolls. She also brought in with her the atmosphere of suppressed excitement. It was more electric now than the previous night, but it didn't affect Max. He sat up in bed, poured the coffee, passed a cup to Frank, who put it on the table at his side.

"They'll be coming for him in a few minutes," Frank said, betraying that he was still thinking of the execution.

"The rolls aren't hot enough," Max grumbled, got out of bed and went into the bathroom.

He had just finished shaving when the trap was sprung. The crash left him unmoved. He continued to clean his razor, his white, cold face expressionless. A moment after the trap was sprung a vast sigh came up from the street in through the open bathroom window, and he looked out and saw the huge crowd standing before the jail.

"Vultures," he thought, and with sudden vicious hatred of them and their morbid curiosity he spat out of the window.

When he returned to the bedroom Frank was quiet. He was still in bed, and his pillow was dark with sweat, and sweat ran down his face so that his skin glistened in the sunlight.

The two men didn't say anything to each other. Max noticed that Frank hadn't touched his coffee or rolls.

While Max dressed the only sound came from the shuffling feet of the crowd as they broke up and returned to their homes. Frank stared up at the ceiling, listening to the shuffling, and sweat continued to darken his pillow.

"I'll be back in a little while," Max said at the door. "You'd better wait for me here."

Frank didn't trust his voice, so he didn't say anything, and Max didn't seem to expect him to say anything.

~§~

"Any news?" Magarth asked as he pushed open the door to the Sheriff's office and entered the dingy little room.

Kamp glanced up.

"I've just got back from the execution," he said. There was still a faint greenish tinge in his brick-red complexion. It was his first execution in five years and it had upset him. He grimaced, went on: "I've had a report that the Packard Clipper we want was seen in Kinston midday yesterday and was headed for Campville, but nothing else has come in—no trace of the girl. Campville's sheriff is keeping his eyes open. We'll hear if anything else turns up."

Magarth sat on the edge of the desk.

"I wonder if they have got her," he said, a worried look in his eyes. "Seems odd they should be leaving the district. I was willing to bet they'd have had a shot at finishing Larson. Of course, if they have got her, they might be taking her some place we wouldn't think to look for her, and then come back here after Larson. Think we should comb the country around Campville?"

"It's being done," Kamp said. "And we're watching all roads into Point Breese for the Packard in case they try to slip back here."

"Good enough," Magarth said approvingly. "Well, there's not much else we can do. I'm going over to Miss Banning's place to see how they're getting on. I saw Doc Kober just now. He thinks Larson has a fighting chance, but he mustn't be worried for a day or so. I sent young Riley up to the farm to look after his foxes."

"Hartman's been in again," Kamp said, pulling a wry face.

"That reminds me," Magarth said. "I told you we were investigating Hartman's background. We've just received a report. He's been playing the markets and has sustained some heavy losses, but he always manages to find enough money to meet his commitments and continues to plunge. No one knows where he gets the money from, but I can guess. It mightn't be a bad idea if the Blandish girl wasn't found until next week. If she comes into her money a thorough investigation could be made, and I bet we'd dig up enough to put Hartman away for a long time."

"You newspaper guys are the most suspicious men in the world," Kamp said, pulling at his moustache. "Anyway, the girl's dangerous. We have to find her as quickly as we can."

"I wonder if she is," Magarth returned. "She seemed normal enough to me when I talked to her."

"Doc Travers explained that to me," Kamp said. "She has a split mind. She may go for weeks acting normal before she has an attack, but when she's that way she's highly dangerous."

"I can't imagine it," Magarth said stubbornly. "I've talked to her; you haven't." He shrugged, slid off the table. "I'll be getting along. Give me a call if anything breaks. You can reach me at Miss Banning's place. I'll be there all morning."

As he ran down the steps of the jail Jedson, the owner of the big service station close by, hailed him by name, crossed the street to speak to him.

Max, standing on the hotel steps, heard Jedson hail Magarth and without appearing to move, edged behind one of the big pillars supporting the hotel porch. He watched Magarth exchange a few words with Jedson, then climb into his battered Cadillac and drive off.

Jedson moved towards the hotel and Max strolled down the steps to meet him.

"Was that Magarth, the newspaper man?" Max asked as Jedson was about to pass him.

Jedson paused, looked Max over, nodded briefly.

"That's right, mister," he said, made to pass on.

"That's my bad luck," Max went on. "I'm supposed to do business with him. It's my first visit to this town. Know where he's gone?"

Jedson shook his head.

"You could put a call through if it's urgent."

"Thanks, buddy," Max said. "It's urgent all right. Who's Miss Banning?"

"She runs a big orange plantation up on Grass Hill," Jedson said; then, realizing he was talking a lot, gave Max a sharp glance.

"Grass Hill?" Max said, and smiled, showing his white pointed teeth. "Thanks."

Jedson watched Max walk quickly into the hotel and up the stairs. He lifted his hat to scratch his head.

"Now, I wonder who he is?" he said to himself.

~§~

While the Sullivans had been trying to sleep in their hotel bedroom, Sam Garland drove his ambulance along the dark highway towards Point Breese. He was excited and jubilant. When his headlights had picked out Carol as she walked along the lonely road, and he caught a glimpse of her red hair, he had automatically slammed on his brakes. *Surely there was no other girl in the district with hair like that?* he said to himself. *She must be Carol Blandish.* And when he turned his spotlight on her he recognized her immediately. She was bruised and exhausted but it was definitely her.

Even now that she was securely locked in the ambulance he could scarcely believe his luck. The five-thousand-dollar reward was still unclaimed, and it would be his—and he could use five thousand dollars.

He wondered suddenly if he shouldn't have strapped Carol to a stretcher. You never knew what tricks a nut would get up to. Garland had been a mental nurse for a number of years before he got sick of it and took on the job of Doc Travers's chauffeur and ambulance-driver. He had learned how to handle dangerous lunatics and wasn't scared of them. He had hesitated whether to stop and fix Carol before going on. Then as there was silence in the ambulance, he decided not to waste time, but to get to Glenview as quickly as he could. He was looking forward to seeing Joe's face when he arrived.

But he wasn't to know of the whispered conversation that was going on inside the ambulance.

The madwoman who was traveling with Carol—her name was Hatty Summers—had been in a home for years. At first she seemed harmless enough, but recently she had developed homicidal tendencies, and arrangements had been made to transfer her from the home in Kinston to Glenview, where the staff were better able to handle dangerous patients.

As soon as Carol set eyes on Hatty Summers she knew she was locked in with a mad woman, and her blood ran cold.

"So they've got you, too," Hatty whispered, and laughed. "Picked you off the road, did they? Now that's what I call real smart: knew you as soon as they saw you."

Carol crouched away from the bright little eyes that seemed to probe right into her mind. Again she experienced the feeling that she was asleep and dreaming.

"They'll take you to Glenview," Hatty went on, "and they'll lock you up. I've heard of Glenview. That's where I'm going, because the nurses are afraid of me at Kinston." She raised her head, added, "And they're right to be afraid of me." She laughed, went on: "Glenview's nice, but I'm sick of being locked up. I want to be free to do what I like. This straight jacket's really cramping my style."

Glenview!

The name stirred a dormant chord in Carol's memory,

conjuring up a shadowy picture of a room with blue walls and a nurse who stared and pointed at her, but said nothing.

"I must get away," she said, speaking her thoughts aloud "I must get away before anything happens..."

She ran to the door and tried to open it, but her fingers slipped over the smooth surface, unable to find a purchase.

"They won't let you get away," Hatty said, giggling with excitement. "You're mad like me. There's nothing you can do about it. Do you want to sing a song?"

"I'm not mad!" Carol cried, twisting round and setting her back against the door. "Don't say that."

"Oh, yes, you are," Hatty said. "I know. You're clever. You can hide it from most people, but not from me. I'm on your frequency."

"Just shut up," Carol said, and hid her face in her hands.

"But you are mad," Hatty whispered. "You may call it by some other name, but you're mad as I am. I can always tell."

"I am not like you," Carol said, but cold fingers seemed to squeeze her heart.

Could she be mad? she asked herself. *Was that the explanation of these extraordinary things that were happening to her? Were they delusions of a diseased mind? Was that why she couldn't remember who she was? Was that the explanation of the odd, infrequent snapping noise that sounded in her head which turned everything into a badly focused film?*

"Losing confidence?" Hatty asked, watching her closely. "Well, don't give up hope. I didn't mean to depress you. We've got each other."

"Oh, stop talking to me!" Carol burst out, and began to beat on the door of the ambulance.

"Hush yourself, you little fool," Hatty said, her tongue darting out like a serpents'. "It won't do any good pretending. He won't let you out until you get to Glenview, and then it'll be too late. Do you want to get away?"

Carol looked at her over her shoulder.

"I must get away..."

"Between us we could manage it. He's smart, but he's overconfident. You'd have to get this jacket off me."

"Oh, no!" Carol said, shrinking back.

"You're not frightened of me?" Hatty asked, and laughed. "We belong to the same breed. We don't hurt each other. You needn't be frightened."

Carol shivered.

"Please don't talk like that; I'm not mad. It's wicked to say I'm mad."

"Don't excite yourself," Hatty said. "If you want to get away you must undo these straps; and you'd better be quick. We can't be far off now. Once they get you inside you'll never get out again."

Carol walked slowly over to her, stood looking down at her.

"And if I do release you, how shall I get away?" she asked, and shivered as she saw the cunning that lurked in the bright little eyes.

"Get me out of this jacket," Hatty whispered, "and then start screaming and banging. He'll come in to see what's the matter. It's his duty to see what's happening. While he's attending to you, I'll go for him. The two of us can fix him easily enough."

Sam Garland was a mile from Point Breese when he heard hammering and screaming from inside the ambulance. He scowled into the darkness, and after a moment's hesitation stopped the ambulance. He didn't want Carol to hurt herself. He wanted to hand her over to Doc Travers in good condition so there'd be no arguing about the five-thousand-dollar reward.

He climbed out of the cab and, cursing under his breath, walked round in the darkness to the back of the ambulance, unlocked the door, opened it and peered into the dimly lit interior.

Carol was flinging herself against the far wall, her screams reverberating in the confined space.

Garland shot a quick look at Hatty Summers. She eyed him from under the blanket, giggled excitedly, but she looked safe enough. He climbed into the ambulance, pulled the door to, but not shut, grabbed hold of Carol, twisting her arms behind her.

"Take it easy," he said. "You lie down, baby. You're getting over-excited."

Carol was terrified when she found how helpless she was in his experienced grip, and although she struggled frantically Garland forced her to a stretcher that hung on a rack opposite to the one on which Hatty lay.

"Let me go!" Carol panted. "Take your hands off me."

"All right, baby," Garland said soothingly. "No need to get worked up. Just lie down. I'll make you comfortable."

He gripped her wrists in one big hand, suddenly stooped and caught her under her knees, lifted her and dropped her on to the stretcher.

At that moment Hatty pushed off the blanket and sat up.

Some instinct warned Garland of his danger, and he looked over his shoulder as Hatty swung her legs off the stretcher.

Still holding Carol's wrists, he faced Hatty.

"Be a good girl and stay where you are," he said gently.

He wasn't flustered, but he knew he would have to get out quick.

He couldn't hope to handle both of them. "Get back on to that stretcher," he ordered, and at the same moment he released Carol's wrists, jumped for the door.

There wasn't enough space for quick movement, and besides, Hatty was already on her feet. She grabbed hold of Garland's arm, swung him round and, laughing gleefully, she shot her hands at his throat.

Carol struggled off the stretcher, tried to force her way past Garland to the door, but he threw her back and, cursing, broke Hatty's stranglehold.

As he broke clear Carol caught hold of his arm, hung on. Hatty flew at him, her eyes blazing. He reeled back under her weight, his shoulders thudding against the stretcher. Then his foot slipped and he was down, and Hatty, screaming with excitement, reached for his throat again.

Garland didn't lose his head. He buried his chin in his chest, kept his neck stiff and hit Hatty with his clenched fist. He hit her very hard, driving her off him, and he twisted round, shoved the ambulance door back, threw himself into the road.

Carol sprang down beside him, began to run. She had only taken two steps when a hand gripped her flying ankle and she pitched forward, coming down heavily on the tarmac, the breath leaving her body.

Hatty sprang out of the ambulance as Garland was getting to his feet. She jumped straight at Garland, her feet thudding into his chest. He went over, rolled clear, struggled up, cursing.

He didn't give a damn if Hatty escaped, but the Blandish girl was not going to get away if he could help it. She represented five thousand dollars to him—and he could use five thousand dollars. He imagined that if he left Hatty alone she would run off and he would only have to worry about Carol, but here he made a mistake. Hatty was after his blood.

And when he again shoved her off, and ran to Carol, Hatty paused for a moment while her blunt fingers scrabbled in the grass by the side of the road for a stone. It took her a moment or so before she found a heavy piece of flint, and in that time Garland had caught hold of Carol and was dragging her back to the ambulance.

Carol screamed frantically, but she was powerless in his grip, and when he swung open the ambulance door she suddenly gave up in despair.

Hatty waited until Garland had lifted Carol, then she ran up behind him on tiptoe and brought the flint down on his head with all her strength. Once he was down she methodically hacked at his neck with the sharp stone.

It was mid-day and the hot sunshine streamed down on the golden plantation and on the big white stucco house that stood on the hill.

Deputy George Staum sat on the white terrace, his hat at the back of his head, a cigarette dangling from his lips. This, he told himself, was the life. Guarding a place like Grass Hill was a cinch, especially when your hostess was as beautiful and as hospitable as Veda Banning. Not only that: there was nothing to do except sit around and nurse a gun and sunbathe. It was a life of ease and luxury: something Staum had always wished to experience. His job was to watch out for the Sullivans, but then he knew the Sullivans didn't exist. Still, if Kamp thought they did and wanted him to sit around in the sun to look out for them, that suited him. In fact, he hoped Kamp would continue to believe in the Sullivan myth so he could stay here for the rest of the fall.

You wouldn't have thought a smart fella like Magarth would have fallen for this boloney about the Sullivans, Staum thought to himself, stretching out his short legs and shaking his head. *It just showed that even a smart guy slipped up every now and then.*

Staum wouldn't have sat in the sunshine so calmly if he had known the Sullivans were lying in the long grass not more than two hundred yards from him, and had been there for the past half hour, their white faces intent, their eyes watching everything that went on around the big house.

"I guess he must be in there," Max said, his thin lips scarcely moving. "If not, why the guard?"

"What are you going to do?" Frank asked uneasily. The sun was burning down on his back and he was thirsty.

"We'll stick around," Max returned. "I want to see just how many guards there are."

~§~

Inside the big cool house Magarth was lolling on a settee, a highball in his hand. Veda, who had just come in from the packing shed smiled her welcome.

"Well, there you are," she said, coming over to him, "I didn't expect to see you this morning. Have you got all you want?"

"You might freshen this up for me," Magarth said, handing over his glass. "I thought I'd look in and see how the patient is. Nurse Davies says he had a good night."

"He is better," Veda returned, sloshing more whisky into Magarth's drink and passing it back. "No news of the Blandish girl yet?"

"No, nor of the Sullivans."

"George Staum doesn't believe in the Sullivans," Veda said, sitting down beside Magarth.

"He doesn't believe in anything. But he will if they ever turn up here—which I hope they won't."

The telephone rang in the hall and a moment later the receiver near Magarth buzzed as the maid switched the call through.

"It's for you, precious," Veda said, handing the receiver to Magarth.

It was Sheriff Kamp on the line.

Magarth listened to the deep growling voice, nodded his head as he listened.

"O.K.... I'll be right down. Thanks, Sheriff," he said, hung up.

"Now what's happened?" Veda asked: "You're always running away just when I think I have you to myself."

"There's another nut loose," Magarth said in disgust. "She was being shipped from Kinston to Glenview last night, but somehow she got loose and murdered the attendant and now they're looking for her. They thought I might like to cover it. I don't want to, but I suppose I'll have to earn my living." He stood up. "I'll be out here tonight if I'm not too busy," he went on. "Think you'd like to have me?"

"I think so," Veda said, slipped her arm through his and walked with him on to the terrace.

"Enjoying yourself?" Magarth asked Staum.

Staum opened one eye, nodded.

"You bet," he said. "It's fine out here."

"Well, don't go to sleep. Your job is to watch for the Sullivans. Got That?"

"Sure," Staum said, and laughed. "I'll watch for them."

"You don't really think they'll come?" Veda asked as Magarth climbed into his car.

"I don't, but we may as well be on the safe side," he returned. "We'd be idiots not to."

"I think they're out of the district by now. So long, sugar. See you tonight."

The Sullivans watched him go.

"That's a nice-looking fraulein," Frank said, staring through a pair of field-glasses at Veda as she made her way along the terrace. "I bet you wouldn't have to be a piano-mover to push her over."

Max fished out a bottle of lemonade, snapped off the cap and drank from the bottle.

"Get your mind off her," he said, passing the bottle to Frank. "You think too much about women."

"Got to think about something," Frank said sullenly. "You intend to kill this guy?"

"If he's there," Max said quietly. "We've got to kill him unless you want to sit in a cell and hear them knock up a scaffold for you."

Frank's face twisted.

"After this we'd better quit," he said in a low voice. "We've had the breaks up to now, and we've got dough. We'd best quit."

Max smiled thinly to himself.

He had been waiting for Frank to say this for some time.

"We're not ready to quit yet," he said.

"Well, I am," Frank said.

There was a long pause.

"I organized this racket. I said when we'd start, and I'll say when we quit," Max said softly.

Frank said nothing. He stared down at the sleeping Deputy Sheriff as he sat slumped in the deck-chair and his face twitched again.

"And we're not quitting yet," Max added.

~§~

Magarth whistled softly under his breath as he drove rapidly along the hilly road leading into Point Breese. It had suddenly occurred to him that if he appointed himself manager of Veda's orange plantation he could live in the house, be near Veda all the time, and yet still have his freedom. It didn't bother him that he knew nothing about the production of oranges. Veda was an expert, and she could look after that end of it. He could ride round on a big white horse and urge the workers to greater effort. Such a job would suit him. He wondered if Veda would react favorably; decided that she would.

If he found the Blandish girl and got her settled, he'd put the idea up to Veda. But the Blandish girl would have to be found first. She had been at liberty now nine days and only five more days remained before she could claim her freedom and her money. Magarth grinned to himself, thinking of Hartman: he would be gnashing his teeth by now.

Then suddenly he slammed on his brakes, skidding the car right across the road, and came to a stop perilously near a ditch.

He sat there staring, not believing his eyes. Then with a suppressed exclamation he threw open the car door, ran to meet Carol as she staggered towards him, her dress in tatters, her hair disheveled, her face drawn with exhaustion.

Magarth grabbed her as she swayed into his arms. Her eyes fluttered as he fought to hold her upright.

"All right, kid," he said, lifting her. "Don't try to talk. You're safe now. Just take it easy."

"Steve... Steve..." she murmured. "Where is he? Is he all right? Please tell me..."

"He's all right," Magarth said, settling her into the car. "He's ill of course, but he's out of danger. I'll take you to him right away."

Carol began to cry weakly.

"I never thought I'd get to him," she said, her head falling against the cushioned back of the seat. "It's been dreadful, I never thought I'd get to him."

Magarth reversed the car, drove furiously back to Grass Hill.

~§~

At one o'clock the same afternoon they caught Hatty Summers as she came out of a saloon bar on the outskirts of Point Breese.

She had always had a liking for neat rum, and with the money she had found on the dead body of Sam Garland she had been indulging her weakness. She spent her few hours of freedom slogging down shots and making new friends with Garland's cash.

She was in an amiable and conciliatory mood when they surrounded her, and she displayed to the horrified crowd the big bloodstained flint with which she had battered Garland's head to pulp, delighted to be the center of attraction.

Dr. Travers and two white-coated attendants took charge of her and hurried her into the waiting ambulance, and there, behind closed doors, expertly put a strait-jacket on her.

Sheriff Kamp, who had been present at the capture, looked around in vain for Magarth.

"That fellow's never where he's wanted," he complained to one of his deputies. "I wanted my picture taken arresting that female. Now where the blazes has the pesky fellow got to?"

Dr. Travers climbed out of the ambulance, hurried over to Kamp, his eyes alight with excitement.

"My patient tells me that Garland picked up Carol Blandish a few miles from Point Breese, and it was to help Carol escape that she murdered poor Garland," he said.

Kamp blinked.

"Does she know what she's talking about?"

"Her description of Carol Blandish is unmistakable. It looks as if the girl's come back to Point Breese."

Kamp lifted his sweat-stained Stetson to scratch his head.

"I'll get working on this right away," he said, but as he prepared to move off, Simon Hartman drove up in a glittering Cadillac.

"Here's Mr. Hartman," Travers said, his face darkening. "You know him, Sheriff?"

"I know him," Kamp growled, and the two men waited for Hartman to join them.

"I hear a lunatic has been captured," Hartman said abruptly. "Is it Carol?"

"No, Mr. Hartman," Travers replied. "It was another of my patients."

"You seem to specialize in losing patients," Hartman grated, his face taut with disappointed anger. "Just when do you propose finding my ward?"

"We have just received news that she has returned to Point Breese," Travers said. "The Sheriff is organizing another search party."

Hartman gave Kamp a contemptuous look. He twisted a pair of leather gloves in his hands in subdued fury. Kamp always felt uneasy in Hartman's presence. His tailored suit and ivory tower attitude rubbed Kamp the wrong way.

"Your search parties, up to now, have been singularly unsuccessful," he said, then abruptly, "Where's Steve Larson? Any news of him?"

Kamp managed to look a little vacant.

"Probably in Waltonville Hospital," he said. "Why?"

"From what I hear from Mrs. Fleming, Carol appears to have fallen in love with him. It's possible she will try to find him. You'd better put a guard at the hospital in case she shows up there."

"I 'spose I could do that," Kamp said, coolly stroking his moustache.

"Then do it," Hartman barked. "The girl should have been found days ago. Get your men to work. She's got to be found before the weekend or I'll see this is the last job you'll have the chance to make mess of!" He turned sharply to Travers. "Come along, Doctor, I want to talk to you."

Kamp watched them go, tipped his hat and winked at his deputy.

"Getting pretty hot under the collar, isn't he?" he said thoughtfully. "Maybe I'd better have a word with that pesky Magarth."

"Want me to go over to the Waltonville Hospital?" the deputy asked.

Kamp shook his head.

"No. Somehow I don't think Larson's there," he returned, winked again and then set off with long, unhurried strides to his office.

~§~

"I think she's a darling," Veda said, as she came into the big room where Magarth was pacing up and down. "She's seen Steve for a moment. He was sleeping, but it was wonderful to see the expression in her eyes as she looked down at him. I only hope I'll be able to look like that if ever you fall ill."

"So do I," Magarth said, "and I hope I won't be too ill to appreciate it. Is she all right?"

"She's had an awful time, but I think she'll be all right after a good rest," Veda returned, sitting on the arm of an easy chair. "Do give me a drink, honey, all this excitement has frayed my nerves."

"What's she doing now?" Magarth asked as he mixed a dry martini. Making drinks always relaxed him.

"She's having a bath," Veda returned. "Don't you think Dr. Kober ought to look at her? He might give her something to help her sleep."

"She won't need anything to help her sleep," Magarth said, carrying the drink over to her. "I don't want any doctors or nurses messing with her. They might scare her into one of her turns. After three years in the Sanatorium she's probably afraid of anyone wearing white."

"I'm quite positive there's nothing the matter with her," Veda said. "Now I've talked to her I think the way you do. She's as normal as I am, and she's such a sweet kid."

Magarth grunted.

"It won't do any harm to keep an eye on her," he said. "But I agree: I can't imagine her being dangerous."

Veda eyed him over the top of the cocktail glass.

"There's something on your mind," he said. "What is it?"

"She said the Sullivans left last night for Point Breese. They intend to finish Larson—silence him," Magarth said quietly. "I'm wondering how they managed to slip through Kamp's cordon. We've been watching for them and all the roads are guarded."

"They can't possibly know he's here, can they?" Veda asked. "You're not worrying about that, are you?"

"Well I am worrying, although I don't think they'll come here," Magarth returned, mixed himself highball. "It won't do to underrate these two." He took a drink, set the glass on the table beside him. "Maybe I'm getting your complaint—frayed nerves. All the, same I'll have a word with Staum. He and his boys will have to wake up their ideas now."

The telephone rang.

"It'll be for you," Veda said, "Everyone in the district seems to know we're living in sin together."

"And I bet they're green with envy," Magarth said with a grin, reached for the receiver.

It was the Sheriff.

"Why didn't you come down like I asked you?" Kamp complained. "I had a nice photograph all lined up for you."

"I've more important things to do than to waste plates on your ugly mug," Magarth returned. "What's eating you?"

"I've got news the Blandish girl is back in town." Kamp went on to tell Magarth what Hatty Summers had told Travers. "And Hartman thinks she'll try to find Larson."

"What are you doing about it?"

"We're searching the district again. I thought I'd tip you off in case she shows up at Grass Hill."

"I'll know what to do."

"Do you still want my deputies up there?"

"You bet I do. They'll have to stick right here until Larson's well enough to give evidence."

"O.K.," Kamp said. "It makes it hard for me, but I guess no one cares what happens to an old guy like me."

"I don't for one," Magarth returned, hung up.

"And what did he want?" Veda asked, finishing her drink. "Not more trouble, I hope?"

"No. I guess he likes the sound of my voice," Magarth said, stood up. "Maybe you'd better see how Carol's getting on. I'm going to have a word with Staum."

The Sullivans, from their hiding-place, saw Magarth come out on to the terrace and sit down by the side of Deputy Staum.

Max was now certain that Steve was in the house. He was also sure he knew which room Steve was in, having caught a glimpse from time to time of a nurse as she moved before a window on the second floor.

But, in spite of the careful watch, he had not seen Magarth arrive with Carol. Magarth, anxious that neither Staum nor his two guards should know that Carol was in the house, had brought her in the back way, a long detour through the plantation, up a little-used by-road.

"As soon as it's dark we'll move in," Max said, and stretched out in the long grass. "We can handle the guards easily enough."

"You mean we've got to kill them?" Frank asked.

"Depends," Max returned. "We've got to make a clean job of this. It could be our last job if we slip up on it."

Frank said: "Let's go some place and eat. I'm sick of watching this joint."

~§~

It was growing dusk when Carol awoke, and she sat up with a start, an uneasy fear brooding over her. For a minute or so she couldn't remember where she was and stared around the luxuriously furnished room with blank, frightened eyes. Then she remembered, and her mind darted to Steve, and she lay back in the big, comfortable bed with a little sigh of relief.

Everything that could be done was being done for Steve. He was out of danger now, but was still very weak. She hoped when she saw him again, he would recognize her, and that her presence would help him get well.

And yet as she lay there, trying to relax, the uneasy fear still brooded over her; a presentiment of danger. But there could be no danger, she tried to assure herself. Magarth had told her that the Sullivans couldn't possibly find Larson or her in this big, comfortable house. He had told her too that the house was guarded night and day. But so great was her fear of the Sullivans that she was willing to credit them with superhuman powers.

She lay for some time watching the dusk creep into darkness, and then suddenly she got out of bed, slipped on a wrap that Veda had lent her, and went to the window.

The big orange plantation spread out before her in the distance; the treetops a darkening blur; the golden fruit invisible now in the twilight. Immediately below was the broad terrace, where she could see one of the guards pacing up and down, a rifle under his arm. From the terrace were steps leading to the sunken garden and the big lawns that stretched away to the rising ground, which in its turn dipped to the plantation.

She stood at the window, fear touching her heart, looking into the darkness, waiting for something she knew would happen.

While she waited the door opened and Veda came in.

"Oh you are awake?" Veda said seeing her at the window. "Shall I turn on the light or would you rather I didn't?"

"Please don't," Carol said, her eyes still searching the darkening grounds.

"Is anything frightening you?" Veda asked gently, crossed the room to stand by Carol's side.

"There's danger out there," Carol said, still as a statue.

"Shall I call Phil?" Veda asked, suddenly alarmed. "Shall I ask him to go and see—" She broke off as Carol gripped her arm.

"Look!" she cried, and began to tremble. "Did you see? Over there by the trees."

Veda stared into the darkness. Nothing moved, no sound came to her; even the wind was still.

"There's nothing," she said soothingly. "Come downstairs. It's nicer down there."

"They're out there... the Sullivans... I'm sure they're out there!" Carol cried.

"I'll tell Phil," Veda said as calmly as she could. "Now get dressed. I've put out clothes for you. I think they'll fit you. Get dressed while I find Phil." She gave Carol a reassuring little pat on her arm, and then hurried through the door and called out Phil's name from the head of the staircase.

Magarth came out of the sitting-room, stared up at her, "Anything up?"

"Yes. Carol thinks the Sullivans have come." There was a slight tremor in Veda's voice.

Magarth came up the stairs two at a time.

"What makes her think that?" he asked sharply.

"She says she saw them. I don't know if she did. I didn't see anything... but she's badly frightened."

"I'll have a word with the guards. Get her dressed and bring her down to the sitting-room," Magarth said shortly, ran downstairs to find Staum.

Outside in the thickening darkness the Sullivans, like two black shadows, moved silently towards the house.

Magarth found Staum in the kitchen. He lad just finished supper and was lying back in his chair, a satisfied sleepy expression on his fat face. The maid, Marie, was preparing to go home and while she put on her hat and coat she chatted to Staum.

Staum looked surprised when Magarth pushed open the kitchen door and came in. He straightened up in his chair.

"Want me?" he asked, getting to his feet.

"Yeah," Magarth returned, and jerked his head to the door, Staum followed him out into the corridor.

"Your boys posted?" Magarth said.

"Sure," Staum returned, frowning. "What's up?"

"Something may be. I want you and me to have a look round the grounds."

"For the love of Mike!" Staum exploded "I've just finished supper. Why can't you take it easy for a while? You're acting like a flea on a hot plate. If you're still worrying about the Sullivans you're wasting my time as well as yours. Don't I keep telling you the Sullivans don't exist? They're just a bogey to frighten kids with."

"If you won't take this business seriously I'll call the Sheriff and have a change made here," Magarth said, suddenly angry.

Staum's face reddened and his eyes glinted unpleasantly.

"No one's going to make a monkey out of me," he returned. "Maybe Kamp's crazy, but I ain't. I tell you the Sullivans don't exist. A guy like you should know better than to be scared by a fairy story like that."

"If that's the way you feel about it, the sooner you go the better," Magarth returned shortly.

"I ain't taking orders from a newspaper reporter," Staum said, although he began to look a little uneasy. "So long as I'm in charge here I'm going to be the boss."

Magarth stepped past him to the telephone.

"We'll see what the Sheriff has to say," he returned, picked up the receiver. He stood for a moment with the receiver to his ear, then he frowned. "The line seems dead," he said, rattled the signal-bar, waited a moment or so, then hung up thoughtfully. "Now, I wonder..."

"Go on, say it," Staum sneered. "You think the Sullivans have cut the line."

"It's likely," Magarth returned, aware of a sudden tension raking his nerves raw. "I want a gun, Staum," he went on abruptly. "If you're not going to do your job, I'll have to do it for you."

"Who said I wasn't going to do my job?" Staum said, flaring up. "You watch your mouth; and you don't get a gun from me. You ain't got a permit."

Magarth controlled his rising temper.

"This bickering won't get us anywhere," he said. "Miss Banning saw two men out in the plantation just now. They scared her. Maybe they're not the Sullivans, but at least we can go out there and see who they are."

"Why didn't you say so before?" Staum returned, led the way to the front door. "If there're guys snooping about out there I'll fix 'em." He added after a pause, "Think the telephone line's cut?"

"Looks like it," Magarth said, worried. He followed Staum on to the terrace.

The lone guard, Mason by name, was lolling against the wall, a cigarette in his mouth, his gun held loosely in the crook of his arm. He wasn't smoking the cigarette but was rolling it from one corner of his mouth to the other out of boredom.

"Hi, George," he called when he saw Staum. "When do I get my supper?"

"You'll have it when I say so," Staum growled. "Seen anyone about?"

"You mean the Sullivans?" Mason asked, "*Haw! Haw!* No, I guess the Sullivans ain't called just yet."

"The lady says she saw two men out in the plantation," Staum went on. "You been keeping your eyes peeled?"

"You bet," the guard returned. "Ain't seen a thing. Maybe the lady was dreaming."

"Yeah, I guess she was," Staum returned bitterly, looked at Magarth. "Satisfied?"

"I'm not," Magarth said. "This fella's half asleep. I tell you two guys were seen out there." He tapped Mason on his chest. "Keep your eyes open, bud, you're fooling with dynamite."

"He thinks the Sullivans are going to pay us a little visit," Staum explained.

"That's terrible," Mason grinned. "I hope they keep off until I've had my supper."

With a hopeless shrug Magarth turned away. Staum followed him.

"Where's the other guard?" Magarth asked.

"Round the back. Want to see him too?"

"I certainly do," Magarth returned. He was feeling a little scared now. If Staum refused to believe that trouble was brewing, anything might happen.

And something was happening right at that moment at the back of the house. It happened so quickly and silently that Magarth and Staum suspected nothing as they moved along in the darkness.

The Sullivans had reached the terrace. Max carried a long thin steel rod at the end of which hung a noose of piano wire. For a moment they watched the unsuspecting man who was guarding the rear of the building. He was seated on the balustrade of the terrace, his legs dangling, his gun lying by his side. He hummed to himself, and every now and then he looked impatiently at his luminous watch. He, too, wanted his supper.

Max touched Frank's arm. Both men knew exactly what to do. Frank remained still: he held his heavy .45 gun loosely in his hand while Max crept forward, his rubber-soled shoes making no sound on the white-paved terrace. He held the steel rod like a man carrying a flag in a procession. When he was within a few yards of the guard he stopped.

The noose of piano wire rose in the air began a silent descent until it was a foot or so above the head of the guard. Max fiddled with the slack of the wire which he held in his hand, adjusting the noose so that it would pass over the wide brim of the guard's hat. Then, with a quick movement like a snake striking, Max swished the noose down and dragged on the slack. At the same moment Frank, moving like a silent, vicious shadow, sprang forward, snatched up the guard's rifle.

The guard, caught round the throat by the strangling wire, could make no sound, and was dragged over backwards, his legs thrashing, his fingers frantically trying to find a purchase on the wire that was cutting into the soft skin of his throat. He struggled for barely ten seconds before his body went limp and blood ran out of his mouth.

Max loosened the noose while Frank eased the wire from the strangled man's throat. Without wasting a moment, Max collapsed the rod, which telescoped into a length of about two feet, and joined Frank in carrying the guard into the dark garden, dumping it behind a row of cabbage.

A moment or so later Magarth and Staum turned the corner and walked along the back terrace.

"I don't see him around," Magarth said abruptly. "I suppose he's gone to bed or something."

"He's around somewhere," Staum snapped. "He wouldn't leave his post unless I told him." Raising his voice, he bawled: "Hey! O'Brien! Where the hell are you."

The two men waited in the darkness. No sound or movement reached them, and while they waited the Sullivans slipped like shadows to the front of the house, crept towards Mason, who had laid down his rifle to light another cigarette.

"Some guard," Magarth said angrily. "I'll raise hell about this when I see the Sheriff.

Staum looked worried.

"He should be here," he muttered, walked to the end of the terrace, bawled again, "O'Brien! Jesus H. Christ!"

"I guess we'll find him in the kitchen," Magarth said bitterly.
He turned sharply, retraced his steps.

The Sullivans had scarcely time to carry Mason away. They had no time to collect his rifle and hat, which had fallen off in his death struggle.

"Now Mason's scrammed," Magarth said, not seeing the glow of a cigarette "You there, guard?" he called, raising his voice.

Staum joined him.

"What are you playing at?" he snarled. "Trying to make out Mason's left his post? My men have more discipline than that."

"Any other explanation?" Magarth said, and felt the hair on the nape of his neck bristle. "I don't see him around. Hear that? Why have the crickets gone quiet?"

Staum fetched out a powerful flashlight, shot the white beam along the terrace.

The two men stood transfixed as they saw the hat and rifle lying on the white flagstones.

"Mason!" Staum shouted, took a step forward. There was a sudden off-key note in his voice.

"Put that light out," Magarth said, snatching up Mason's rifle. "Come on; inside, quick!"

Staum didn't need any urging. Neither of them said anything until Magarth had closed and barred the front door.

"What's happened to them?" Staum asked, shaken.

"I told you the Sullivans were here—do you want more proof?" Magarth said, pushed past the gaping Deputy, ran to the kitchen, which was deserted. He locked and bolted the back door, returned to the hall. "You stay here and keep your eyes peeled," he said to Staum. "I'm going upstairs. They're after Larson, but they're not going to get him. You're the first line of defense. See they don't get you," and he left Staum, who was now looking scared, and ran up the stairs.

Veda met him on the landing.

"Is it all right?" she asked, then clutched his arm when she saw the expression in his eyes. "What's happened?"

"Plenty," he said, keeping his voice low. "They're out there all right, and they've got the two guards. That leaves Staum and me, you, Carol and the nurse. They've cut the telephone wires, so we're sealed off unless—"

"I'll go," Veda said promptly. "I could get across the plantation and get the overseer and his men up here."

Magarth slipped his arm round her.

"That's fine," he said, "but not yet. We can't afford to take chances. If they get you, we're sunk. We'd best wait until they try to get into the house, then you slip out the back way."

"It may be too late then," Veda said. "It'll take me ten minutes at least to get across the plantation. I'd better go now."

"You're not going until I know where they are," Magarth said firmly. "Where's Carol?"

"She's with Steve."

"All right; we'll keep near Steve. They're after him, and it'll be to his room they'll come if they get into the house."

"You ain't leaving me down here alone, are you?" Staum called up plaintively from the foot of the stairs.

"Why not?" Magarth returned. "The Sullivans are just a bogey you frighten children with—remember? You're not a child, are you?" He took Veda's arm and together they walked quickly down the passage to Steve's room.

They found Carol, looking lovely in one of Veda's simple linen dresses, seated by Steve's side. Nurse Davies, a tall, grey-haired woman, was sewing near the window.

Carol looked up quickly as Magarth and Veda came in, and made a quick sign to them not to say anything.

Steve, looking white and drawn, opened his eyes as Magarth came quietly to his side.

"Hello, you big, lazy dope," Magarth said, smiling. "Got your girl now, have you?"

Steve nodded.

"Thanks to you, Phil," he said, reached out for Carol's hand. "Just seeing her makes me feel good."

"Mr. Larson shouldn't talk," Nurse Davies said, shaking her head at Magarth. "He's still very weak."

"Sure," Magarth said, stepped back, signaled to Carol.

"I'll be back in a moment," she said to Steve, patted his hand, joined Magarth and Veda in the passage.

"Look, kid," Magarth said quickly, "you were right. They're out there and they've got the two guards. You stay with Steve. I'll stick right here outside the door. Staum's watching the stairs. They can't reach him except up the stairs, so lock yourself in and don't get scared. They're not going to get him."

Carol's face paled, but her eyes were determined.

"No," she said. "They're not going to get him."

"Good kid," Magarth said. "You get back to Steve and leave this to me." He pushed her gently back into Steve's room, turned to Veda. "That's about all we can do," he went on. "The next move is up to them."

"I'm going, Phil" Veda said. "I know every inch of the way in the dark. It's madness to wait for them to make the first move. We need to get help."

"Maybe I'd better go," Magarth said, running his fingers through his hair. "I don't like the idea of you going out there."

"I'm going, so stop arguing. Come and see me off."

The Sullivans were waiting for just such a move. Frank stood in the shadows near the back door; Max leaned against the wall a foot or so from the front door. They were in no hurry. They knew that the plantation workers had their living quarters on the other side of the plantation, and the only way Magarth could raise the alarm and get help was to send someone to make the journey.

"We'll try the back way," Magarth said, "but I'm going out first to see if the coast's clear. Then run, Veda, run like hell."

"I'll run," she said, going with him down the stairs.

"Miss Banning's going for help," Magarth said to Staum who was backed up against the wall, his fat face glistening with sweat. "You stick where you are. I'll be back a moment."

"Think she'll make it?" Staum asked.

"She'll make it," Magarth returned, but he wasn't any too confident.

Together Veda and he went into the kitchen. Magarth didn't turn on the light, and they groped their way across the dark room to the window.

"Keep out of sight," Magarth whispered, and he peered through the glass, trying to see any movement on the dark terrace. He stood there for several minutes, but saw nothing to alarm him.

Frank, peering through the pillars of the balustrade, saw Magarth looking through the window, and he grinned, ducked down, waited.

Magarth opened the back door, stepped onto the terrace, looked up and down. He crossed to the balustrade, his nerves jumpy, and stood within a couple of feet of the invisible Frank. Satisfied that nothing stirred, he returned, beckoned to Veda.

"It's all right," he whispered, his lips close to her ear. "I guess they're round the front. Run, kid, and try not to make a noise." He kissed her suddenly, held her for a moment, then watched her move swiftly and silently down the steps. The darkness swallowed her up.

~§~

The big house was quiet. The nurse had left Carol to watch Steve and had gone to her room next door.

Magarth sat on the top of the stairs, his rifle across his knees. Staum sat on the bottom stair. The hall, stairs and landings were ablaze with light. The hands of the big hall clock pointed to ten minutes past eleven. Veda had been gone now a quarter of an hour. In a few more minutes, Magarth thought hopefully, help would be with them, then they could go out into the darkness and hunt the Sullivans instead of sitting here waiting for their attack.

In the bedroom Steve opened his eyes. He had been sleeping, and now, refreshed, he smiled at Carol, reached for her hand.

"I've been thinking so much about you," he said. "All the time I've been hurt you've never been far from my thoughts. You know I love you, don't you, Carol? I haven't much to offer you... there's the farm. It's nice up there, and in a while—"

"I don't think you should talk," Carol interrupted him, leaned forward to kiss him. "You must rest, darling. I want you to get well quickly."

"I'm all right," Steve said firmly. "I'm feeling much stronger. I want to talk. We've got to find out who you are, Carol, We've got to find out why you were in that truck... where you were going..."

A feeling of fear ran through Carol.

"Oh, no," she said. "Please don't talk about that. I'm afraid... I'm afraid of finding out about myself. That woman said I was mad." She slipped from her chair, put her arms round his neck, held his head against her breast. "Do you think I'm mad? Is that why I don't know who I am? It frightens me so. You see if... I couldn't marry you, Steve"

"Of course you're not mad," he returned. "You've had a bad crack on your head. It's something that can be put right, I'm sure of it, then your memory will come back. You mustn't worry about it, Carol."

Holding him to her, Carol thought of the Sullivans waiting out in the dark, and she shivered.

"What's frightening you, kid?" Steve asked. "It's all going to be all right. As soon as I get well we're going to have a swell time... just you and me. I've got it all doped out. That's all I've been thinking about while I've waited for you."

Carol held him closer so he shouldn't see she was crying.

~§~

"Give them another ring" Sheriff Kamp said impatiently to the operator. "I know there's someone there." He glanced at his assistant deputy: a lean, hard-bitten man whom they called Lofty. "She says there's no answer."

"I bet she's calling a wrong number," Lofty said and spat accurately into the spittoon. "You know how these dames are. You got to watch them."

After a delay the operator said the line was out of order.

"Get it tested and report back," Kamp snapped and hung up. He looked worried.

"Think something's wrong?" Lofty asked, lighting a cigarette. He squinted at Kamp through the haze of smoke.

"I don't know," Kamp said uneasily. "George ain't too bright. He's not very resourceful. I told him to call me every two hours, and he hasn't followed orders. These Sullivans—" He broke off, pulled at his moustache.

"I wouldn't like anything to happen to Miss Banning," Lofty said. "She's a swell dame. Think we should go up there?"

"It's a long run," Kamp said, "and it's getting late. I ain't keen—"

The telephone rang.

Kamp listened to the operator's voice, grunted, hung up.

"She says the line is down."

Lofty reached for his revolver belt.

"Let's go," he said, looking sharply at Kamp as he buckled up.

"I guess you're right," Kamp said, got to his feet, lifted down a rifle from the rack behind his desk. "Looks like there's trouble up there."

~§~

The night was moonless, and as Veda sped down the narrow path towards the plantation she felt as if she were in a dark tunnel miles underground.

She paused for a moment to look back at the lighted windows of the house, and as she did so she caught sight of a dark figure moving towards her as stealthily as a ghost.

Veda had plenty of courage, but for a second or so her heart seemed to stop beating, then with a little cry she whirled round and ran blindly down the path.

She had gone only a few yards when Frank caught up with her. His short fat fingers clamped onto her shoulder and spun her round. All she could see of him was a dim outline. She was aware of the smell of his hair oil. She was too frightened to scream, and stood motionless, unable to do more than stare at this menacing shadowy figure.

Frank reached out, touched her face with his left hand, then, moving so fast that she didn't see his right hand flash up, he struck her on the side of her head with his rubber hose.

~§~

George Staum stood up, stretched himself. He had no stomach for being alone in the big hall and he was scared. The smooth, silent way in which his two guards had vanished had completely unnerved him, and he expected the Sullivans to materialize out of the walls at any moment.

His hands, slippery with sweat, gripped his rifle so tightly that the muscles in his arms ached. His eyes darted this way and that, and he felt a little sick.

He could hear Magarth moving about on the upper landing, and every so often he would call up to him. He wished now he hadn't been picked for this job, and would have given a month's pay to find himself in the safety of the Sheriff's office.

In the sitting-room, a few feet from him, Max watched him through the crack of the slightly open door. Down the passage in the darkness, Frank pressed himself against the wall, edged slowly toward him.

Staum felt danger in the air. It was as if the atmosphere around him were tightening, and he stood still, listening, his face ugly with fear.

A slight sound, no louder than the scratching of a mouse, made him jerk his head round to look down the passage. Frank had reached the fuse box and the main switch lever squeaked as he pressed it down.

"Who's there?" Staum croaked, stepping forward.

Then the whole house plunged into darkness.

Magarth ran to the head of the stairs, stopped.

"Staum!" he shouted. "You all right?"

"There's someone near me," Staum whimpered. "Quick! Come down here...!"

Magarth didn't move.

There was a sudden startled gasp from Staum; then out of the darkness came the gruesome sound of a man being strangled with piano wire.

There was nothing Magarth could do for Staum. He wanted to warn Carol of what was happening, but he dared not leave the head of the staircase. It was up these stairs that the Sullivans would have to come if they were to get Steve, and the stairs could not be left unguarded for a moment. He dropped on hands and knees, pushed his rifle forward and waited, helplessly aware that he was now the last barrier left between the Sullivans and their intended victim.

Carol and Steve were talking together when the light went out. Realizing what it meant, Carol nearly fainted; only the thought that she must protect Steve kept her conscious.

Steve was unperturbed.

"A fuse must have blown," he said. "Relax. They'll fix it in a moment."

Carol knew then that she must tell him.

"It isn't a fuse, darling," she said, catching hold of him. "It's the Sullivans. They're in the house."

"And you knew it all the time?" Steve asked, his fingers touching her hair. "I had a feeling something was frightening you. Is Magarth out there?"

"Yes, and the Sheriff's deputy," Carol said, trying to control the quaver in her voice. "I'm so frightened, Steve..."

"Go to the door and see what's happening," Steve said. "Call to Magarth."

Below, in the sitting-room, the door closed, Max was talking to Frank. They were calmly standing in the shadows like a pair of black pillars.

"The newspaper guy's guarding the head of the stairs," he was saying. "You keep him busy. I'm going around the back. I can get on the roof and then I'll take him in the rear. You make enough noise to hold his attention."

Carol unlocked the bedroom door, opened it a few inches.

"Magarth, are you there?" she whispered.

"Stay where you are," Magarth whispered back. "They're in the hall somewhere. They've got Staum."

Carol felt her heart contract.

"Then... you're alone?"

"Don't worry about me," Magarth said. "I can take care of myself. You keep that door locked."

"Don't let them get near him," Carol pleaded.

"I won't," Magarth said grimly. "Veda's gone for help. You two keep under cover."

A faint sound in the hall below caused him to stiffen and peer into the darkness. He shifted forward, waited. All he heard was the somber ticking of the clock.

Outside, Max swung himself onto the low roof, climbed up a stack-pipe as easily as if it were a staircase, hooked his fingers into the windowsill a foot or so above his head. He balanced himself for a moment, then drew himself up.

Carol groped her way back to Steve. He flinched when she touched him but relaxed when he caught the scent of her hair.

"He's out there alone," she said, taking Steve's hand in hers, "but he says they can't get in here."

"I'm not going to let him fight my battles," Steve said, pushed back the blanket.

"No!" Carol said frantically. "You mustn't, darling, you're ill... please stay where you are...!"

Steve swung his legs out of bed, gripped her arm as he levered himself to his feet.

"I'm not lying here... they want me... I know that."

He caught her to him. "If this doesn't work out, Carol, remember I love you. You're the loveliest, the most precious thing that has ever happened to me—"

"Steve, darling," Carol said, clinging to him. "Please stay with me... don't go out there... it's what they want..."

"Say you love me, Carol."

"Of course I do," she sobbed. "But you mustn't go out there. You'll be playing right into their hands."

Magarth, lying flat, staring into the darkness, never knew what hit him. Max had crept down on him, saw the outline of his head against the black pit of the staircase, and had struck before Magarth could twist round to protect himself. As he went limp, Max took out a flashlight, signaled to Frank, who came swiftly up the stairs.

~§~

The battered Ford V8 roared out of Point Breese and headed for the mountain road. Lofty sat at the wheel, his eyes bright with excitement. He took the corner out of Point Breese on two wheels, slithered the car half across the road, wrestled with the steering wheel for a moment, then slammed his foot down on the gas pedal again.

"Hey!" Kamp spluttered, appalled. "Careful how you go. I want to arrive in one piece."

"Don't want anything to happen to Miss Banning," Lofty returned, whipped the Ford past an oncoming truck, missing the truck's fender by inches. "We got to get up there fast, Sheriff. You leave this to me. I could drive these roads with my eyes shut."

Kamp clutched the side of the car, hung on like grim death.

"She won't stand the racket, Lofty," he gasped. "She'll blow her top if you drive her like this."

"That's too bad," Lofty said grimly. "Then you're due for a new car, Sheriff. We're getting up there fast."

Kamp closed his eyes, groaned.

"She'll boil," he muttered feverishly. "She'll boil her head off."

"Then let her boil," Lofty returned, the gas pedal flat on the boards. "Get on, you big lump of lazy iron," he bawled, sitting forward. "Gimme a bit of speed!"

~§~

Carol's legs suddenly refused to support her. She sank limply on the bed, the darkness in the room stifling her. Then something extraordinary seemed to happen inside her head.

Her brain seemed to expand and contract as if it were breathing, and she gripped her temples between her hands. She was now scarcely aware that Steve had left her and was groping his way across the room to the door. He walked slowly; every step he made a tremendous effort, moving as if he were fighting a gale.

"Steve..." Carol whimpered. "Don't leave me."

But he had reached the door now, fumbled at the lock, opened it.

The Sullivans were waiting just outside. The white hard light of Max's flashlight centered on Steve's chest. For a moment nothing happened, no one moved, then Steve stiffened, put up his hands in a fighting stance: a helpless gesture of defiance.

"Here it is, Larson," Max said softly.

A red, spiteful flash lit up the dark room; then another and another. Gunfire rattled the windows.

Steve took a step forward, hit out blindly, began to fall. Max fired again.

The crack of the gun synchronized with the sudden loud *snap!* that exploded inside Carol's head.

For a split second everything that moved in the room— Steve falling, Max's gun hand, Frank's head as it flinched back, the wavering light of the flashlight—came to a sudden standstill. For that split second the scene looked like a photograph, then movement began again, but to Carol it was no longer the same. It was out of focus, dim-edged, almost soundless.

Her fear slid out of her like a dropping cloak. She stood up, moved along the wall, glided towards the Sullivans as they bent over Steve.

Max's experienced hand touched Steve's chest.

"We're done," he said, straightened. "Let's get out of here."

Frank gave a little shiver and said: "This is our last job, Max. I quit after this. I've lost my taste for death."

"Let's get out of here," Max repeated, ignoring him.

Outside the night was made hideous by a roaring car engine, and a squealing of brakes as Lofty pulled up before the house.

"Back way," Max said, moved swiftly down the corridor. As Frank followed him an invisible hand came out of the darkness and gripped his arm. For one ghastly moment he thought Larson had come alive again, and he turned, his mouth drying with horror.

There was nothing to see except a black wall of darkness, but he could hear someone breathing close to him, and fingers like talons pinched his arm muscles.

"Max!" he cried shrilly, lunged forward, his fist sweeping up viciously, striking empty air, throwing him off balance.

Cold groping fingers passed across his face, swiftly and lightly like a draft of air. So light was the touch it was as if a cobweb had settled over his features, and he started back, terror paralyzing him.

"Come on," Max called impatiently from the head of the stairs.

"There's someone here." Frank quavered, groped into the darkness.

"Come on, you fool!" Max said sharply, then stiffened as Frank suddenly gave a blood-curdling scream.

Even Max's iron nerves flinched at the sound, and he stood for a moment in dread. Something brushed past him and instinctively he jumped back. Hooked fingers grazed his neck, and he fired blindly: the crash of the gun reverberated through the house, and he heard footsteps running lightly down the stairs. He fired shot after shot, blindly and with growing panic. In the hall gunfire cracked, in reply as Kamp and Lofty tumbled through the front doorway.

Max wheeled, crashed into Frank, caught hold of him as he began to scream again. Without hesitation, Max shortened his grip on his gun, hit Frank across the face with the barrel, stooped, slung him across his shoulder, darted along the passage.

He reached a window, lowered Frank to the sloping roof, scrambled through the window himself.

Frank lay on the tiles, only half conscious.

"I'm blind !" he moaned. "My eyes... she got my eyes...!"

CHAPTER VI

ON a dull, airless afternoon, a month after the death of Steve Larson, a battered Cadillac swept up the drive and came to rest before the front door of the house on Grass Hill.

Veda, who had been watching from a window for the past half-hour, came quickly out on to the terrace and ran to meet Magarth as he climbed from the car.

"Hello, honey," he said, pulled her to him and kissed her. "I've got it all fixed up for her, and it's been some job." He linked his arm through hers and walked with her into the house. "How has she been?"

"Just the same," Veda returned unhappily. "You'd never believe it was the same girl, Phil. She's grown so hard and strange. She rather frightens me."

"That's bad. Does she still sit around brooding and doing nothing?" Magarth asked, taking off his hat and coat and following Veda into the sitting-room.

"Yes, and I can't interest her in anything. I tried to keep the newspapers from her, but she managed to get hold of them, so she knows now about herself. It's awful, Phil. After she read the papers she locked herself in her room, and I heard her pacing up and down for hours. I've tried to persuade her to confide in me, but she so obviously wants to be left alone that I haven't the heart to worry her."

"She was bound to find out sooner or later, but it's bad she had to find out through the papers. My colleagues didn't pull any punches," Magarth said, frowning. "Well, I've fixed everything up for her now. The money's hers. She'll have about four million bucks, which isn't so bad. Hartman has been helping himself, but we were in time to save the bulk of it. She's lucky we intervened when we did."

"Any news of him?"

"He's skipped. He knew the game was up when we began the investigation. The Federal agents are after him, but I bet he's out of the country by now. Well, I'd better go up and see her."

"Now she has her freedom and her money I have a feeling she plans to leave us," Veda said. "I do hope she won't go just yet. Will you try to persuade her to stay a little longer? She's not fit to be on her own, and she has no friends and nowhere to go. Do be firm with her, Phil."

"I'll do my best, but I have no hold on her. She's free to do what she likes now, you know."

"Well, do try. It'd worry me to death to think of her on her own with all that money and no one to advise her."

"I'll see what I can do," Magarth returned. "Has Dr. Kober seen her?"

"Only for a few minutes. He's uneasy about her and suspects bone pressure after that truck accident, but she refused to be examined. Dr. Travers has also been here, but I wouldn't let him see her. He says he won't be responsible for what may happen if she is allowed to be free. I told him I didn't believe she's dangerous. But I do think she's become a little queer, Phil. She's not a bit like she was when we first saw her."

"I'll go up."

He found Carol alone in her big, restful room. She was sitting by the window, and she didn't turn her head as he came in. There was a cold stillness about her that made Magarth uneasy. He pulled up a chair near her, sat down and said with forced brightness: "I have good news for you, Carol. You're a rich young woman now."

At the sound of his voice she gave a little start, turned. Her large green eyes stared mechanically at him.

"I didn't hear you come in," she said in a flat, hard voice. "Did you say good news?"

Magarth gave her a quick searching glance. The changeless stillness on her white face and the icy blankness in her eyes perplexed and worried him.

"Yes, very good news. The money is now in your name. I have all the papers with me. Would you like to go through them with me?"

She shook her head.

"Oh, no," she said emphatically, paused, then went on: "You say I'm rich? How much is there?"

"Four million dollars. It is a lot of money."

Her mouth tightened.

"Yes," she said, laced her slim fingers and stared out of the window. There was a bitter, brooding look in her eyes now, and she remained so still and silent that Magarth said quietly:

"Are you pleased?"

"I've been reading about myself in the papers," she said abruptly. "It's not pretty reading."

"Now, look, Carol, you mustn't believe everything you read in the newspapers..." he began, but she silenced him with a movement of her hand.

"I've learned things about myself," she said, still staring out of the window. "I am insane. That was news to me. I am also the daughter of a homicidal degenerate who caused the death of my mother. I have been in an asylum for three years, and if it wasn't for the law of this State I'd be there now." She suddenly clenched her hands. "I'm dangerous. They call me the homicidal redhead. They write of my love for Steve, and say that, if he had lived, I could never have married him. They describe that as a lunatic's tragic love affair—" She broke off, bit down on her lip and the knuckles of her hands showed white.

"Please, Carol," Magarth said. "Don't torture yourself."

"But you tell me you have good news... that I'm worth four million dollars, and you ask me if I'm pleased. Yes, I am; very, very pleased," and she laughed, a cold bitter laugh that sent a chill up Magarth's spine.

"You mustn't go on like this," he said firmly. "It'll get you nowhere. Veda and I want to help you—"

She turned, caught hold of his wrist.

"Aren't you afraid I'll do something evil to you?" she demanded. "They say I am dangerous... like my father. Do you know what they say of my father? It's here in the paper. I'll read it to you." She picked up a creased and badly folded newspaper that was lying on the floor by her side. "This is what they say:

"Slim Grissom was a killer: born a mental degenerate, his love of cruelty got him into trouble at an early age. His schoolmaster caught him cutting up a live kitten with a pair of rusty scissors, and he was expelled from school. When he was fifteen, he abducted a little girl, who was found a week later half crazed with terror. She had been a victim of a particularly brutal assault. But Grisson was never caught, for his mother, the notorious Ma Grissom, smuggled him out of the town.

"Ma Grissom built her son into a gangster. At first he made mistakes and drifted in and out of prison on short sentences, but Ma Grisson would wait patiently until he was free and then continue her coaching. He learned not to make mistakes and got in with a powerful gang, working bank hold-ups. He climbed slowly into the saddle of leadership by the simple method of killing anyone who opposed him, until the gang finally settled down and accepted him as their leader. There has never been in the history of American crime a more vicious, more deadly, more degenerate criminal than Slim Grisson—"

"Stop," Magarth said sharply. "I don't want to listen to any more of that. Carol, do be sensible. Where is all this getting you?"

She dropped the newspaper with a little shudder.

"And he was my father... I have his blood in my veins. You talk about helping me. How can you help me? How can anyone help me with a heritage like that?" She got to her feet and began, to pace up and down. "No... please don't say anything. I know you mean to be kind. I'm very grateful to you both. But now..." She paused, looked at him from under her eyelids. There was a cold menace in her stillness that startled Magarth. "Now I must be alone. Perhaps I am dangerous as my father was. Do you think I want to endanger the lives of people like you and Veda?"

"But this is nonsense, Carol," Magarth said sharply. "You have been with us for more than a month, and nothing has happened. It only makes things worse if you—"

"I have made up my mind," Carol said, interrupting him. "I leave here tomorrow. But before I go there are things I want you to do."

"But you mustn't go... not yet, anyway," Magarth protested. "You're still suffering from shock..."

She made a quick, angry gesture of impatience and the right side of her mouth began to twitch.

"I have made my plans and no one will stop me," she said, a curious grating note in her voice. "For a month I have sat here making plans. I would have gone sooner if I had money. Now I am ready to go."

Magarth saw it was useless to argue with her. She was in an implacable mood, and, looking at her, he realized that Dr. Travers had some foundation when he said she was dangerous.

"But where are you going?" he asked. "You have no friends, except Veda and I. You have no home. You can't go off into the blue, you know."

Again she made the angry, impatient gesture.

"We are wasting time. Will you take over my affairs? I know nothing about money and I don't want to know anything about it. I have talked with the lawyer. He tells me I should appoint someone to look after my investments and to represent me. My grandfather had a number of business activities that have come to me. Will you represent me?"

Magarth was startled.

"I'll gladly do what I can," he said, "but I have my other work—"

"You will be well paid. I have made all the arrangements with the lawyer," she went on in the same cold, impersonal voice. "You can give up your newspaper work. You and Veda can marry. You want to marry her, don't you?"

"I guess so," Magarth said, ran his fingers through his hair. The turn of the conversation embarrassed him. He didn't like the intimate details of his life being brought out into the open.

"Then you will see my lawyer? You'll discuss it with him? He has all the details."

He hesitated a moment, then nodded.

"All right," he said, added, "but what do you intend to do?"

"When can I have some money?" she asked abruptly, ignoring his question.

"As soon as you like... now, if you want it."

"Yes, now. I want two thousand dollars, and I want you to arrange that I can draw cash anywhere in the country at a moment's notice. I want you to buy me a car and have it here by tomorrow morning. Go and see the lawyer and bring me the necessary papers to sign so you can take over my affairs immediately. You can set your own salary. I wish to leave here tomorrow morning."

"Won't you wait a little longer?" he asked. "You'll be all alone...."

A sudden glow like fever came into her cheeks.

"Please do what I say or I must find someone else," she said with raised voice. "Where I am going and what I intend to do is my affair."

Magarth shrugged.

"All right," he said unhappily, got to his feet. "I'll do it."

She put her hand on his arm, and for a moment the hardness in her eyes softened.

"You are very kind," she said in a low tone. "Don't think I'm ungrateful. I don't know what I should have done without you and Veda. I hope you will both be very happy."

"That's O.K.," he said, and managed to smile. "You know how I feel about you. I do wish you'd think again. Veda and I want you to stay with us. I don't know what you are planning to do, but I have a hunch nothing good will come of it."

"I have made up my mind," she said quietly and turned away. "Will you leave me now? Will you please tell Veda that I am leaving tomorrow morning? I don't want to see anyone tonight."

Magarth made a final appeal.

"Won't you take me into your confidence, Carol?" he pleaded. "I might be able to help you. Why do you insist on going off on your own, when you have two people who would do anything for you? Tell me what you plan to do, and I'll help you."

She shook her head.

"No one can help me," she said. "What I have to do can only be done by myself, and alone. Please leave me now."

"All right," Magarth said, admitting defeat, and he crossed to the door.

When he had gone Carol went to the window and sat down. She remained motionless for some moments, her cold, clenched hands pressing against her temples.

"Wherever you are, Steve, my darling, love me," she said softly. "I am so lonely and afraid, but I will find them. They will not escape me, and I will make them pay for what they did to you. I will be as ruthless and as cruel to them as they were to us. I have nothing left to live for but to make them pay."

She was still sitting before the window when the pale autumn light faded, and rain, which had been threatening all the afternoon, began to fall.

~§~

Rain was still falling the next day. Dirty grey clouds, lying low on the hills, formed belts of mist that brought darkness to the late afternoon. Fading shafts of sunlight slanted through the blackened tree boughs.

A black Chrysler coupé, its fenders splashed with mud, nosed its way up the steeply rising by-road which led to the old plantation house so recently occupied by Tex Sherill.

Carol stopped the car before the crumbling porch, got out and stood for a moment while she surveyed the dark building for any sign of life. The dark checkered curtains covered a faint light inside.

The rain dripped dismally from the eaves on to the wooden stoop and made a soft whispering sound. The blank face of 'the house was tight in darkness, and Carol wondered if it were empty.

She mounted the wooden steps and tried the door-handle. The door was locked. She rapped with her knuckles on the hard panel and waited. She had to rap several times before she heard a faint step on the other side of the door. She rapped again insistently, and the voice of Miss Lolly came through the letter- box, "Who is it?"

"Carol Blandish. I want to speak to you."

She heard Miss Lolly catch her breath, then the door opened a few inches, stopped as the chain on the inside prevented it opening further.

"Why have you come back?" Miss Lolly asked out of the darkness. "I took a big risk setting you free."

"I'm here because I need some information," Carol said, leaning against the door-post and speaking close to the narrow opening.

"But you can't come in," Miss Lolly said. "I want to be left alone. Leave me in peace."

"You helped me before. I was hoping you would help me now. I am looking for the Sullivans."

Miss Lolly drew in a sharp breath.

"What do you want with them?" she asked fiercely. "They are hunting for you, you little fool. Leave them alone!"

"They shot my lover," Carol said in her hard flat voice. "Do you think I'm going to leave them alone after that?"

There was a moment's silence.

"Revenge?" Miss Lolly said, a new and eager note in her voice. "Is that what you want?"

"I want to find them," Carol said. "And deal with them."

The chain grated, then the door opened.

"Come in," Miss Lolly said out of the darkness. "I am alone here now. Mr. Sherill left soon after you did."

Carol followed her down the long dark passage into the back room, where a lamp burned brightly on the table. The room was full of old, shabby furniture, and it was not easy to move about without touching something.

Miss Lolly kept in the shadows. Carol could see her big tragic eyes looking at her. Around her throat was twisted a white scarf, hiding her beard.

"Sit down," Miss Lolly said. "So you are looking for them? If I were younger I would look for them, too."

Carol opened her light dust-coat, pulled off her close-fitting hat. She shook out her hair with a quick movement of her head.

"Do you know where they are?" she asked as she sat down on a sagging chair.

"But what can you do to them if you do find them?" Miss Lolly said, a note of despair in her voice. "What could I do? They are so cunning, so quick, so strong. No one can do anything to them."

Carol turned her head, and for a moment the two women looked at each other. Miss Lolly was startled to see the hard, bitter expression on Carol's face, and the icy bleakness of her eyes.

"I will make them pay," Carol said softly, "no matter how cunning and quick and strong they are. I will make them pay if it takes me the rest of my life. I have nothing else to live for."

Miss Lolly nodded, and her fingers touched the scarf at her throat.

"I feel like that too," she said, and two tears ran out of her eyes and dropped on to her hand. "You see, Max cut off my beard."

Carol didn't move nor did her expression change.

"Why did he do that?" she asked.

"Because I let you go," Miss Lolly said, clasping her hands. "I would rather they had killed me. I'm a vain old woman, my dear: it may seem horrible to you, but I loved my beard. I have had it a long time."

"Tell me what happened."

Miss Lolly drew up a chair, again adjusted the scarf round her chin, sat down. She put out a hand hopefully, but Carol drew away, her face cold and hard.

"Tell me," she repeated.

"They came back two days after you had gone. Frank remained in the car and Max came in here. I was a little frightened, but I sat where you are sitting now and waited to see what he would do to me. He seemed to know you had gone, for he didn't ask for you. He asked for Mr. Sherill, and I told him he had left here. He stood looking at me for a long time, then he asked why I hadn't gone too, and I told him there was nowhere for me to go." Miss Lolly fidgeted with her scarf, then went on after a long pause: "He hit me over the head, and later when I came to they had gone. He had cut off my beard. You may remember it?" She looked wistfully at Carol. "It was a very beautiful beard, and he burnt it. He's a devil," she said, raising her voice. "He knew nothing would give me more pain than that."

"And Frank?" Carol asked.

"He remained in the car," Miss Lolly said, looking bewildered. "I don't know why, for he is cruel, and it is not like him to keep away when someone is going to be hurt, but he remained in the car."

Carol smiled. Looking at her, Miss Lolly felt a chill run down her spine.

"He stayed in the car because he is blind," Carol said. "I blinded him after he had killed Steve."

Miss Lolly remained still. She was surprised that she felt a shocked kind of pity for Frank.

"Blind? I wouldn't wish anyone to be blind," she said. "It's a terrible thing to endure."

Carol made an impatient movement.

"Where are they?" she asked, a harsh note creeping into her voice. "If you know, tell me, but don't waste my time. Every moment I remain here means they are getting further away from me. Where are they?"

Miss Lolly shrank back, alarmed at the suppressed venom in the green eyes.

"I don't know," she said, "but they had a room upstairs where they kept their things. They took everything when they left except a photograph which had slipped between the floorboards. That may tell you something."

"Where is it?" Carol demanded.

"I have it here. I was looking at it when you knocked." Miss Lolly opened a drawer, took out a photograph and laid it on the table under the white light of the lamp.

It was a photograph of a girl whose dark hair was parted in the middle; the broad white line between the parting was pronounced. It was a curious face: a little coarse, full-lipped, wide-eyed and fleshy. There was something magnetic about it: sensual, animal quality; an uncontrolled wantonness; a badness that was scarcely concealed by the veneer of polished sophistication. Under the brazenly skimpy swimsuit she wore was a shape to set a man crazy. Across the bottom of the photograph, scrawled in white ink and in a big sprawling hand, was the inscription:

To darling Frank from Linda

Without change of expression, Carol turned the photograph and read the name of the photographer stamped on the back:

Kenneth Carr, 397 Main Street, Santa Rio

Then she once more turned the photograph to study the girl's face. Miss Lolly watched her closely.

"She is the kind of woman a man wouldn't forget easily," she said, leaning forward to peer over Carol's shoulder. "She's bad, but attractive. A man would return to her again and again. Find her, and I think you will find Frank."

"Yes," Carol said. "I believe you're right."

And then she turned and left without saying goodbye.

~§~

Santo Rio is a small, compact little town on the Pacific Coast: a millionaire's playground. It has no industry unless you call every form of lavish and luxurious entertainment an industry; in which case Santo Rio's industry is a thriving one. The main bulk of its citizens earn their living by entertaining the rich visitors who come in their thousands to Santo Rio all the year round, but the town had an underbelly the size of a beached whale. Gambling, racing, yachting, dancing, ordinary and extraordinary forms of vice, night clubs, theatres, cinemas and so on employ those people who are not smart enough to stand on their own feet and rim their own rackets.

The smart ones—of whom Eddie Regan was a leading member—make a comfortable living out of blackmail, con jobs, being gigolos or practicing any other nefarious racket that brings in easy money.

Eddie Regan was tall, wide and handsome. He had black curly hair, a tanned complexion, excellent teeth as white as orange pith, and sparkling blue eyes that proved irresistible to rich, elderly women who came to Santo Rio to kick over the traces, probably for the last time.

Eddie made a reasonable income as a dancing partner to these elderly women, and supplemented this income from time to time by blackmailing them when they were foolish enough (as they often were) to furnish him with evidence which they would be reluctant for their husbands to see.

Making love to elderly women was not Eddie's idea of a good time, but he was smart enough to realize his talents were only suited to such a career, and so, being a man of considerable vitality, he consoled himself with youthful beauty in his off-duty hours.

His present consolation was Miss Linda Lee, the subject of the photograph that had been overlooked by the Sullivans when they had packed up and left the old plantation house for good.

Eddie had come upon Linda quite by chance. He had been lounging on the beach one afternoon keeping an eye open for any elderly woman who happened to look lonely when he observed Linda coming out of the sea for a sun bath. Now, Linda had the kind of figure that looked its best in a wet swimsuit: anyway, Eddie thought so, and he was, in his way, an expert on such matters. Elderly women were immediately banished from his mind as he gave his undivided attention to the sensational torso that was moving his way.

Eddie had seen nothing like it before, and in his long life of amorous experiences he had seen many pleasing sights. Without hesitation he decided it was imperative that he should become closer acquainted with this torso, and as soon as its dark-haired owner had settled down on a beach wrap and handed herself over to the hot rays of the sun, he crossed the strip of sand dividing them and sat down by her side.

Linda was quite pleased to have company. Maybe Eddie's handsome face and sunburned, manly chest had something to do with it, but whatever it was, she received his advances graciously, and in a minute or so they had become old friends:

in under an hour they were lovers. That was the way Eddie liked his women: smooth, polished, quick and willing.

Eddie, who was a cynic, fully expected that by the end of the week Linda's charms would have palled as the charms of so many other young women who had also been quick and willing had palled in the past. But, instead, he found himself thinking about Linda night and day; neglecting his "work" to be with her; and even passing up a golden opportunity to levy a little blackmail just to take her out to an expensive night club and impress her.

Their association had now lasted three weeks, and so far as Eddie was concerned he was eager and as amorous as the day the association first began. He was even willing to secure proprietary rights over Linda, a step he had avoided in the past as not only unnecessary, but as a direct menace to his freedom.

Linda, however, had no wish to lose her independence and freedom. Receiving Eddie every day and two or three nights a week as a lover was one thing; but Eddie as a complete lord and master, to say nothing of being a permanent lodger, was something else besides.

So Eddie was kept in check and was not allowed all the freedom he might wish. He was baffled by the luxurious standard by which Linda lived. She owned a charming little villa which boasted its own private beach and a small tropical garden which a negro gardener attended to with colorful and fertile results, and—which was hidden away in a quiet secluded spot along the coastline.

The villa was furnished in style and comfort; the meals provided by the negro cook were excellent. The upkeep of such an establishment must have been considerable: where then did the money come from? Where did the money come from to keep Linda supplied with the smartest clothes, the smartest shoes and the smartest hats to be seen in Santo Rio? Where did the money come from that bought the glittering blue Road Master Buick in which Linda drove around town or out into the country when the spirit moved her?

Linda had explained away her wealth as a legacy received from an uncle who had made a fortune in oil. But Eddie was a little too smart to believe that, although he allowed her to think he accepted the story. Linda was just not the type to have an uncle in oil.

The obvious explanation never occurred to him. He was confident that Linda could be in love only with him. He decided that Linda had devised some new kind of racket to keep herself in luxury, and he was curious to discover what the racket was.

But the obvious, explanation was the answer. Linda had a lover, who was so besotted by her that he had set her up in this, magnificent luxury although he seldom saw her, as his business took him all over the country. But never for a moment did he forget her, nor, even when associating with other women, did he cease to imagine that it was Linda he held in his arms.

Linda was quite content to let this man supply her with money, to keep her in luxury and to demand so little of her. She thought him a bore and a ghastly little sensualist (as he was), but far too useful to break with. The fact that he so seldom visited the villa (he saw her only four or five times during the year) more than compensated her for what she had to put up with when he did make his visit. He was generous and wealthy, and in her opinion harmless, but here she made a serious error of judgment. But then she had never heard of the Sullivan brothers, and if she had she wouldn't have believed that this fat-faced man she called Frank was one of the dreaded brothers. She might have been a little less careless and a little more faithful to him had she known this fact.

She had met Max once or twice and had taken a dislike to him. He was the only man she had ever met who was not influenced by her beauty and who had not looked a second time at her sensual and sensational figure.

Max had scared her. His eyes had the same glittering stillness as a snake's; and Linda was terrified of snakes.

It is doubtful, too, whether Eddie would have been quite so enchanted with Linda had he known that she was the mistress of one of the Sullivan brothers. Eddie had heard a lot about the Sullivans, although he had never seen either of them. But what he had heard of them would have been quite sufficient to have cooled his ardor for Linda if he had learned the truth at the beginning of his whirlwind courtship. Now, however, he was rather far gone, and even the threat of the Sullivans might not have deterred him.

This day, then, on a hot, sunny afternoon, Eddie drove along Ocean Boulevard in his cream and scarlet roadster (a parting gift of silence from one of his elderly women friends) and felt that all was well with the world.

He made a dashing, handsome figure in his close-fitting white singlet and immaculate white flannel trousers. His, big muscular arms, the color of mahogany, were bare, his large smooth brown hands rested on the cream-colored steering-wheel and his carefully manicured nails glittered in the sun.

He drove with a wide smile on his face because he was exceedingly proud of his big white teeth and he saw no reason why he should not show them. Many a female heart fluttered as he drove along and many a female head turned to look after him. Eddie was aware of the sensation he caused and was gratified.

He arrived at Linda's villa a few minutes after 3:30 and found Linda pottering in the garden, in which flowers of every hue and shade put Technicolor to shame. Linda was wearing white duck slacks, red and white open-toed sandals over bare feet and scarlet toenails, a scarlet halter that, accurately speaking, should have been a size larger to conceal what it attempted to conceal, although Eddie found no fault with it, and on her pretty nose she wore a pair of red horn sunglasses with the lenses the size of doughnuts.

As she moved her curves swayed before her, and her smooth hips flowed like molten metal under her close-fitting slacks.

Eddie sprang from the car, ran across the lawn and jumped a flower-bed with athletic ease as she turned to greet him.

"I was wondering if you were coming," she said in her carefully cultivated deep-throated drawl. "I thought it would be fun to go for a swim this afternoon."

But Eddie had other ideas. He glanced down the long hallway to the bedroom.

"Not yet," he said firmly, and touched her wrist with his brown fingers and then moved them along her arm to her shoulders and behind her neck. "By six the water will be perfect. We'll wait until six."

She relaxed to the touch of his fingers. No one she had ever met had such an exciting touch as Eddie. His fingers seemed to emit sparks of electricity that flowed down her skin.

"Then come inside and have tea," she said, linking her arm through his. "Would you like that?"

Eddie thought it was as good an excuse as any to get her into the house, and together they wandered into the cool, sun-screened lounge, which looked on to the garden through folding glass doors.

Linda took off her sunglasses and dropped on to the white, suede-covered divan with a little exclamation of pleasure. She raised her shapely brown arms above her head and regarded Eddie with a cool smile. She looked a little older than the photograph that had been left in the old plantation house; her eyes were harder and her lips not quite so ready to smile, although they smiled for Eddie; but then Eddie was favored and he knew it.

"Ring the bell, darling," she said, closing her eyes. "And they'll bring tea. I've asked them to cut you some of those tricky little sandwiches you like so much— remember?"

But at the moment tricky little sandwiches were not of the slightest interest to Eddie. He stood over this voluptuous creature and experienced a sudden difficulty in breathing. Blood pounded in his ears and his heart raced uncomfortably. He knew what he wanted and it wasn't tricky little sandwiches.

"I think we'll skip tea," he said, and bending over her, caught her up in his arms and began to walk swiftly across the big room to the door.

Linda was worldly enough to realize that, unless she took immediate evasive action, she would miss her tea, so she began to kick and struggle, but Eddie had not developed his muscles for nothing, and he continued on his way without any considerable inconvenience, climbed the stairs, kicked open the door of Linda's luxurious if over-ornate bedroom, and laid her, still struggling, on the bed.

"Really, Eddie," she gasped as soon as she could get her breath, "you are the most disgusting man I have ever met. No! Don't you dare touch me! You're not always going to have your own way. I mean it this time! We're going right back to the lounge, and we're going to have tea, and then we're going to have a bath..."

Eddie drew the blue and white curtains across the windows without paying the slightest attention to this diatribe. Having satisfied himself that the room was now cloaked in a dimness that created a more intimate atmosphere, he returned in time to prevent Linda from getting off the bed.

"Everything in its proper order," he said firmly, "Tea and a bath later," and he took Linda in his arms with the intention of smothering her resistance with kisses, which, from experience, he was confident would quickly bring her to unconditional surrender.

But this afternoon Linda felt perverse, and had no inclination to submit to Eddie's rough, violent wooing. She was getting a little tired of being taken for granted. Cavemen were all very well once in a while, but too much of that kind of thing was too great a strain on a girl's nerves; so when Eddie, a confident gleam in his eyes, grabbed hold of her, she gave him a resounding box on his ears.

"I said no!" she told him angrily.

For a second or so Eddie sat staring at her, his big hands still gripping her back, his face still close to hers, but his eyes were no longer confident: they were angry and a little spiteful, and the desire in them was by no means checked.

"So you want a fight, do you?" he said. "Well, you've certainly come to the right guy if that's what you want."

Linda scrambled hastily off the bed and made a dart for the door. She had had one fight with Eddie in the early days of their tempestuous wooing, and the following morning found her not only covered with unsightly bruises but also feeling that she had been fed through a wringer. She had no desire to repeat the experience.

Eddie's long arm shot out, grabbed her and jerked her across the bed. She bounced on the mattress. He pinned her wrists down and lightly bit her neck, sending a shiver through her.

"Now, please, darling," Linda begged as she found herself helpless in his grip. "Please, darling, let me go. Don't you dare hit me... you know how I bruise. Eddie! You're not to... Oh! You jerk! Oh! Oh! Eddie, stop it! The servants will hear you!"

A few moments later, bruised, smarting and breathless, she surrendered.

"You are a devil, Eddie," she panted, digging her fingers into his hard, smooth shoulders. "You've hurt me... you've bruised me... but, damn you, it felt good."

He grinned down at her, ran his fingers through her thick hair, his finger-tips exploring the shape of her hard little skull. He smelled the coconut scent of her hair.

Her arms strained him to her, and she crushed her mouth against his.

There was a long stillness in the room while they were caught up in the vortex of their passion. The hands of the little clock by the bedside moved forward, its blank face seeing nothing of what went on in the dim-lighted room. The evening sun slowly crept round the house and reflected on the blue and white curtains.

Eddie was the first to awake. He moved his head, stretched his thick arms luxuriously, sighed, opened his eyes. Then suddenly his stomach turned a somersault and his heart stopped beating for a split second and then began to race. A man was sitting on the foot of the bed, watching him.

For a full minute Eddie stared at this intruder, believing he was still asleep and dreaming. The man was a nightmare figure, dressed in black, whose white, lean, granite-hard face hung over Eddie like an apparition from a horror play.

Eddie clutched Linda, who woke with a start. Terror struck her speechless, for she instantly recognized the figure in black. She was so paralyzed with fear that she could make no move to cover her nakedness, and lay still as a statue, her heart scarcely beating.

"Tell your two-bit gigolo to get out of here," Max said softly. "I want to talk to you."

The sound of Max's voice broke the hypnotic spell that had gripped both Linda and Eddie.

Linda gave a horrified scream and snatched up a big cushion with which to cover herself. Eddie sat up with an oath, his eyes blazing with embarrassed fury, his great hands closed into fists; but that was as far as he got.

There was a flash of steel as a knife jumped into Max's hand. He leaned forward and with incredible swiftness traced the point of the knife lightly down Eddie's face, down his neck and chest to his stomach. It was as if a feather had touched Eddie, but instantly a thin line of blood appeared where the knife-point had touched him.

At the sight of the knife and the line of blood Eddie's fury and courage oozed out of him like oil from a leaky can.

He was tough enough when it came to handling elderly rich women, and even to fighting with Linda, but cold steel made him sick to his stomach.

"Don't touch me!" he gasped, his fine brown complexion turning to a muddy white. "I'm going... don't touch me with that knife."

"Get out!" Max said, his dead eyes bearing down on Eddie's terrified face.

"Sure," Eddie spluttered, scrambled off the bed and huddled into his clothes. He had no thought for Linda and he didn't
even look her way. His one burning desire was to get away from this dangerous thug, and he couldn't get away fast enough. "I'm going... just take it easy."

Max leaned forward and wiped the blood from the knife off on to Linda's thigh; as he did so he looked at her and his thin lips curled in contempt.

She shuddered, but made no move. The knife terrified her.

"Don't leave me, Eddie," she whimpered, but Eddie was already on his way; the door slammed behind him.

Max rose to his feet, put away his knife and picked up a silk wrap that was lying across a chair. He flung it at Linda.

"Put it on, you whore," he said.

Utterly demoralized, Linda put on the wrap with trembling hands. This awful man was certain to tell Frank. Then what would Frank do? Kick her out? Would she have to go back to being a showgirl again? Lose all this luxury, her freedom, her car and her beautiful clothes? She felt so bad that when she had put on the wrap she slumped back on to the bed.

Max leaned against the wall. He had tilted his hat over his nose, and now he lit a cigarette, looking at her from over the flame of the match.

"So you couldn't take his money without cheating," he said contemptuously. "I warned him, but he's a sucker for a bitch like you. Well, from now on it's going to be different. From now on you're going to earn your money."

Linda flinched.

"Don't tell him," she implored, holding her wrap close to her. "It won't ever happen again. I promise. Frank loves me. Why spoil his life?"

Max blew a long stream of tobacco smoke down his pinched nostrils.

"You're damn right it won't happen again," he said. "And I'm not spoiling his life because I'm not telling him. I don't see the point of distracting him with the truth."

Linda stared at him, began to control her trembling limbs.

"I don't trust you," she said. "I know meanness when I see it. You couldn't keep quiet—"

"Shut up!" he returned. "He's come home now for good. And you're going to stay with him, do what he tells you, sleep with him when he feels that way, take him around, shave him, keep his clothes in order, read to him. You're going to be always at his side to help him. You're going to be his eyes."

Linda thought he had gone crazy.

"What do you mean—be his eyes? He has his own eyes, hasn't he?"

Max smiled thinly. He crossed over to her, caught a handful of her hair in his fingers, dragged her head back. She made no effort to break his hold, but stared back at him, her eyes dark with terror.

"And if you try any tricks I'll fix you," he said. "I warn once, never twice. If you run away, if you're unfaithful to him, I'll find you wherever you are and I'll burn his name across your face with acid." He released her and raising his hand he hit her heavily across her mouth, knocking her flat across the bed. "What he can see in a tramp like you I don't know, but he was always a sucker. Well, he wants you, and he's going to have you: there's nothing else left for him."

As he went to the door Linda sat up, her hand on her lips. He opened the door, went out on to the landing. She heard him call, "Frank; she's waiting for you."

She remained sitting on the bed, unable to move, staring at the open door, listening to a slow shuffling step on the stairs with growing horror.

Then Frank came in, his sightless eyes hidden behind dark glasses, a stick in his hand guided him to the bed. He wasn't used to using the cane and waved it around like an antenna.

He looked sightlessly over the top of Linda's head. There were pent-up desire, self-pity, urgent animal longing in his fat white face.

"Hello, Linda, honey?" he said, his hand groping for her. "Daddy's home."

~§~

The next two weeks were a nightmare for Linda. Never, as long as she lived, would she forget them. She had no leisure from Frank's incessant demands. When he wasn't making mauling, hateful love to her, he was wanting to be read to; to be taken for rides in the car, to be waited on hand and foot. His blindness soured his already vicious temper and he vented his spleen on her. Now he could no longer see her beauty   she quickly lost her influence over him. He refused to let her buy clothes (and in the past Linda never let a day pass without replenishing her already bursting wardrobe). "Wear what you've got," he would snarl. "I can't see you in new things, so what the hell?" Worse still, he controlled the money now, and became miserly; cutting down expenses, keeping Linda without a nickel.

She was driven to distraction, for she feared to leave him, knowing that Max was capable of carrying out his threat. She had no privacy and could not move a step without hearing the tap of his stick and the plaintive whine of his voice asking where she was.

She longed to see Eddie again, and poured out an account of her sufferings to him in long and hysterical letters.

Eddie was also suffering. He had not realized how crazy he was about Linda until their separation. Now that he dared not go near the villa he became moody, slept badly and thought continually of Linda's charms. His racket and consequently his income suffered.

One afternoon, some sixteen days after Max's dramatic appearance in Linda's bedroom, Eddie was sitting in a drug store idling an hour away before he called on one of his elderly clients when he noticed a girl come in and sit on a stool not far from him.

It was a slack hour of the day, and Eddie and the girl were the only two people in the place. More from habit than interest, Eddie looked the girl over. She was shabbily but neatly dressed. Under a dowdy little hat a mass of raven black hair struggled for freedom. She wore horn spectacles, and in spite of her lack of make-up she was attractive. But Eddie had seen so many beautiful and glamorous women that such a poorly dressed, unsophisticated object was of no interest to him. He observed, however, that in spite of the shabby clothes, the girl had an exceptionally good figure, and her long, slender legs held his attention for a moment before he resumed reading his news paper.

He heard the girl speaking to the soda-jerk, a little bald-headed guy whose name was Andrews and with whom Eddie was friendly.

"I'm looking for part-time work," the girl said in a quiet, well-modulated voice. "You wouldn't know anyone who wants a companion for the evening or someone to mind the children, would you?"

Andrews, who liked to help people when he could, swabbed down the counter, wrinkled his forehead and considered the question.

"Can't say I do," he said at last, "Most folks around this little town don't have children and don't need companions. It's a kind of gay little town, if you know what I mean."

"Every town has children."

"This ain't every town."

"I've got a job," the girl explained as she stirred her coffee, "but it doesn't pay too well and I thought something in the evening might help out."

"Yeah, I see how it is," Andrews said, scratched his head. "Well, I don't know of anyone, but if I hear of something I'll pass it on."

"Oh, will you?" the girl said, brightening. "I should be very grateful. Mary Prentiss is the name. May I write it down? I live on East Street."

Andrews found her a pencil and paper. She quickly scribbled down her address.

"If there's a blind person who, needs a companion," the girl went on as she was writing, "I have had training with blind people—"

"Sure, but there ain't many blind people in Santo Rio, in fact, I don't know any at all," Andrews said. "But I'll keep my eyes open for you."

Eddie watched her go, tipped his hat over his handsome nose and considered the idea that had suddenly entered his head. With a feeling of growing excitement he decided the idea was inspired.

"Let's have that dame's name and address, Andy," he said, sliding off his stool. "I know a blind guy who's aching for a little female society."

~§~

At eleven o'clock the same evening Eddie found Linda waiting for him at the secluded and prearranged rendezvous, a quarter of a mile or so from the villa.

Their first wild, passionate greeting over, Eddie drew her down beside him on the sand and, holding her close, began to talk.

"Now, listen, honey, we haven't much time. That dope I sent you won't keep him quiet for long, but long enough for me to tell you I've got an idea."

"I've been waiting for you to get an idea," Linda said, clasping his hands. "If I hadn't been certain you'd have thought of something I think I would have killed myself."

Eddie made sympathetic noises, although he was as sure as Linda was herself she would not have done anything as drastic as that.

"We've both been through hell," he said, "but, although this idea isn't the complete cure, it'll help. I've found a girl who wants a job as a companion. You must persuade Frank that a change now and then will be good for him—a change of company, I mean. Persuade him to hire this girl to come in two or three evenings a week to read to him."

Linda twisted round, her eyes stormy.

"Do you call that a good idea?" she demanded. "Where will it get me? Do you think he'll let me out of his hearing even if he does have a companion?"

Eddie smiled down at her.

"That's where you're kidding yourself, honey," he said. "You're forgetting one thing: the guy's blind. He can't see how lovely you are, and his interest is going to flag unless you help him to keep the memory green, which, of course, you won't. Sooner or later he'll want to hear a new voice, to have someone different around no matter how crazy he is about you at the moment. I've talked to this girl. She's got a good voice, although she's not much to look at. And, more important still, she has a swell shape. (Not so good as yours, precious, but good enough.) I've given her the nudge that she might have to be more than a companion to this guy, but that she'll be paid well. She didn't bat an eyelid. I'll bet you in a while Frank will want to be alone with her. From what you've told me about him he won't be content to sit and listen to a girl reading to him every evening. He'll want to make a pass at her, and you'll be in the way. Soon he'll be suggesting you take a walk, or do a movie or, something, and with a lot of persuasion you'll go." He pressed her to him. "And you'll find me waiting right here for you whenever you can get away. Now, don't interrupt. Let me finish. It'll take time, but there's no other way round it. We don't want this guy Max shoving his oar in. He scares me. I don't scare easily," Eddie added, not wanting her to think he was yellow, "but when a guy uses a sticker the way he does, I'm scared and I stay scared. Once we get Frank used to the idea, we can find him any amount of girls to keep him amused. It'll cost dough, but right now I'm making plenty, and to get you to myself even for a day is worth all the money in the world. In a couple of months, if you play your hand right, don't let him get near you; snarl and snap at him, he'll be glad to be rid of you. Then you and me can get out of this burg without Max turning sour. How do you like it?"

Linda turned it over in her mind. She was sufficiently stupid to dislike the idea of setting up a rival in her home. There was a dog-in-the-manger streak in her nature that rebelled against the thought of another woman enjoying the luxuries of the villa, but if she were to escape from Frank this seemed the only logical way, unless...

"I wish he was dead," she said between her teeth. "I wish someone would rid me of him forever. Wouldn't that be the best solution of all? He could easily fall down the stairs or drink the wrong thing."

"You can get that idea right out of your pretty little head," Eddie said with great firmness. "If it wasn't for Max it might be arranged, but if anything happened to Frank, Max would know who to look for. I'm not taking that risk for you or anyone else."

And so, reluctantly, Linda agreed to give Eddie's idea a trial. Rather to her surprise, the idea worked out exactly as Eddie had predicted.

After a week of carefully preparing the ground, Linda suggested to Frank that he might care to have someone in to read to him, and went on to describe Mary Prentiss (whom she had not as yet seen) in such glowing terms that Frank rose immediately to the bait.

Linda had been irritable and sharp-tempered during the past week, had avoided Frank's questing hands, snapped and snarled at him along the lines suggested by Eddie, until Frank was growing tired of the sound of her querulous voice. She wasn't so hot now that he was around her all day. The idea of having someone fresh in the house appealed to him.

Mary Prentiss called the following evening, and Linda made it her business to meet her at the gate so she should have an opportunity of talking with her before she met Frank.

Linda was agreeably surprised when she saw the shabbily dressed figure coming along the narrow beach path. This was no dangerous rival, she consoled herself. If Frank could but see her, he wouldn't look at her twice. It amused Linda to know that he was all worked up, imagining his new companion to be as glamorous as herself.

The fat fool would get a shock if he could see her, she thought spitefully.

Mary Prentiss did manage to look very plain, although her big green eyes were undoubtedly beautiful. But the dowdy clothes, the lack of make-up and the awful hair style seemed to neutralize the effect of her eyes.

Linda was a little puzzled to see how white and haggard she became when she introduced her to Frank. She thought for a moment the girl was going to faint, but she appeared to control herself, and, still puzzled, Linda left them alone together.

She noticed an immediate change in Frank when the girl had gone. He was more cheerful, less trying and openly enthusiastic.

Each evening for the next week Mary Prentiss came after dinner to read to him, and, acting on Eddie's instructions.

Linda was always present. She watched Frank, noted his growing restlessness, his lack of interest in the books Mary Prentiss selected for her reading. The girl was as impersonal as a nurse. Whenever Frank's groping hand reached out for her, Linda asked him sharply if there was anything he needed, and the hand was quickly withdrawn, and Frank's fat, sensual face darkened with frustrated disappointment.

A week later Eddie's prediction came true.

"I've been thinking," Frank said abruptly one afternoon. "You don't get out enough. It's not right that you should stay in night after night when I have someone to read to me. Take yourself to a movie tonight. The change will do you good."

So that night, when the girl who called herself Mary Prentiss came as usual to read to Frank, she found him alone.

"Isn't Miss Lee here tonight?" she asked quietly, as she drew up a chair and selected a book to read.

"No," Frank said, and smiled. "I've been wanting to be with you for some time—alone. You know why, don't you?"

"I think so," Mary Prentiss said, and laid the book down on her lap.

"Come here," Frank said, his face suddenly congested.

She stood close to his chair and allowed his hand to stray over her. There was a look on her face of intense loathing and horror, but she remained still, with closed eyes and set mouth. It was, to her, as if a filthy, repulsive spider with obscene and hairy legs were crawling over her bare skin.

Then suddenly she drew back out of his reach.

"Please don't," she said sharply. "Not here. I have a code of honor. Not in the same house. I'm thinking of Miss Lee."

Frank could scarcely believe his ears.

"What's she got to do with it?" he demanded thickly.

"This is her home," Mary Prentiss said in a low voice, and yet he eyes were watching Frank's face with desperate intentness as if she were trying to read his mind. "But at my place..."

She stopped, gave a little sigh.

"Don't be a dope," Frank said, heaving himself out of his chair. "This is my home, too. To hell with her. What did she ever do for me, except spend my money? Come here. I want you."

"No," she said firmly; "but if you will come with me it would be different. I would have no scruples then, but it is being in this house..."

"All right," Frank said, and laughed. "I haven't been out for a long time. Let's go. She won't be back until midnight. Where's your place?"

"East Street," she told him, her green eyes lighting up. "I have a car. It won't take us long."

Frank caught hold of her, tried to find her face with his lips, and for a moment she nearly lost control of herself, but she drew away, shuddering, and said, without betraying the sick horror that gripped her, "Not yet... soon, but not yet."

"Well, come on then," Frank said impatiently. He was not used to being dictated to by his women. He caught hold of her arm and let her lead him from the house and along the narrow beach path. She guided him into the seat of a black Chrysler coupé that was parked in the shadows, out of sight of the villa.

"How can you afford to run a car like this?" he asked suspiciously, as his fingers touched the fabric of the seat and he felt the springing and the leg room.

"I borrowed it," she said in the same cold, flat voice, started the engine and drove quickly towards the lights of the town. Her window was cracked open and the wind tossed her hair.

"How I miss my eyes!" Frank snarled suddenly. "You wouldn't know what it feels like to be driven without seeing or knowing where you are going." He brooded for a moment, added, "It's a feeling of total helplessness."

"Is it?" she said, gripping the steering-wheel until her knuckles showed white.

He ran his hand down her leg.

"Hurry, sweetheart," he urged. "You'll find me a very satisfactory lover." And then he asked in a lower tone, "Have you any experience?"

She shuddered away from him.

"You'll see," she said. "You'll know soon enough."

She drove rapidly along Ocean Boulevard, pulled up under a street lamp in the main street. The theatre traffic roared past them, the sidewalks were crowded.

"Why do you stop?" he asked impatiently, listening to the traffic and the murmur of the crowd passing by. "Are we there?"

"Yes; this is the end of your journey," she said.

There was a jarring note in her voice that made him jerk his head round and stare sightlessly at her.

"What's the matter?" he demanded, reached out and caught her wrist. "If you think you can back out of it now... no one plays tricks with me—" He broke off as his sensitive fingers felt the puckered scar on her wrist. "What's this?" he asked sharply, a chord in his memory stirring.

"A scar," she said, watching him closely. "I cut myself."

His memory groped into the past. Then he remembered seeing such a scar on the wrist of the Blandish girl, and he stiffened. His highly developed instinct for danger warned him to get away, but his desire for her swamped it. Why think of Carol Blandish? She was miles away. Still, the uneasiness of the situation suddenly sat coldly on his shoulders. He paused for a moment longer and then spoke.

"I once knew a girl who had a scar like this," he muttered, his fat face tightening. "She was mad. Damn her! She blinded me with her claws."

"I know," Carol said softly, and wrenched her wrist away, "and now, I am going to kill you."

An icy chill ran through Frank's body.

"Who are you?" he quavered, groping for the door-handle.

"You know who," she said. "I've waited a long time for this moment. First you, and then Max," and her fingers closed round his wrist in a grip of steel.

Blind panic seized Frank. If he could have seen her, could have been sure she wasn't pointing a gun at him, could be sure that in a second or so no bullet would smash into him, he wouldn't have acted as he did, and as Carol had hoped he would act. But the suffocating darkness that pressed in on him, the knowledge that he was trapped in a car with a dangerous, revengeful, mad woman, paralyzed his mind. His one thought was to get away from her and into the crowd so she could not reach him.

He broke free from her grip, threw open the car door and stumbled blindly into the street. The moment his feet touched the ground he began to run.

Carol slammed the car door, gripped the steering-wheel as she leaned forward to watch the dark figure run blindly into the headlights of the oncoming traffic.

"Look, Steve," she said with a sob in her voice, "there he goes. I hand him over to you."

Frank heard sudden shouts around him and the squealing of car brakes. He floundered forward in his blindness, thrusting out his hands into a darkness that was so thick he could almost feel it, and he heard himself screaming.

The onrushing traffic frantically tried to avoid him. Cars swerved, crashed into one another. Women screamed. A policeman blew his whistle.

A cream and scarlet roadster suddenly shot out of the inter-section and hurtled across the road. Eddie, a little drunk, his arm round Linda, had no chance of avoiding Frank. For a brief second he saw Frank facing him, the bright headlights of the car beat on his sweating, terrified face. He heard Linda scream, "It's Frank!" and he swerved, crammed on his brakes. The fender of the car hit Frank a glancing blow, threw him across the road and under the wheels of a speeding truck.

In the confusion that followed no one noticed the black Chrysler coupé pull away from the curb and drive silently away into the darkness.

~§~

Max followed the nurse along the rubber-covered corridor of the Waltonville Hospital. His face was expressionless, but his thin nostrils were white and pinched.

The nurse signed to him to wait and went into a room, closed the door after her.

Max leaned against the wall, thrust his hands into his pockets. There was a bored look in his eyes: he wanted to smoke, but it wasn't allowed.

The nurse came to the door after a few moments, beckoned to him.

"No more than two minutes," she said. "His injuries are very severe."

"Dying?"

"Yes."

"Then why not say so? Think I'll cry?" Max said impatiently. He walked into the room, stood by the bed and looked down at Frank. The fat face was yellow, the lips were blue. He scarcely seemed to breathe. Even so, nothing stirred in Max's heart for his old partner.

"Here I am," Max said curtly, wanting to get it over.

Frank struggled to speak, and Max had to bend over him to catch the halting words. He was reluctant to do this because Frank's breath was bad.

"It was Carol Blandish," Frank gasped. "She said I was the first, then you. I knew her by the scar on her wrist."

Max straightened.

"You were always a sucker for women, you fat fool," he said bitterly. "You asked for it." Then he added, "She won't get me. I'm not weak like you are."

Frank's breath suddenly heaved up in a gasping rattle. Max looked at him, lifted his shoulders.

"So long, sucker," he said.

The nurse came in, looked quickly at Frank, then drew the sheet over his face.

Max was studying her. She was young and pretty, and he tapped Frank's dead shoulder.

"That's one of 'em you won't make a pass at," he said, tilted his hat over his eyes and went out.

CHAPTER VII

THERE was a satisfied, almost cheerful expression on Max's face as he walked down the broad steps that led from the hospital. It had suddenly dawned on him that he was now twice as rich as he had been before entering the hospital. Frank was hardly a memory now.

Neither of the Sullivans had kept his substantial savings in a bank. They knew it was easy for the police to tie up a banking account, and they kept their money where they could get at it quickly. Max's father had charge of it; and now Frank was dead his share would automatically come to Max, for no one else knew about it: except, of course, Max's father, but he didn't count. It meant, then, that Max could retire, give up this murder racket and buy a bird store as he had always wished to do. The idea appealed to him.

He paused beside the black Packard Clipper, lit a cigarette, tossed the match into the gutter. For a moment or so his mind dwelt on Carol. Frank had said, "First me, then you." There could be no doubt that she had engineered Frank's death. Max had talked with Linda, had heard about the mysterious Mary Prentiss and had put two and two together. Mary Prentiss had been Carol Blandish, and she was out for revenge. But Frank had always been a sucker for women. It would have been easy for any woman to have tripped him up. In Max's case it was different. Women meant nothing to him. If Carol Blandish tried her tricks with him, she would be sorry. He would smash her as ruthlessly as he had smashed others who had got in his way.

He was so confident of his ability to look after himself that he dismissed Carol from his mind as not worth further thought. No, the death of Frank was the end of the episode; the end, too, of the Sullivan brothers. Max Geza was about to give up his professional status as a killer and become a bird fancier. It would be interesting to see how it worked out.

He tossed the half-burned cigarette into the street, pulled his soft hat further over his eyes, opened the car door. Then he paused, his narrow eyebrows coming together in a puzzled frown.

Lying on the front seat immediately under the driving-wheel was a single, but magnificent, scarlet orchid.

Max stared at the flower, his face expressionless, his eyes a little startled. Then he picked it up, turned it between his fingers as he studied it. An expensive bloom for someone to have dropped through the car window for no reason at all; or was there a reason? *Did it mean anything?* he asked himself, his mind attuned always to danger. He glanced up and down the street, saw nothing to raise his suspicions, shrugged his shoulders.

Then he dropped the orchid into the gutter, got into the car and trod on the starter. But he did not engage the gear. He sat staring through the windshield, his eyes still thoughtful. He didn't like mysteries: not that you could call this a mystery, but it was odd. At one time he and Frank used to hang two little black crows made of wool on the doorknockers of their intended victims. Once or twice it saved them trouble, as the recipient of the woolen crows had shot himself, but it was a cheap theatrical trick and Max soon put a stop to it. Warning symbols seemed to him to be undignified. *Was the scarlet orchid a warning symbol?* he asked himself. If it was, then whoever had dropped it into the car had better watch out. Max didn't appreciate such tricks. He pulled at his thin, pinched nose, got out of the car and picked up the bloom. After a moment's hesitation he stuck it in his buttonhole. Then he engaged gear and drove away.

~§~

On a hill overlooking Santo Rio's magnificent harbor and bay stood a two-story pinewood house surrounded by a wilderness of palm trees and flowering shrubs. It was a forlorn-looking place, weather-beaten, shabby and lonely. On the wooden gate hung a nameplate which read: *Kozikot.* Max had never bothered to remove the plate, although each time he came to the house he sneered at it.

This wooden structure was his home. He rarely visited it, but it was convenient to have some place where he could keep his few personal possessions and his money. It also afforded a home for his father, Ismi Geza, who was getting to be an old man. Ismi had been a circus clown for forty of his sixty-five years. He still looked like a clown as he moved slowly alone the garden path towards the house. He was bent and bald and sad looking. His skin was pitted and as rough as sandpaper from the constant application of cheap grease-paint: the uniform of his profession. His left leg dragged a little: the heritage of a stroke which had ended, his circus career. There was no likeness to his son in his round, fleshy, sad face, and Ismi wouldn't have wished it.

He was frightened of Max: as he had been frightened of Max's mother, Max had taken after his mother, in looks and in nature. It was not in Ismi to be cruel. He was a simple, peace-loving creature and only at ease when he was alone.

As he was about to enter the house he heard a car coming up the road, and he paused, looked over his shoulder, his eyes uneasy. No car had been up this lonely road for three months or more, and the sound startled him. The road dust swallowed the approaching car and made it look like a demon tearing up the hill.

The black Packard Clipper pulled up outside the gate and Max climbed out. He stood with his hands in his overcoat pockets, his hat tilted over his nose and the scarlet orchid in his buttonhole. There was an air of purpose and menace about him, and Ismi watched him intently. He lived in dread of these visits, when Max appeared without warning; not knowing what was going to happen, how Max would treat him.

Max stared at the nameplate on the gate for a moment or so, then with a slight shrug pushed the gate open and walked up the garden path.

Ismi immediately noticed the orchid, and he stared at it, feeling that something was wrong, that something unpleasant was about to happen to upset the quiet and uneventful flow of his life. Max had never before worn a flower in his buttonhole. Surely, the old man thought, something had happened to make his son wear a flower.

Father and son eyed each other as Max arrived at the bottom of the steps leading to the house.

"Frank's dead," Max said briefly. "He was run over by a truck."

Although Ismi had hated Frank, he was shocked. He was too close to death himself to hear it spoken of without a twinge of apprehension.

"I hope he didn't suffer," was all he could think of to say.

"The truck smashed his chest and it took him two hours to croak," Max returned, sniffed at the orchid. "You can draw your own conclusions."

It then dawned on the old man what Frank's death could mean.

"Will this be the end of it all?" he asked eagerly. He knew Max and Frank were the Sullivan brothers. It had amused Max to tell him, to describe the various murders they had committed, to watch the old man's politely controlled horror.

"Yes," Max said. "I have his money now as well as my own. It was agreed that if one of us died, the one left should take over the other's money. I'm rich."

Ismi rubbed his bald head nervously.

"Will it make any difference to me?"

"I don't know," Max returned indifferently. "I have had no time to think of you. I'll come to your little problems later." He came up the steps, stood opposite the old man. They were the same height, even though Ismi was bent. "I'm going into business," he went on. "If I can find anything for you to do, you can have the job. If not, you can stay here. Do you want to stay here?"

"I like it here," Ismi said, nodding, "but, of course, if I can be useful to you..."

Max leaned against the wooden post of the verandah.

"You're getting senile," he said softly. "Your brain's dull. Doesn't it surprise you that Frank of all people should get himself run over by a truck?"

Ismi considered this, saw at once that he should have been surprised; was dismayed to realize that what Max had said was true. He was getting senile; his brain was dull.

"I hadn't thought," he said, looking at Max furtively. "Yes, something must have happened. I should have realized that the moment you told me."

Max told him about Roy Larson, how they had had to kill Steve to silence him; how Carol had blinded Frank, had tracked him to Santo Rio and had engineered his death.

Ismi stood silent and still in the hot sunshine, his eyes on the ground, his veined hands folded, and listened.

Max spoke briefly and softly.

"Frank's last words were to warn me that I should be next," he concluded. "She is here in town. What do you think of it?"

"I wish you hadn't told me," Ismi said, and walked into the house.

Max pursed his thin lips, shrugged, returned to the car. He collected his two suitcases and entered the house, went up the dusty carpeted stairs to his room, kicked open the door and set down the bags.

It was a big room, sparsely furnished, and with a view of the distant harbor. There was an unlived-in, bleak atmosphere in the room that might have affected anyone but Max: such things meant nothing to him.

He stood for a moment listening at the door, then he shut and locked it. He crossed the room to a big old-fashioned wardrobe, opened it and slid back a panel in the floor. From this cunningly concealed locker he pulled out two leather brief-cases. For the next half-hour he was busily counting stacks of five and ten dollar bills: each stack tied and labeled, each containing a hundred notes. When he was through, he returned the money to its hiding place and shut the wardrobe. He was rich, he told himself; he was free to do what he liked, and although his face remained expressionless, his eyes lit up with suppressed excitement.

As he was going downstairs he heard the telephone ring, and he paused, listening to his father's voice as he answered.

Ismi came into the passage after a moment or so, looked up at Max as he stood on the stairs.

"They're calling about Frank's funeral," he said, an odd look in his eyes. "Perhaps you'd better speak to them."

"They? Who?" Max snapped impatiently.

"The mortician. It's something to do with flowers."

"What do I care?" Max returned, and came down the stairs. "Tell them to shove him away as they think best. I don't want to be bothered. I gave them money. What else do they want?"

"Do you want the flowers put on the grave?" Ismi said without looking at his son.

Max's eyes grew thoughtful.

"What kind of flowers?" he asked, his voice soft.

"Orchids... scarlet orchids. They say they didn't think they were very suitable for a funeral."

Max took his cigarette from his lips, regarded the glowing end for a moment. He knew his father had something else to say; and he could tell by his face that he was scared to say it.

"Go on," he said sharply.

"They said there was a card with the flowers," Ismi muttered, and again stopped dead.

"And what was on the card?" Max asked.

"From Carol Blandish and Steve Larson," Ismi returned.

Max pitched his cigarette into the garden, moved to the front door. There was a far-away look in his eyes. At the door he turned.

"Tell them I'm not interested," he said briefly, and walked out of the house, down the steps to the Packard. The smell of briny pier rocks drifted over the lot.

Without appearing to do so he looked searchingly around the garden, down into the Bay. There was a cat-like stillness and watchfulness in his attitude and his eyes glittered.

Nothing moved, and yet he had a feeling that he was being watched. He was not uneasy, but he was viciously angry, and he took the orchid from his buttonhole and slowly tore the bloom into, small pieces, which he scattered on the sandy path. Then he climbed into the Packard and drove it round to the garage at the back of the house.

~§~

"I'll be leaving tomorrow," Max said as Ismi cleared the supper things. "I think I'll settle in Chicago. There's a guy there who wants to sell out, and if his price is right I'll buy. Last time I was there he had a hundred different kinds of birds, and there's good living accommodation over the shop. You could come out there and run the house if you want to."

Ismi stacked the plates and dishes on a tray.

"I wouldn't like to live in a town again," he said, after hesitation. "Would it be all right if I stayed here?"

Max yawned, stretched his legs to the log fire.

"Please yourself," he said, thinking maybe it was as well to shake the old man off now. He was getting old: before long he'd be a nuisance, and he had no intension of actually caring for him.

"Then I guess I'll stay here," Ismi said, picked up the tray, and as he turned to the door a dog began to howl mournfully somewhere in the garden. The wind was rising and it caught the sound, carried it past the house towards the Bay.

Max glanced over his shoulder towards the door, listened too.

"What's he howling about?" he demanded irritably.

Ismi shook his head, carried the tray into the kitchen. While he washed the dishes he listened to the continual howling. It got on his nerves. He had never heard the dog howl like this before, and after he had put away the dishes he went out into the garden.

The moon floated high above the pine trees, its yellow face partly obscured by light clouds. The wind rustled the shrubs, and the garden was alive with whispered sounds.

Ismi walked down the path to the kennel. At the sound of his approach the dog stopped howling and whined.

"What is it?" Ismi asked, bending to look into the dark kennel. He could just make out the dog as it crouched on the floor, and he struck a match. The tiny flame showed him the dog, its hair in ridges all along its back, its eyes blank with fright.

Ismi suddenly felt uneasy and he straightened, looked over

his shoulder into the half-darkness. He fancied he saw a movement near the house, and he peered forward as the dog whined again. A mass of black shadows confronted him and he told himself uneasily that he had imagined the movement, but he waited, wondering if he would see it again. After a few minutes he gave up and returned to the house. He was relieved to shut and bolt the door.

Max was still lolling before the fire when the old man came into the living room. He neither spoke nor looked up. There was a long silence in the room. The only sounds came from the wind as it moaned round the house and the faint whining from the dog. But Ismi sat tense and listened, and after a while he thought be heard soft footsteps overhead. He looked quickly at Max, but he showed no sign of hearing anything, and the old man hesitated to speak.

A board creaked somewhere in the house and this sound was followed by a scraping noise which, if Ismi hadn't been listening for it, he would not have heard.

He glanced up quickly and met Max's eyes. He, too, was listening.

"Do you hear anything?" Max asked, squirming in his chair.

"I thought so," Ismi said doubtfully. "This old house moans in the wind."

Max raised his hand, and the two men listened again.

Seconds ticked by and they heard nothing. The wind had died down, and the silence was so acute that Max could hear the faint wheezing sound of Ismi's breathing.

He made an impatient movement.

"What the hell's the matter with me?" he muttered angrily, and bent to pick up the poker to stir the fire, but a sign from Ismi stopped him.

Both men heard the faint footfall this time, and with set face Max slipped his hand inside his coat, drew his gun.

"Stay here," he whispered to Ismi, and crept to the door. He moved like a shadow, and before opening the door he snapped off the electric light.

Out in the dark passage he paused to listen. He heard nothing and began to edge up the stairs. He still wasn't convinced that anyone was in the house, but he wasn't taking chances. The house was old, and the wind could play tricks; boards that were dry and rotten could creak without being trodden on, but he was going to make sure.

He reached the head of the stairs, paused to listen again, then he turned on the electric light and walked swiftly to his room, threw open the door and went in. The room was empty and nothing seemed disturbed. As he moved to the wardrobe he heard the dog howling again, and he ran to the window. For a moment or so he could see nothing, then the moon breaking through the clouds shed a faint light over the garden. He thought he saw a shadow moving below, and he stared fixedly, but at that moment the clouds drifted once more across the face of the moon.

He turned back to the wardrobe, suddenly frightened, and opened it. One glance was enough. The locker was open and all the money he possessed was gone.

He stood staring at the open locker, paralyzed with shock. His breath seemed to roar at the back of his throat and blood rushed to his head, making him feel lightheaded and faint.

He moved forward slowly like an old man, groped inside the locker with fingers that had turned cold. He touched something soft, lifted it, and knew what it was as he carried it to the light. Then with a sudden, croaking cry, like that of a savage animal in pain, he flung the orchid to the floor, ground it under his heel, while he smashed his clenched fists against the sides of his head with uncontrolled fury.

Ismi found him rolling on the floor in a kind of fit, his face scratched and bleeding, white foam at his lips.

The only thing of distinction about Palm Bay Hotel was its enormous neon sign which could be seen from practically any point in Santo Rio. Because of this sign visitors to the town, arriving by night, were constantly mistaking Palm Bay for a luxury, or at least a high class, hotel.

In daylight this rambling, four-story brick building looked what it was—third rate, dirty and disreputable; but at night it hid its dinginess behind its brilliant neon sign and caught unwary customers. Of course, the customers didn't stay for more than a night, but you can run a hotel on one-nighters if you get enough of them and if your charges are exorbitant.

Palm Bay had also a number of permanent residents. They represented the lower strata of Santa Rio's society, but they did occasionally pay their bills, and with their support, and with the scientific fleecing of the one-nighters, the hotel got along well enough in spite of being in direct competition with some of the most exclusive and luxurious hotels in the country.

When Eddie Regan first came to Santo Rio, like so many of the other visitors, he had been deceived by Palm Bay's neon sign and had taken a room. He very soon discovered that the hotel was third rate, but being, at that time, a little third rate himself, he stayed on. By the time he had made a success of his racket he had become so used to Palm Bay that he decided to make it his permanent headquarters, and took over one of the few of the hotel's suites and furnished it on the proceeds of his first attempt at blackmail. The suite was transformed into an oasis of luxury compared with the other bleakly furnished rooms, and Eddie was immediately regarded as the star boarder by the management and was treated accordingly.

This night, half an hour or so after Max had discovered the loss of his savings, Eddie was sitting in the dusty, fusty bar, drinking Scotch and feeling lonely.

Everyone in the hotel knew he had been the direct cause of Frank's death. They also knew that Frank had been keeping Linda in luxury and that Eddie had been sleeping with her on the sly. There wasn't much that the staff and residents of Palm Bay didn't know about one another, and Eddie knew they knew all about him.

They even knew that the police were trying to make up their minds whether or not Eddie had deliberately killed Frank. The D.A. felt that a jury wouldn't believe that Eddie had managed to arrive in his car at the identical moment when Frank had run blindly into the street; although the D.A. himself was ready to believe anything was possible when dealing with a smart guy like Eddie. The motive was obvious, but the evidence too flimsy.

Neither Linda nor Eddie had told the D.A. about Mary Prentiss. They felt that if they mentioned that mysterious young woman the police might easily and unjustly suspect that they had worked in collaboration with her. When questioned by the D.A., Linda had explained that Frank had told her to go to the movies, and she had gone ("Very unwillingly," she assured the D.A. with tears in her eyes) and had left him alone.

On her way downtown she had met Eddie, and what could be more natural than for them to join company? No, she had no idea why Frank had come into town, nor could she explain how he had got there. She came through the searching examination very well, and when inconvenient questions were asked concerning her relations with Frank and Eddie, she staged such a noisy attack of hysterics that the D.A. was glad to get her out of his office.

Frank's death presented a nice little problem, and the D.A. was still busy scratching his head over it.

Eddie decided it would be wiser for Linda and himself to separate until the police no longer took any interest in them. It was obvious to both of them that they could not continue to live in Santo Rio, and Linda was busy packing her clothes and selecting the best of the furniture so that when the police did give them a clean bill they could leave town immediately. They would have to rent a van and depart after dark.

Eddie was shocked and dismayed when he learned that Frank had left no money for Linda. Up to the time of Frank's death Eddie had been in the pleasant position of enjoying Linda's charms without having to pay for them. Now he had not only to support himself, but Linda as well, and Linda's extravagant tastes were already startling him.

While he idled over a double whisky and soda he considered various ideas of how to increase his earning powers, but eventually came to the conclusion that unless he managed to hit on a scheme whereby he came into a large sum of money, things were going to be difficult. In spite of considerable concentration, no such scheme materialized. With a sudden grunt of disgust he pushed his empty glass towards the bartender and lit a cigarette.

As the bartender was refilling the glass he said under his breath, "Take a gander at that blossom who's just drifted in."

Eddie swung round on his stool and looked into the main entrance lobby. He caught sight of a girl as she crossed to the reception desk and he whistled softly.

She was tall and slender and lovely to look at, with the most amazing red hair that Eddie had ever seen. Dressed from head to foot in black, with a long black cloak banging from her shoulders and which was fastened at her throat by a gold chain, she made an arresting and somewhat startling picture. She wore no hat, and the only splash of color came from a scarlet orchid which she wore pinned high up on the cloak.

"Hold everything, Bud," Eddie said to the bartender. "This wants looking into," and he slid off the stool, walked quietly to the bar entrance where he could see across the lobby to the reception desk.

Gus, the reception clerk, a lean, hard-featured man with quick, restless eyes, winked at Eddie as the girl bent to sign the register. Eddie winked back.

The bellhop, who had appeared by magic, took the girl's suitcase and conducted her with obvious enthusiasm to the ancient elevator. Eddie noticed the girl carried two leather brief-cases, and he wondered idly what they contained.

He had a good look at the girl as she walked to the elevator. She was pale and moved listlessly, and Eddie had a sudden feeling that be had seen her somewhere before. This puzzled him, for he was sure that he would never have forgotten that head of hair if he had seen her before; but, for all that, the feeling persisted.

When she had disappeared into the elevator Eddie went over to the reception desk.

"Who's the gorgeous redhead, Gus?" he asked.

Gus shot his grimy shirt cuffs, ran his hand over his thinning hair.

"She signs herself 'Carol Blandish'," he returned, eying the register. "Hot dish, ain't she? It wouldn't give me a clot on the brain to give her a tumble." He shook his head, sighed. "That big old neon sign's the brightest idea we've ever had. I bet we wouldn't have caught her if it hadn't been for the old sign, and I bet she stays only for one night."

"Carol Blandish," Eddie repeated, frowning, "Now, where have I heard that name before?"

"Search me. Have you heard it before?"

Eddie stared at Gus, his blue eyes suddenly very big.

"For God's sake!" he exclaimed. "That's the dame who's been in the newspapers—the heiress. Why, she's worth millions! You've read about her, haven't you?"

"Not me," Gus said, shaking his head. "I only read the sports column. What do you mean—heiress?"

"That's right. She's worth millions; and she's supposed to be crazy."

"That don't mean anything," Gus said scornfully. "The way folks act around here I guess half the town's crazy, and they ain't got millions, either." He brooded for a moment, added, "She's got a swell shape hung over her bones, hasn't she? Just imagine the possibilities."

"What the hell is she doing here?" Eddie asked, running his fingers through his hair. "What a bird to pluck! That's what I call business and pleasure." He suddenly snapped his fingers. "What's the number of her room, Gus? I'm going to work on her. It's a chance of a lifetime."

"No. 247," Gus said, added helpfully, "I got the passkey if you want it."

Eddie shook his head.

"None of that stuff," he said. "This has got to be handled right. It's got to be as smooth as silk. For the first time in my life I've a real beauty to work on, and am I going to enjoy myself!"

"It should come a lot sweeter after working on those old grey mares of yours," Gus said, and sighed. "I envy you, pal."

"Yeah," Eddie said, straightening his tie. "I'm damned if I don't envy myself."

~§~

The bellhop dumped the suitcase by the bed, pulled the yellow blinds down, shutting out the rain-splashed and dirty windows, threw open the bathroom door with an apologetic smirk, punched the bed as if to prove it still had springs, and stood away, his right hand expectant, his eyes bright with hope.

Carol was scarcely aware of him. Her head ached and her body cried out for rest. She moved listlessly to the solitary, shabby armchair and sank into it, dropping the briefcases at her feet.

The bellhop, a worldly young man of seventeen summers, eyed her doubtfully. He thought she looked good enough to eat, but he was reserving his final judgment until he had seen the size of his tip.

"Was there anything else you wanted?" he asked a little sharply, as she seemed to have forgotten him. "You can have dinner up here if you like, and a fire. They'll charge you plenty for the fire, but if you fancy it I'll get it fixed."

She started and peered up at him as if she were short-sighted. To her he seemed far away, a blurred image in black and white, and yet his voice grated loudly in her ears.

"Yes, a fire," she said, drawing her cloak round her. "And dinner, please."

Still he waited, a pained expression on his face.

"I'll send the waiter," he said, "or will the set dinner do? It ain't bad. I eat it myself."

"Yes—anything. Please leave me alone now," she said, pressing her temples between her fingers.

"Don't you feel well?" the bellhop asked, curious. There was something odd about her, and he felt suddenly uneasy to be alone with her. "Is there something I can get you?"

Quickly and impatiently she opened her handbag and threw a dollar note at him.

"No!" she said. "Leave me alone!"

He picked up the note, eyed her, a startled expression on his face, and went away. He was glad to shut the door on her.

"If you ask me," he said to no one in particular, "that girl's got a bat in her attic."

For some time Carol sat motionless. She was cold and the sharp stabbing pains inside her head frightened her. She had planned to leave Santo Rio after taking Max's money, but during the drive down from the house on the hill she had developed this agonizing pain in her head, and unable to drive further she had decided to break the journey at Palm Bay. She had no idea what kind of a hotel it was, but the brilliant neon sign had attracted her.

A negro porter came in at this moment to light the fire, and his entrance disturbed her train of thought. She got up and went into the bathroom while he was building the fire. In the overheated dingy room, with its leaky shower and stained bath, she suddenly felt faint, and had to clutch onto the towel rail to prevent herself from falling.

She realized then that she was starving. She had had no food from the moment she had seen Max leave the hospital and had followed him to his home. She sat on the edge of the bath, holding her head, until she heard the porter leave, closing the door sharply behind him.

Eddie was in the corridor when the waiter came along pushing the trolley containing the set dinner to Carol's room.

Eddie was on good terms with all the hotel staff, and this waiter, Bregstein by name, was a particular crony of his.

"That little lot for No. 247?" he asked, taking out a five-dollar bill and folding if between his fingers.

Bregstein eyed the five-spot, beamed and said it was.

"O.K., Bud," Eddie said, slipping the note into Bregstein's pocket, "go buy yourself a drink. I'll take it in. Redheads are right up my alley."

"That alley of yours must be getting a little overcrowded, Mr. Regan," Bregstein said with a leer.

"Yeah, but there's always room for one more," Eddie returned, straightened his immaculate tuxedo. "Think she'll take me for a waiter?"

"The kind you see on the movies," Bregstein sighed. "Those guys who don't have to pay for their own laundry." He eyed Eddie uneasily, went on: "The management won't like this, Mr. Regan. You won't start anything I couldn't finish, will you?"

"The management won't know unless you tell them," Eddie said carelessly, pushed the trolley to the door of 247, knocked, opened the door and went in.

He was a little startled to see Carol crouching over the fire, her head in her hands.

He wheeled the trolley to the table.

Clearing his throat, he said: "Your dinner, madam. Would you like it served by the fire?"

"Leave it there, please," Carol said without turning.

"May I draw the chair up for you?" Eddie asked, a little uncertain and not anything like as confident as he had been before entering the room.

"No... leave me alone and go," Carol said, a grating note in her voice.

Then Eddie saw the two briefcases lying on the floor and he stood transfixed as he read the gold letters stamped on the side of each case. On one was: *Frank Kurt;* on the other: *Max Geza.* He gaped at Carol with startled eyes, and as he did so she happened to move her arm and he caught sight of the white puckered scar on her wrist. He gave a convulsive start as he realized that she was Mary Prentiss.

This discovery so startled him that he hastily left the room before she might look up and recognize him. When he was once more in the corridor he stood for a moment thinking, his eyes bright and his breathing heavy. What a sweet set-up, he thought: Carol Blandish, the millionairess, masquerading as Mary Prentiss and responsible for the death of Frank, and in possession of Frank's and Max's property. If he couldn't turn that to good account then he might as well give up his racket and take up knitting.

When Carol had finished the dinner, which she ate ravenously, she felt better and the pain in her head slowly receded. Taking off her cloak, she pulled the chair up to the fire and sat down to review the past days with cold triumph. She had already settled Frank's account, and had made good strides in the settling of Max's. From the time Max had left the hospital she had been on his heels and he had had no suspicion. She had even followed him up the stairs of the old wooden house and had watched him through a chink in the door panel as he counted the money he had taken from the wardrobe. She had seen in his hard eyes the intense pleasure the money had given him, and she knew that by taking it she would inflict on him a hurt as great as the one he had inflicted on Miss Lolly when he had cut off her beard.

She had decided to give him a few days longer in which to grieve over his loss and then she would finish him. Her eyes burned feverishly when she thought of that moment and her long white fingers turned into claws.

Then she remembered the briefcases lying at her feet, and she picked up one of them, opened it, looked at the neatly stacked money with an expression of horror in her eyes. Each note seemed to her to reek of the Sullivans, and she seemed to hear the faint echo of their metallic voices seeping out of the leather case. With a shiver of disgust she threw the case from her and its contents came tumbling out on to the dingy carpet.

At this moment the door opened and Eddie, now prepared to deal with the situation, came in. His opening sentence died in his throat when he saw the stacks of dollar bills on the floor. He spotted the briefcase and he realized at once that this money belonged to Frank and Max. He also jumped to the conclusion that Frank's money, anyway, was now Linda's property, and what was Linda's was, of course, his as well.

Carol turned quickly in her chair when she heard the door close, saw Eddie and recognized him. She remained still; her big green eyes watchful.

Eddie stirred the money with his foot, looked at her.

"Know me?" he asked, and smiled.

"Get out," Carol said quietly.

Now, sure of himself, Eddie lounged to the fireplace and propped himself up against the mantelpiece.

"The police are looking for a dame who calls herself Mary Prentiss," he said, reached for a cigarette, lit it. "The charge is murder, and they have a good enough case, if they find her, to make it stick."

"Get out," Carol repeated, and her hands closed into fists.

"They wouldn't hang you. They'd put you away, sweetheart, for twenty years." He regarded the glowing end of his cigarette, glanced at her, went on: "You wouldn't like prison life, you know. You've had a dose of asylum life, but they treat you tough in prison. There aren't any padded rooms and sedatives to numb your days."

"Why are you telling me this?" she asked, suddenly relaxing back in her chair.

"Look, baby, we don't have to wrap this up in cotton wool. Don't try and bluff. I know you are Mary Prentiss because of that scar. You were the girl who agreed to be Frank's companion, who took my money to keep him amused, and who engineered his death. I don't know why you did it, but I can soon find out. You are also Carol Blandish, the millionairess, late of Glenview Mental Sanatorium. You and me are going to do a deal. I'm taking this money for a start, and then you'll give me a certified check for half a million, otherwise I'm going to hand you over to the police. What do you say to all that?"

"I don't like you," Carol said, and her mouth twitched. "You'd better go."

"Don't rush it, baby," Eddie said, and showed his big white teeth in a sneering smile. "I'm not going until you've paid up. Come on, get wise. I've got you where I want you, and there's no wriggling out of it."

She looked up at him, her eyes like holes burned in white paper.

"Get out!" she said violently, "and leave me alone."

"I'll give you a couple of hours to think it over," Eddie said, a little startled. "But I'll take this dough while I'm at it. It doesn't belong to you."

As he bent to pick up the money Carol snatched up the poker and struck at his head with all her strength.

Eddie had just time to drop flat. The poker missed his head but caught his shoulder, and the pain stunned him for a second or so.

But as Carol jumped to her feet he rolled clear and, cursing, swung his legs round, catching her just below her knees, bringing her down on top of him. He grabbed her arms, rolled her over on her back and pinned her to the floor.

"Now, you hell-cat," he said viciously, "I'll teach you to start something like this," and releasing one of her arms he slapped her heavily across her face.

It was a mistake to release her arm, for she struck back like lightning. Instinct rather than sight warned Eddie and he jerked back his head in time to save his eyes. Her fingernails ploughed four deep scratches down his jaw, drawing blood. Before he could recover from the first shock of pain she was up and had darted to the door. He snatched at the skirt of her black silk dress, brought her up with a jerk, then the dress ripped and he lost his hold.

She reached the door, set her back against it, her hands behind her. As he got slowly to his feet he heard the key turn in the lock.

"That won't get you anywhere," he said, breathing heavily. Blood from the scratches dripped on to his white shirt-front. "Unlock that door or I'll give you the thrashing of your life."

Carol removed the key, bent and slipped it under the door.

"Now neither of us can get away," she said softly.

"I'll make you pay for this," Eddie said, not liking the cold, vicious expression on her face nor the burning light in her eyes. "I'm three times as strong as you and I'll skin you if you start anything funny."

She gave a soft metallic laugh which set his nerves tingling.

"You're afraid of me," she said, sidled across the room towards him.

"Stay where you are," Eddie said sharply, and he remembered with a little chill what the newspapers had said about her. *Homicidal... wildcat... dangerous.*

But she came on, her hands hanging loosely at her sides, her eyes burning.

"So you're going to have me locked up," she jeered at him. "I don't think so. I don't like being locked up."

Eddie backed away until he came up against the wall, She struck before he was properly set and her finger-nails, missing his eyes by a hair's-breadth, slashed his cheek. Furious with pain, Eddie grabbed her, and for a minute or so they fought like animals. It was all Eddie could do to keep the flying fingernails out of his eyes. Each time he grabbed at her wrists she evaded him, and although she did not reach his eyes, she scratched and tore at his face until it was a mask of blood.

Eddie hit her in the body, but she clung on to him, He got hold of her arms, twisted them behind her, turned her and threw her down on the bed. Her dress was ripped into shreds and he couldn't hold her, his hands sliding off her smooth, slippery young body. She managed to turn and bite at his wrists, and as he lost his hold her knees came up and she kicked him away.

He jumped her before she could get off the bed, and by sheer weight flattened her.

"I'll teach you, you wildcat!" he panted, and raised his fist to club her, but her hands flew up to his throat and he only just caught her wrists in time. They lay like that, their faces close, each struggling to exert sufficient strength to overpower the other.

She was stronger than he thought possible, and he could feel her cold fingers creeping up his neck towards his eyes again.

Panic now seized him and, releasing her, he sprang away, rushed to the door, turned as he heard her savage little cry. She came at him, her eyes blazing and her white face working. He grabbed up a chair and smashed it down across her shoulders so that the chair splintered in his hands.

She pitched forward, and as she was falling he hit her with all his strength on the back of her head. The chair-back snapped, and he stood staring down at her limp body, a piece of the chair firmly clenched in his hand, blood running down his face, horror in his eyes.

"I've killed her!" he thought and turned cold.

For almost a minute he stood staring down at her as she lay before him; practically naked above the waist; her face waxen, her black dress in shreds, one stocking down to her ankle. Her arms and neck were smeared with his blood. The sight of her turned him sick.

If the cops find her here, he thought wildly, *they'll crucify me! They won't believe I hit her in self-defense.*

Then he thought of Gus. Gus would have to get him out of this mess. If there was anyone who could do it—Gus was the guy.

He blundered to the telephone, and when Gus answered he gasped, "Come up here, quick!" Then he flopped onto the bed and kept his eyes averted from the still figure on the floor. The horror of it all swept over him.

After a while the rattle of a key in the lock aroused him, and he got unsteadily to his feet as Gus came in.

Gus stopped short, caught his breath sharply.

"For God's sake!" he exclaimed, his eyes hardening. Then he came into the room, closed the door. "Is she dead?"

"I don't know," Eddie quavered. He looked ghastly with blood still trickling down his face and soaking into his collar and coat. "Look what she did to me. She's crazy! She came at me like a wild animal. If I hadn't hit her..."

But Gus wasn't listening. The dollar bills scattered all over the room held his attention. He shot a quick, hard glance at Eddie, then knelt beside Carol, felt her pulse, lifted her head, grimaced as he got blood on his fingers. He lowered her head very gently to the floor, wiped his fingers on her torn dress and stood up with a little grunt.

"Is she...?" Eddie began, gulped, waited.

"You've smashed her skull," Gus said brutally. "Why did you have to hit her so hard, you crazy bastard?"

"Is she dead?" Eddie jerked out, his knees buckling. He had to sit on the bed.

"She won't last long," Gus said grimly. "The back of her head's caved in."

Eddie shuddered.

"She'd've killed me, Gus," he moaned. "I had to do it. I swear she'd have killed me... look what she did to me."

Eddie pointed at his bloodied face.

"Tell it to the cops," Gus said. "If you can't cook up a better yarn than that they'll fling you into the gas chamber so fast you'll be dizzy in the head till the pellets drop."

"Don't..." Eddie cried, starting to his feet. "I tell you—"

"Save it," Gus returned; "You don't have to tell me a thing. I'm thinking of the hotel, not you. The cops would slam us shut if they heard about this. Can't you stop that bleeding?" he went on irritably. "You're ruining the carpet."

Eddie went into the bathroom, came back holding a towel to his face.

"We've got to get her out of here before she croaks," he said desperately. "No one knows she's in town. For the love of Mike, Gus, get her out of here and dump her somewhere."

"Me?" Gus exclaimed. "And get an accessory rap tied to my tail? That's a laugh. I ain't as dumb as that."

Eddie clutched his arm.

"You can fix it, Gus. I'll make it worth your while, Look, take that dough. There's more than twenty grand there."

Gus gave an exaggerated start and appeared to see for the first time the money that was scattered, over the floor.

"You two been robbing a bank?" he asked.

"It's mine," Eddie said hysterically. "Get her out of here and you can have the lot. Come on, Gus, you know you can fix it for me."

Gus ran his hand over his thinning hair.

"Yeah, I guess I could," he said, slowly. "You'll give me this dough if I get rid of her?"

"Yes... only get her out quick."

"I'll chance it," Gus said, making up his mind, and he bent to pick up the money, pushing Carol aside with his foot to get at some of the notes.

"Get her out first," Eddie said, wringing his hands.

"Take it easy," Gus said. "I'll take her down in the service elevator. She's got a car in the garage; may as well use that. I'll dump her outside the hospital if the coast's clear. You'd better get out of town, Eddie," he went on, stuffing the last of the notes into the briefcase. "If the cops see your mug they'll haul you in as a suspect."

"I'm going," Eddie gasped. "Thanks, Gus, you're a pal."

"Think nothing of it," Gus returned, closed the briefcase. "I was always a sucker for a smart guy like you."

Eddie went unsteadily across the room to where the other briefcase lay hidden behind the overturned armchair. As he picked it up Gus joined him with three quick, silent strides.

"Wait a minute, pal," he said. "I'll have that too."

Eddie snarled at him.

"It's mine," he said, clutching on to the case. "She stole it."

"Too bad," Gus sneered. "Remind me to cry when I have a moment. Hand it over."

"It's mine," Eddie repeated weakly. "You wouldn't skin me, Gus? It's all the dough I have in the world. I've gotta have dough if I'm to get away."

"You're breaking my heart," Gus said. "Hand it over unless you want me to call the cops."

Eddie flung the case on the floor.

"You dirty rat!" he cried. "Take it then, and I hope it poisons your life."

"It won't," Gus said, and winked. "So long, Eddie. Get out of town quick. I don't want to see that scratched-up puss of yours for a long time. It makes me feel sad," and he laughed.

Not trusting himself to speak, Eddie half ran, half staggered from the room.

~§~

Ismi Geza sat in the waiting room of the Montgomery Ward of the Santo Rio Memorial Hospital. It was a pleasant room; light, airy and comfortably furnished. The armchair in which he sat rested him, and he thought, rather to his surprise, how nice it would be to have an armchair as comfortable as this at home.

He thought about the armchair because he was afraid to think about Max. They had taken him away in an ambulance, and hadn't allowed Ismi to travel with him. Ismi had been forced to follow behind in Max's Packard. He hadn't driven a car for years, and the journey had shaken his nerves.

Ismi guessed that Max had had a stroke. Apoplexy seemed to run in the family. Ismi had had a stroke when he had seen an old friend of his mauled by a lion. Max had had his stroke when he had found he had lost his money. The causes had been so different, Ismi thought sadly, but the results could be the same. He hoped not. He hoped that Max would recover. Ismi dragging leg bothered him: it would be an even greater trial to an energetic, impatient man like Max.

The door opened quietly and the Head Sister came in. Ismi liked her immediately. She had a grave, kind face. She was, he thought, a sensible-looking woman: a woman he could trust.

He was so frightened of what she was going to tell him that when she began to speak he went suddenly deaf, and only a few disjointed sentences got through to his bemused mind. She was saying something about hemorrhage from rupture of the cerebral artery... evidence of paralysis affecting the left side of the body... reflexes inactive.

"I see," Ismi said when she paused. "But is he hurt bad? Will he die?"

She saw at once that he hadn't understood what she had said, and that he was frightened. She tried to make it as easy as she could for him.

No, he wouldn't die, she told him quietly, but he might be paralyzed; unable to walk again. It was too early to say just yet; later they would know for certain.

"He won't like it," Ismi said miserably. "He is not a patient boy." He fidgeted with his battered felt hat. "You'll do what you can for him? I don't mind the expense. I've saved—"

"You can see him for a few minutes," she said, feeling an unexpected sorrow for him. "Say nothing to worry him. He must be kept very quiet."

Ismi found Max lying in bed in a small, neat room, his head and shoulders slightly raised. The old man scarcely recognized his son. The left side of Max's face was pulled out of shape, giving him a grotesque, frightening appearance. The left corner of his lip was drawn down, and Ismi could see his white teeth set in a perpetual snarl.

Max's eyes burned like two small embers. They fastened on Ismi as he came slowly up to the bed: terrible eyes, full of hatred, fury and viciousness.

By the window was Nurse Hennekey, a tall, dark girl with a curiously flat, expressionless face. She looked up with surprised interest when she saw Ismi come into the room, but she didn't move nor speak.

"They'll do everything they can for you, son" Ismi said, touching the cold white bed-rail a little helplessly. "You'll soon be better. I will come and see you every day."

Max just stared at him, unable to speak, but the brooding look in his eyes did not change, nor did the hatred die out of them.

"I won't stay now," Ismi said, uneasy and afraid. "It is getting late, but I'll come tomorrow."

Max's lips moved as he tried to say something, but no sound came from them. His dull black eyes seemed to convey a message.

"You mustn't talk," Ismi said. "They told me you must keep very quiet." He was surprised to feel a tear run down his fleshy cheek He was remembering Max when he was a little boy. He had had great hopes of him then.

Max's lips moved again. They formed the words "Get out!" but Ismi didn't realize what he was trying to say.

Nurse Hennekey, who was watching, read the words as they were formed by Max's lips and she signaled Ismi to go.

"I'll be back," Ismi promised, touched the tear away with his finger. "Don't worry about anything." He hesitated, added: "Don't worry about money. I have enough. I've saved..."

Nurse Hennekey touched his arm, led him to the door.

"Look after him please, nurse," he said. "He's my son."

She nodded briefly, looked away so he couldn't see her little frown of distaste. She felt there was something horrible about Max; hated him for no reason at all; had a creepy sensation when she touched him.

Ismi walked slowly along the corridor with its double line of doors on each side of him. On each door was a small nameplate, and Ismi paused to read one of them. Then he turned back to satisfy himself that Max was receiving similar treatment. He wanted his son to have the best of everything. Yes, there was his son's name printed on the plate. How quick and efficient these people were, he thought. The boy hadn't been in the hospital more than a few hours and they had his name already on the door.

He heard footsteps, and glancing round saw a tall young fellow and a pretty girl coming along the corridor. They paused at a door opposite, knocked softly and waited.

Ismi liked the look of them, and he continued to watch until they entered the room and closed the door behind them. Curious, he went over to read the nameplate, and when he saw the name he started back with a shudder as if he had trodden on a snake.

~§~

Veda and Magarth stood looking down at Carol as she lay, white and unconscious, in the hospital bed. The resident doctor, Dr. Cantor, had his fingers on her pulse.

"I hope I did right in sending for you," he was saying to Magarth. "I've read about Miss Blandish, of course, and when we found out who she was, I remembered you had been appointed as her business executive and thought I'd better put a call through to you right away."

Magarth nodded.

"She's pretty bad, isn't she?"

"I would have said her case was hopeless," Cantor returned, "but by the luckiest chance Dr. Kraplien, the greatest brain specialist in the country, is visiting us at the moment, and he has decided to operate. He thinks he can save her."

Veda gripped Magarth's hand.

"Dr. Kraplien doesn't think any serious damage has been done to the brain," Dr. Cantor went on. "The fracture is severe, of course, but we believe the brain itself is uninjured. There is pressure there, due probably to the injury she received in the truck accident. If the operation is successful, the patient's memory will be restored to the moment of the trauma." Dr. Cantor gave Magarth a significant glance. "That will mean she will have no knowledge at all of what has happened to her since the truck accident occurred."

Magarth looked startled.

"You mean she won't even remember me?" he asked. "That'll be hard to take."

"She'll remember no one or any event that happened after the truck accident," Dr. Cantor said. "Dr. Kraplien has taken a great interest in the case. He has spoken to Dr. Travers of the Glenview Mental Sanatorium, and has gone into Miss Blandish's case history with him. He thinks her condition may be entirely due to cerebral compression, and that he may be able to cure her of these fits of violence."

"I do hope he does. She's been through so much," Veda said, and bent and kissed Carol's still white face. "But is it possible?"

Cantor lifted his shoulders. It was rather obvious that he wasn't optimistic.

"The operation will be in less than half an hour now," he said. "Perhaps, when you have seen the police, you'll come back? I should have news for you."

~§~

Many odd visitors have come to Santo Rio at one time or another. Old Joe, who sells newspapers at the entrance to the railway station, has seen them all. Old Joe is an authority on the visitors to Santo Rio. He remembers the old lady with the three Persian cats walking sedately behind her, the pretty actress who arrived very drunk and hit a red-cap over the head with a bottle of gin. He remembers the rich and the sly, the innocent and the evil, but he will tell you that the most extraordinary visitor of them all was Miss Lolly Meadows.

Miss Lolly arrived at Santo Rio on the same train that brought Veda and Magarth to this pacific coast town. It had taken considerable courage for Miss Lolly to have made the journey, but make it she did.

Ever since Carol had visited her, and she had shown Carol the photograph of Linda Lee, Miss Lolly had been uneasy in her conscience. She felt it was disgraceful that she had allowed a young girl like Carol to go off on her own to tackle two such dangerous brutes as the Sullivans. Carol wanted to avenge herself on them, but so did Miss Lolly. Then why had Miss Lolly let her go off by herself? Why hadn't she, at least, offered to go with her?

After three or four days of this kind of thinking Miss Lolly had decided to go to Santo Rio and see if she could find Carol. The decision was made not without a great deal of misgivings and fear, for it was many years since Miss Lolly had traveled in a train, had mixed with strangers and had felt curious, morbid eyes staring at her.

Old Joe will tell you that he saw Miss Lolly as she came out of the railway station in her black shabby dress that she had worn last some twenty years ago and on her head a vast black hat trimmed with artificial cherries and grapes. The close-trimmed beard, of course, completed the picture and startled Old Joe half out of his senses.

Miss Lolly stood close to Old Joe and surveyed the teeming traffic, the pushing crowds, the languid and scantily dressed young women in their beach suits, and was horrified.

Old Joe had a kind nature, and although a little embarrassed to be seen talking to such an odd freak, he asked her if he could help her in any way, and Miss Lolly, recognizing kindness in his face, told him she had come to find Carol Blandish.

For a moment or so Old Joe eyed her doubtfully. He decided she was crazy but harmless, and without a word he handed her the midday newspaper, pointed to the paragraph that told of the finding of the famous heiress unconscious in her car outside the Santo Rio Memorial Hospital, and that an operation was to be performed on her immediately.

Miss Lolly had scarcely time to absorb this item of news when, looking up, she saw, walking on the other side of the street, the limping figure of Ismi Geza.

Miss Lolly recognized Ismi immediately although she hadn't seen him for more than fifteen years. She realized at once where Ismi was, Max was most likely to be, and thanking Old Joe for his kindness, she hurried after Ismi, overtook him easily enough, touched his arm.

Ismi stared at her for several seconds before clasping her hand. This meeting between the bearded lady and the circus clown practically disorganized the traffic and caused a vast crowd to collect: and realizing the sensation they were causing, Ismi hurriedly hailed a taxi, pushed Miss Lolly in and bundled himself in beside her.

The crowd raised a cheer as the taxi drove away.

~§~

Max lay in his bed, his cruel twisted mind a torment of pain and frustrated fury. That this could have happened to him, he thought: to be struck down—to be helpless, paralyzed for life. And Carol Blandish was responsible! It was she who had killed Frank! She who had taken their money! She who had turned him into a helpless cripple! He snarled to himself as he realized that he could do nothing to her now. She was out of his reach.

For the past eight hours he had remained motionless, his eyes closed, thinking of Carol. He had been aware of the nurse as she moved about the room, but he had refused to open his eyes or to show any sign of life. He wanted to be alone, with his thoughts; to create in his mind a revenge that would satisfy him, but every horrible, outrageous act he conceived to inflict on Carol was not bad enough to please him.

He heard the door open, and looking between his eyelashes he saw another nurse come in; and he guessed rightly she was the night nurse.

He heard Nurse Hennekey say: "Thank heaven you've come. This dreadful little man has been giving me the creeps."

"Is he asleep?" the other nurse asked, and giggled.

"Yes," Nurse Hennekey returned. "He's been asleep for hours. That's the only good thing about him. But even to look at him gives me the horrors."

Max felt rather than saw the other nurse draw near. His hard, twisted face remained expressionless, but he listened intently.

"He won't give me the horrors," the other nurse said firmly. "Although he isn't exactly an oil-painting."

"You wait until you see his eyes," Nurse Hennekey said, "You'll change your mind about him then. I wouldn't be surprised if he hadn't murdered someone. I've never seen such hateful and vicious eyes. You should have seen how he looked at his poor old father."

"You'll make me burst into tears in a moment," the other nurse, Bradford by name, returned with a laugh. "But tell me about the other patient. Is it true? Is she really Carol Blandish?"

It was only by exerting a tremendous effort that Max did not betray that be was listening. Under the cover of the blanket his right hand closed into a fist.

"Yes. The heiress. She's lovely to look at. I've never seen such marvelous hair," Nurse Hennekey said. "Her case papers are in her room. You'd better have a look at them. Dr. Cantor will be around during the night. The operation was successful.

They say Dr. Kraplien was magnificent. It means she'll be normal again. The operation took five hours. I wish I'd seen it, but I had to look after this thing," and she waved to the still, silent Max.

"I'll go and look at her now," Nurse Bradford said. "You get off, and don't be late in the morning."

The two nurses left the room, and Max opened his eyes. He listened intently, heard a murmur of voices outside, heard a door open and Nurse Bradford say, "Isn't she lovely!"

So Carol Blandish was opposite: within a few yards of him, Max thought, and a little red spark of murder lit up in his brain. If only he could move! If only he could get at her! His lips came off his teeth in a snarl. But the nurse... he would have to settle the nurse first.

What was he thinking of? He was already making plans as if he could carry them out. Perhaps he could carry them out. He tried to raise himself on his right arm, but the left side of his body, dead and cold, was too heavy. He tried again, exerting all his strength, succeeded in rolling over on his left side. From that position he could look down on to the floor. If he let himself fall, he might be able to drag himself to the door. He rolled back again as the door opened and Nurse Bradford came in.

She was young with corn-colored hair, and big, rather stupid blue eyes.

"Oh, you're awake," she said brightly. "I'm the night nurse. I'm going to make you comfortable."

Max closed his eyes in case she should see intended murder in them.

"Let me straighten the bed," she went on cheerfully.

He was going to do it, Max told himself. With this nurse out of the way, he would get at Carol Blandish if it killed him. But first, the nurse...

As she began to rearrange the blanket and sheet, Max lifted his right hand, beckoned to her.

"Do you want anything?" she asked, looking at him with apprehension.

Again he beckoned, tried to speak, and she leaned down, her face close to his to catch the mumbled words.

With a snarl Max grabbed her throat in his right hand, dragged her down, kicked his right leg free from the blanket and hooked it across her struggling body, pinning her to the bed. She was stronger than he expected, and it wasn't easy to keep his grip, which she tore at with both hands.

He hung on, cursing silently, feeling his fingers sliding off her smooth throat as she scratched and pulled at his hand. He squeezed harder.

She's going to get away, he thought frantically. *She'll scream!* Her terrified eyes stared into his; her cap had fallen off in the struggle and her corn-colored hair fell about her shoulders. He would have to do something quickly. She was nearly free. He released his grip, tore his hand free, and raising his clenched fist smashed it down on her upturned face as if he were hammering a nail into wood.

Stunned now, she could only struggle feebly, and once again his fingers fastened on her throat. Then his shoulders seemed to grow lumpy and sweat ran down his twisted face. The nurse's face turned blue and her eyes protruded, blind. Still cursing, Max exerted all his strength. The nurse's slender body writhed. One hand began to beat on the bed mechanically, without force.

Max closed his eyes and strained. The nurse's hand suddenly stopped beating, opened and closed and opened again, hung limp. There was a muffled crack, almost immediately followed by a sharper one, and he let the nurse slide from the bed to the floor.

Max lay still; his breath came in great shuddering gasps. The struggle had been almost too much for him, and he realized, in alarm and rage, how weak he had become. But the red spark of murder that burned in his brain urged him on. There was no time to lose. Someone might come in: you never knew who was coming in when you were a prisoner in a hospital. If he was to finish Carol, he must act at once. But he made no move in spite of the urgency. He felt as if he were suffocating, and blood pounded in his head, turning him sick and dizzy.

So he waited, his right fist clenched, his nails digging into his sweating palm until his breathing became easier. As new strength began to creep back into his twisted body he heard someone coming down the passage and his heart began to bump like a disturbed pendulum against his side. But the footfalls passed, died away.

It was an almost impossible task he had set himself, he thought. He would have to crawl across the passage, and anyone passing would immediately see him and raise the alarm. If only he had a gun! No one would stop him if he had a gun!

But he refused to give up. It was too late to give up, anyway. He would go through with it.

He threw off the blanket, slowly worked himself to the edge of the bed. Looking down, he stared into the dead face of the nurse, and he drew back his lips in a grimace. She looked hideous. The mottled blue of her complexion clashed horribly with her corn-colored hair.

Slowly, he leaned out of bed until his right hand touched the floor, then he let his body slide off the bed, and he checked his progress with his hand. But as his heavy, dead leg began to move there was nothing he could do to control it, and suddenly he felt himself falling and thudded on to the floor the breath driven out of his body and pain surging over him like a white hot wave, drowning him in a sea of darkness.

He had no idea how long he remained on the floor, but gradually he recovered consciousness to find his head resting on the nurse's hair, his right arm across her body. He rolled away from her, shuddering, began to drag himself across the smooth polished floor towards the door.

To his surprise he found that he made quick progress in spite of having to drag his left arm and leg, which had no feeling in. them. He reached the door, stretched up and turned the handle, pulled the door open a few inches, then paused to rest. He was feeling bad now. The blood pounding in his head threatened to burst a blood-vessel and his breathing made a loud snoring noise at the back of his throat. Again he waited, knowing that if he went out into the passage someone would be certain to hear him.

And, while he waited his brain slowly became inflamed with vicious fury at the thought of being so close to Carol, and, in a little while, of being able to lay his hands on her.

As he was about to move again he heard someone coming, and he quickly pushed the door to and waited, trying to hold his breath, snarling at the possibility of discovery.

He heard something going on outside, and cautiously he pulled the door open an inch or so and glanced out.

A nurse was standing opposite him. She was taking a number of bed sheets from a cupboard. She was a tall, good-looking girl and she hummed softly under her breath. For no reason at all Max stared at the long ladder in her stocking. It was the only thing about her that held his attention. With a pile of sheets in her arms, she closed the cupboard door with her foot, walked quickly away down the corridor.

Max felt sweat running down his face. It was as if his face was a sponge full of water, and he could feel the sweat in his hair. He looked across the corridor at the opposite door, tried to read the nameplate, but the printing was too small. There were two other doors a little farther up the corridor, and he wondered with sudden panic in which room Carol lay.

He would have no time to crawl up and down the corridor, for he moved too slowly. He would have to go straight into the room opposite and chance to luck that she was in there. He placed his ear to the floor and listened. The vast building seemed for that moment to be stilled, then the soft whirring sound of the express elevators as they raced between the floors came to him; but no other sound.

Drawing a deep breath, he pushed open the door and crawled into the passage.

~§~

"If you saw him now," Ismi said, "you wouldn't worry like this. I know he hasn't been a good boy, but now." He broke off, shook his head sadly.

Miss Lolly continued to pace up and down, her hands clasped, her gaunt face set.

These two were in the shabby little hotel room which Ismi had taken to be near Max. They had been together now for more than six hours, and they had talked of Max practically without ceasing.

"I know him better than you do," Miss Lolly said. "He is your son. You have a father's feeling towards him. You try to excuse him." Her hand touched her shorn beard. "He is evil bad. So was Frank."

"Frank's dead," Ismi said, and crossed himself.

"Would that the other were dead too," Miss Lolly muttered. "So long as he can breathe she's in danger. I feel it in my bones. I can't help it, Ismi. I feel it."

"He is paralyzed," the old man insisted. "You don't know what you're saying. You haven't seen him. He can't even speak."

"He is Max," Miss Lolly said. "I'm frightened. To think she is opposite his room. It's too close, Ismi. If he finds out..."

Ismi groaned.

"You go on and on," he said. "I tell you he can't move. He'll never be able to walk again. I know. Look what happened to me, and Max is twenty times as bad as I was."

Miss Lolly went to her suitcase, opened it, took out a heavy throwing-knife.

"There's nothing he can't do with a knife," she said, showing it to Ismi. "I kept this. It is his—one of many. He could throw a knife even if he couldn't walk. There's nothing he can't do with it."

Ismi wrung his hands.

"You're wearing me out," he groaned. "You go on and on. He hasn't a knife. He hasn't any weapon. Nothing... please stop. Nothing can happen to her."

Miss Lolly eyed him.

"I'm going to the hospital," she said. "I couldn't rest. I should have gone before now if it hadn't been for you."

Ismi started to his feet.

"What are you going to do? You're not going to tell them who he is—what he's done? You wouldn't do that?"

"I must warn them," she said firmly. "I don't trust him."

Ismi caught her hands in his.

"Don't tell them," he pleaded. "They wouldn't treat him so well if they knew. They have his name on the door and a special nurse. He is very ill. Have a little mercy, Lolly. He is my son."

"He had no mercy for me," Miss Lolly said quietly. "Why should I feel for him now?"

"Because he is so helpless now," Ismi said. "Go and see for yourself. He can't do anything evil. This may be the making of him. When he is well enough I'll take him away. I'll begin a new life for him. Don't tell them."

"Why did you have such a son?" Miss Lolly burst out. "I warned you. Why did you marry such a woman? I told you she was no good, and you found that out soon enough. Why didn't you listen to me?"

Ismi sat down again.

"You were right," he said. "I wish I had listened to you. What am I going to do, Lolly? There's no future for me now. I have little money." He put his hands over his eyes. "It won't last long. Every nickel will have to go to Max. He needs it now." He rocked himself backwards and forwards. "I feel so old and useless, Lolly."

While he was speaking Miss Lolly moved silently to the door. She opened it, stood looking back at the old clown as he moaned to himself.

"What's to become of us?" he went on. "I know you're right. He is evil. He'll go on doing evil no matter how helpless he is, because he is wicked to the core."

But Miss Lolly didn't hear. She was already running down the stairs, and it wasn't until she reached the main lobby of this shoddy little hotel that she realized that she was still grasping the heavy throwing-knife, and hastily she hid it from sight under her coat.

A couple of drummers, fat, oily-faced men, nudged each other as Miss Lolly crossed the lobby.

"That's the kind of hotel this is," one of them said to the other. "Even the dames have beards."

But Miss Lolly paid no attention, although she heard what was said. She went into the dark street, and after a minute or so hailed a passing taxi.

She arrived at the Santo Rio Memorial Hospital as the tower clock chimed eleven.

The porter at the gate eyed her with a mixture of disgust and contempt on his round fat face.

"You can't see anyone now," he said firmly. "Come tomorrow. The Head Sister's off duty and the resident doctor's on his rounds. It's no use wagging your head at me. You can't come in," and he turned back to his office, closing the door firmly in Miss Lolly's face.

She looked up at the immense building with its thousands of lighted windows. Somewhere in this building was Max: opposite his room was Carol.

She had a presentiment of danger. She knew Max. If he learned that Carol was so close to him he would move heaven and earth to get at her. Setting her ridiculous hat more firmly on her head, she walked quietly past the porter's lodge and moved quickly, like a lost shadow, towards the main hospital building.

~§~

Max reached the opposite door, paused for a moment to lift himself up on his arm to read the nameplate. A hot wave of vicious exaltation ran through him when he saw the name: *Carol Blandish*. So she was there; behind that door, now within his reach. He fumbled at the handle, pushed the door open, dragged himself along the floor into the room, closed the door.

The room was in semi-darkness, lit only by a small blue pilot light immediately over the bed. For a moment or so Max could see nothing, blinded by the contrast between this dim light and the harsh light of the corridor. Then things in the room began to take shape. He became aware of the bed, set in the middle of the room, the white enameled table by the bed and the armchair. But his whole vicious attention was concentrated on the bed.

He crawled towards it, paused when he reached it. It was a high bed, and reaching up he could only just get his fingers on the top of the edge of the mattress. When he raised himself on his right arm he could see Carol lying in the bed, but as his left arm was useless he could not reach her.

She lay on her back, the sheet drawn up to her chin, her face the color of snow in the bluish light. She looked as if she were dead—very lovely and calm—but he could see the slight rise and fall of her breasts as she breathed. Her head was swathed in bandages, and only a wisp of her beautiful red hair showed beneath the bandages.

Max saw nothing of this: all he saw was someone to kill just out of his reach, and, trembling with fury, he caught hold of the bed-rail and tried to lever himself up, but the dead side of his body proved too heavy.

He thought for a moment that he was going to have another stroke. To be so close to her; to have had to suffer so much to get to her and for her still to be safe and beyond his reach was more than he could endure. He relaxed on the floor, shut his eyes, tried to control the pounding of blood in his head. He must think. There must be some way in which he could reach her.

Perhaps if he pushed the armchair against the bed he could hoist himself on to it and be within reach. He began to drag himself across the floor to the armchair when his ears, never ceasing to listen for an alarming sound, warned him that some-one was coming.

He paused, listened intently.

Miss Lolly came scurrying down the passage, breathless and alarmed. No one had seen her enter the hospital, although she had had several narrow escapes. She had found the Montgomery Ward with difficulty, remembered Ismi had said that Max was on the third floor, and she had toiled up the emergency staircase, knowing that it was unlikely that she would meet anyone.

But once on the third floor there were nurses busy in the rooms leading on to the landing, and Miss Lolly had to wait her opportunity to make a dash down the corridor. She succeeded, and was now half walking, half running along the broad corridor, her eyes searching each nameplate to show her Max's room.

She had decided to see him first. If he was as ill and as helpless as Ismi had said, she wouldn't betray him. But she knew Max: had long distrusted him. Ismi was simple, believed well of anyone. It seemed unlikely to her that Max could ever be harmless.

She suddenly paused as Max's name caught her eye. There it was, printed neatly on a white card. *To think they should make such a fuss over such a brute,* she thought indignantly. She listened outside the door, heard nothing and found she was suddenly trembling. She remembered the last time she had seen him; remembered the cold viciousness in his eyes and the vindictive way be had looked at her. How he had deliberately struck her, so quickly that she had had no chance of protecting herself.

Her hand instinctively gripped the handle of the knife she kept hidden under her coat, and turning the door handle she looked into the room.

For a moment or so the shock of seeing the dead nurse huddled on the floor brought Miss Lolly's heart almost to a bumping standstill. She saw the empty bed, realized instantly what it meant. Had she arrived in time? She knew there wasn't a second to lose, and pulling herself together she whirled on her heel and sprang across the corridor to the opposite door.

She had now no thought, for herself; her one aim was to save Carol and throwing open the door she blundered into the semi-dark room.

Max, crouching in the darkness, recognized her immediately, and suppressed a cry of fury as she came blundering into the room. He knew she wouldn't be able to see him for a moment or so until her eyes became accustomed to the dim light. In that time he must settle her, if he was going through with his vengeance. He dragged himself towards her, holding his breath, but as he reached her Miss Lolly saw him.

She didn't know what it was that was moving towards her. She could just make out a dark menacing mass that was reaching out for her, and she guessed immediately it was Max.

Catching her breath in horror, she stepped back, felt his hand grip the hem of her dress, hang on. Blind terror seized her, and bending over him she struck at him with the knife: struck with all her strength.

The blade of the knife cut into Max's side, seared through his flesh and buried itself into the hard wood of the floor. For a second or so these two looked at each other, then swinging his fist Max hit Miss Lolly on the side of the head, knocking her flat.

But he was alarmed, feeling the blood running down his side, and he wondered if she had cut an artery. It had been a wild, stupid stroke. To Max, who was an expert, such a stroke was inexcusable. She had had him at her mercy: she should have finished him.

He gripped the knife-handle, his lips coming off his teeth. He scarcely felt the cold edge of the knife as it hit into him. He had now what he wanted. The old fool had brought him the one weapon with which he was expert.

But she had driven it so firmly into the floor that be could not move it. He became aware that his strength was very gradually slipping away from him as his blood flowed from his side. In a sudden frenzy he tugged and jerked at the knife, saw Miss Lolly struggling slowly to her feet. Everything was going wrong, he thought furiously, and shouted at her, although no sound came from his twitching, twisted lips.

She was on her feet now, her grotesque hat on the side of her head, her eyes wild with fear. Supporting herself by the bedrail, she placed herself between him and the silent, unconscious Carol.

He took a new grip on the knife-handle, began to work, it backwards and forwards, feeling it slowly loosening, and his face lit up with ghastly triumph.

"No!" Miss Lolly said breathlessly. "Leave it alone. Take your hand off it."

He snarled at her, wrenched and jerked at the knife-handle, feeling it slowly, and as if reluctantly, coming free.

Miss Lolly saw his look of triumph, knew what would happen if he once got possession of the knife, and looked around wildly for a weapon. Standing in a corner was an iron cylinder of oxygen. She ran to it, snatched it up and turned.

Even as she did so the knife came loose, and rolling over, Max sent it flying through the air.

Miss Lolly gave a hoarse scream, swung up the cylinder as the knife struck her in the middle of her narrow, bony chest. She stood for a moment, the cylinder above her head, the knife growing out of her outmoded black dress, her eyes sightless; then her knees buckled, the cylinder crashed to the floor, narrowly missing Max, and she dropped.

Slowly now, he crawled over to her, and leaning over her he spat in her face. He knew she had finished him. He could tell that he was bleeding to death, and a cold drowsiness was already creeping over him. He could feel his blood running down his side, flowing out of him, carrying away his evil spirit.

But there was still a chance, he thought, if he were quick. If he could get the knife out of Miss Lolly's body he might still have enough strength to throw it. From where he lay Carol made a perfect target.

He again gripped the knife-handle, again pulled at the knife. The handle was slippery with blood, but he kept at it until it was free. But then he found he had become so weak that he could scarcely lift the knife. He turned on his side, looked across the dim room.

Suddenly his mind was projected back to the days when he and Frank worked in the circus. The girl in the bed, lit by the blue light, reminded him of a girl who once stood against a board and let him throw phosphorus-painted knives at her. He remembered the time he had so carefully aimed the knife at her throat. It had been a clever throw, for it had been done in the dark. He could still do it: even now, when he was dying.

His father had said, over and over again: "There is no knife-thrower like you in the world. I have never known you to miss any target once you have made up your mind to hit it."

That was true, Max thought, and gathered together his last remaining strength.

It was not a difficult target. He could see Carol's throat just above the white sheet, but it was a pity that the knife was now so heavy. He raised it with an effort, balanced it, then paused.

There suddenly seemed to be a cold breath of air in the room, and he saw a shadow move; then a figure came out of a corner and glided toward him. Although sunlight streamed through the open blinds the figure's face was dark and out of focus.

He gripped the knife tightly, feeling the hair rise on the back of his neck, and a chill run up his spine.

But it was Frank standing there, only Frank, smiling his tight smile. Fat smug Frank in his black overcoat and black hat and black concertina-shaped trousers.

"You've waited too long, Max," Frank said. "You'll never do it now," and he laughed.

Max snarled at him, again balanced the knife, and his brain commanded his muscles to throw. Nothing happened. The knife began to slip out of his cold fingers.

"Thing of it is," Frank whispered to him from out of the shadows, "there ain't nothing left for you here, old boy."

The knife clattered to the floor and Max's arm dropped. His fingers curled and drew into the sleeve of his hospital gown.

"Come on, Max," Frank urged. "I'm waiting for you."

Before Max died, he thought with satisfaction that he had not spoilt his reputation: he had not missed his target, for he hadn't made the throw.

A little later Carol sighed and opened her eyes. From where she lay she could not see the horror that surrounded her on the floor, and she lay still, her mind washed clear of the past, and waited for someone to come to her.

NOW AVAILABLE FROM BRUIN CRIMEWORKS:

No Orchids for Miss Blandish

James Hadley Chase

Widely recognized as one of the top thrillers of the 20th century, NO ORCHIDS FOR MISS BLANDISH set the standard for crime fiction and has gone on to sell over four million copies worldwide. *—A kidnapped heiress becomes a helpless pawn in an underworld of sexual perversion, murder and mayhem.*

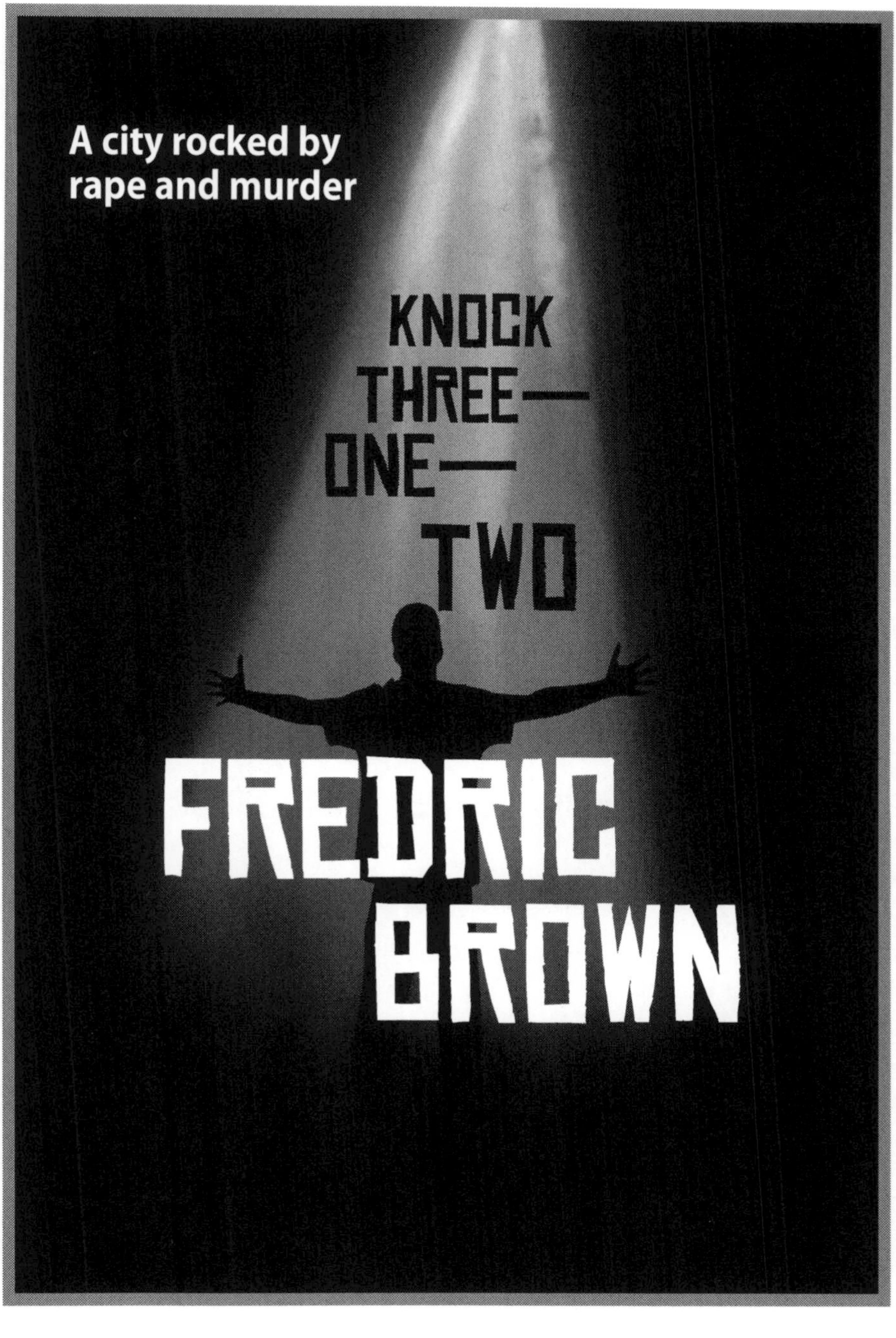
A city rocked by
rape and murder
KNOCK
THREE—
ONE—
TWO
FREDRIC
BROWN

Now Available from Bruin Books Originals

CARDINAL BISHOP, INC.

BY JONATHAN EEDS

A FALLEN HERO. . .A JADED GIRLFRIEND. . .

A MISSING HEIRESS. . .AN EVIL RELIC. . .

CARDINAL BISHOP IS OPEN FOR BUSINESS

A STORY OF LOVE, MYSTERY, TIME TRAVEL. . ..

AND A REALLY PISSED-OFF PIGEON

What readers are saying—

"Not since 'Hitchhiker's Guide to the Galaxy' have I read such a humorous book...made me laugh out loud."

"...a likable scoundrel whom I could not help but cheer on."

"The dialog is wonderful..."

Coming soon from Bruin Crimeworks:

…two thrilling novels by the
by one of the top crime writers of
any generation— *David Dodge*

DEATH & TAXES

Noir-town San Francisco is the backdrop for this fast-paced, fresh and flat-out enjoyable novel about tax evasion, shattered loyalties and, of course, murder. Whit Whitney is one the most endearing characters to appear in American crime fiction.

To Catch a Thief

Immortalized on film by Alfred Hitchcock, *TO CATCH A THIEF* is a classic romantic crime caper. This timeless story of love and honor unfolds amidst a high stakes game of cat-and-mouse. Out of print and scarce for many years, Bruin Crimeworks is proud to make it available again.

Printed in Poland
by Amazon Fulfillment
Poland Sp. z o.o., Wrocław

59024406R00143